Since Alberta was coo[...] her recipe, so Vinny's words didn't make much sense, as she didn't know what he was referring to. "What are you talking about? I'm in the middle of making gravy, there's nothing clever about that."

"You were right about Lucy."

Few things could distract Alberta from her cooking, but Vinny's comment turned out to be one of them.

"What did you find out?"

"Well the first thing I learned was *Il cuor non spaglia*," he replied. "Trust your instincts."

Letting out a deep breath, Alberta looked out the window over the kitchen sink. A soft breeze filtered into the room making the yellow and white gingham curtains flutter. In the distance was Memory Lake, the lake that just yesterday had a dead body floating on top of it. The body was no longer there, but the lake contained its stain, was contaminated by it, and would be for a long time to come. Suddenly Alberta became very nervous and wasn't sure she wanted to ask what else Vinny had found out, because once you hear something you can't unhear it, you can't forget about the truth no matter how hard you try, but she knew she had to ask.

"And what's the second thing you learned?"

"Lucy didn't commit suicide, nor did she die from an accidental drowning," Vinny announced. "She was stabbed once right through the heart.

"*Dio mio*," Alberta said softly.

"Lucy Agostino was definitely murdered."

# MURDER
## on MEMORY
# LAKE

## J. D. GRIFFO

# KENSINGTON PUBLISHING CORP.
www.kensingtonbooks.com

KENSINGTON BOOKS are published by

Kensington Publishing Corp.
119 West 40th Street
New York, NY 10018

All Kensington titles, imprints, and distributed lines are available at special quantity discounts for bulk purchases for sales promotions, premiums, fund-raising, educational, or institutional use. Special book excerpts or customized print-ings can also be created to fit specific needs. For details, write or phone the office of the Kensington sales manager: Kensington Publishing Corp., 119 West 40th Street, New York, NY 10018, attn: Sales Department; phone 1-800-221-2647.

KENSINGTON BOOKS and the K logo are Reg. U.S. Pat. & TM Off.

ISBN-13: 978-1-4967-1394-0
ISBN-10: 1-4967-1394-X

First printing: August 2018

10  9  8  7  6  5  4  3  2  1

Printed in the United States of America

First electronic edition: August 2018

ISBN-13: 978-1-4967-1395-7
ISBN-10: 1-4967-1395-8

*This book and its characters are dedicated to my own loud, loving, crazy, and hilariously funny Italian family, as well as the real-life Ferraras, who —if you can believe it— are even louder and crazier.*

# ACKNOWLEDGMENTS

Special thanks to my copy editor, Cynthia Durand, for her meticulous attention to detail; my editor, John Scognamiglio, for seeing my inner Jessica Fletcher before I did; my agent, Evan Marshall, for making this happen yet again; and Linda and Audrey Ferrara (no relation to Alberta!), for acting as my unwitting muses.

# CHAPTER 1—*Alberta*

*Finchè c'e vita c'è speranza.*

There's an old Italian saying—*Finchè c'è vita c'è speranza*—that translates to *Where there's life, there's hope.*

It's a sweet, optimistic thought, one that is memorized by Italians of all ages, stored in the back of the brain, and forgotten until the difficult times arrive. Then when life becomes unbearable, when the rug, the flooring, and the earth itself, are ripped from underfoot, when the view below is all jagged rocks and open flames, it's recited as if its words contained magic.

Being an old Italian lady, Alberta knew that old Italian saying by heart. She heard her mother say it defiantly while tears gathered in her eyes, she overheard her grandmother say it to even older relatives as they simultaneously made the sign of the cross, she even heard her father mumble it once when he thought he was alone. Throughout her lifetime she had uttered it herself, more often than she could remember, each time believing with a little less fervor that its miracle properties existed. Because, unfortunately, when disappointment is the constant companion of hope, it becomes hard to believe in the power of words, even those words that are handed down from generation to generation.

After one too many disappointments, disillusion replaced faith and Alberta had to accept the hard truth that the comfort those words were supposed to bring was never going to arrive. The gift of hope, the joy of a better tomorrow, was not going to be handed to her in a beautifully wrapped package with a shiny bow. Her mother, her grandmother, even her father, who knew everything about everything, were wrong, and that well-worn saying was nothing more than *pio desiderio*—wishful thinking. Or more bluntly, a waste of time.

"I'd rather believe in the power of a good lasagna," Alberta would say, "than some *pazzo* string of words that mean nothing."

This realization struck Alberta early on in her life, in her mid-twenties, when she was a wife and mother and the world around her should have been filled with joy and wonder, when the future should have invoked feelings of curiosity instead of apathy, and the past should have made her smile instead of question her choices. But even though it was a devastating turning point, Alberta was grateful for the strength to understand the truth. Had she ignored this knowledge and kept on repeating the words *Finchè c'è vita c'è speranza*, it would have been like reciting the rosary without believing in prayer. So instead of deceiving her soul, Alberta decided to live her life without having any expectations.

Knowing her change of heart would be met with

disapproval and pity, she kept her plan of action to herself. And her silence served her well.

Day after day she toiled on in private, pushing forward, but not expecting to arrive at a place superior to the one from where she began. Surprisingly, most days were fine. Some were better than others, some were harder, just like the days experienced by everyone else around her, even those who clung to the old saying with desperate, greedy hands. The only difference was that she saw how the hopeful were constantly dejected when their lives never changed and was thankful that she didn't allow blind faith to lay heavy on her chest like an invited albatross.

Most days she had even forgotten that she had chosen to live a life devoid of hope and carried on with the chores of the living as if it were business as usual. Moments arrived, memories faded, anniversaries flew by all on their own volition without Alberta's permission or involvement. Sometimes she felt as if she were living someone else's life and fulfilling someone else's destiny, and on the rare occasions when she stopped to think about her own life's possibilities, she felt powerless to change what she considered to be inevitable. So, when those thoughts came into her head, she rolled her eyes and did something practical, like try, for the umpteenth time, to perfect one of her grandmother's recipes.

Then one day a few weeks before her sixty-fourth birthday, when Alberta was no longer a wife, but a widow, and long after her children needed a mother to survive, something quite unexpected happened— the gift of hope that decades earlier Alberta dismissed as nothing more than *pio desiderio*, as unhealthy and wasteful fantasy, finally arrived. Not on the wings of an angel, but the heels of a hearse.

At eighty-eight years old and as a nine-year resident of the Sisters of Mercy nursing home, Carmela's death wasn't unexpected, but it still caught Alberta by surprise because she thought her aunt should've died a long time ago and was surprised she had hung on for so long.

To say that Carmela was no longer engaged in life was an understatement. For the past five years she hadn't spoken a word, nor had she been able to take care of her basic bodily functions. She was being held a prisoner on earth by her own stubbornness. She slept her days away or stared out the window at the world she was no longer a part of, and during each visit Alberta couldn't understand why this woman clung on to a life she no longer was living.

"Just go already," Alberta would whisper in Carmela's ear when it was just the two of them in the room. "There is nothing left for you here, so just die for Crise sake."

If anyone overheard Alberta they would have labeled her a cruel, evil woman, but quite the opposite was true. Alberta loved her Aunt Carmela and thought she was the most courageous woman she knew, who had lived a long, if not necessarily fulfilling, life and was now doing nothing more than taking up space. A cruel thought, perhaps, but a realistic one nonetheless.

When the shock of Aunt Carmela's death wore off, Alberta hoped her words and the compassion behind them in some way helped her aunt decide it was time to stop fighting the inevitable. The only thing that shocked her more than hearing the news about her aunt's death was receiving a call from Giancarlo Mastrantonio, Jr.

"Is this Alberta Ferrara Scaglione?"

The voice on the other end of the call sounded as if it belonged to someone who had a minor role in *The Godfather*, so Alberta was immediately suspicious. It could either be a long-lost relative or some duplicitous scam artist/telemarketer, and she didn't know which was worse.

"Who's asking?"

"This is Giancarlo Mastrantonio, Jr."

The caller announced his name with such confidence, a proclamation of sorts, as if the mere mention of it should impress the listener, or at least instill a sense of recognition. It did neither.

"Who?" Alberta replied, not even trying to conceal her annoyance.

"Giancarlo Mastrantonio, Jr.," he repeated. "Esquire."

"*Ah, Madon!*" Alberta swore. "I am done talking with lawyers. My husband didn't leave me any money, so go find yourself another patsy!"

A minute after she hung up the phone it rang again, and before she could tell Mr. Mastrantonio, Jr., exactly how she felt about lawyers and exactly what he could do with his slimy law degree, he said six words that changed her life forever.

"You're inna your Aunt Carmela's will."

"What?"

"You know yourra Aunt Carmela . . . yourra father's sister . . . she, uh, she passed away," Giancarlo said delicately, as he wasn't sure if he was conveying previously unheard news.

"Of course I know my aunt died!" Alberta shouted.

"Who do you think picked out the dress she was buried in? It was her favorite, she wore it to my son Rocco's wedding."

"Oh, that was a very pretty dress," Giancarlo replied. "The yellow was a . . . how do you say . . . a *flattering* color."

"It made her look sallow!" she bellowed, then softened a bit when a memory returned. "But she loved the color and didn't care less what anyone thought, so I figured it would be perfect."

"I think you made a . . . *bene* choice, *molto bene.*"

"Yeah? Well, not everybody thought it was a good choice," Alberta replied. "My sister, Helen, thought it made her look Asian, which I told her it absolutely did not, but you know my sister, she always has to be right even when she's wrong. Wait a minute? What do you mean, I'm in Carmela's will? My aunt didn't have a will, she didn't have anything."

Then Giancarlo informed Alberta of how wrong she was about her aunt, and Alberta realized how very little she knew about the woman.

"She had how much money?!"

Alberta screamed so loudly that Giancarlo, who was wearing hearing aids, had to pull the phone away from his ear and let the high-pitched ringing noise subside before answering the question.

"I canna explain to you everything atta the reading of the will, but assa I said to you, it's a substantial sum of money," Giancarlo started. "Plussa, you have the house."

"What house?!"

Again Giancarlo let the ringing subside, while on

the other end of the line Alberta paced her kitchen as far as the phone cord would allow her to.

"The lake house," Giancarlo said. "It'sa so pretty, you gonna love it."

When Alberta hung up the phone, she thought she dreamed it all. She chalked it up to stress and didn't believe a word Giancarlo had said until she found herself a few days later sitting in his office in a black leather club chair that looked like it was more expensive than every piece of furniture she ever bought in her life. Giancarlo did look like an extra from *The Godfather*, but thankfully one who was on the good side of Don Corleone. Although Giancarlo had sounded much older than Alberta on the phone, in person he looked about forty years old.

*This one must've been born on the boat coming over,* Alberta thought. Then she looked around the office and added, *However he got to this country, he's doing a lot better than me.*

His office looked like one of those dens she saw in old movies. The walls were lined with bookshelves, stocked with rows of thick books that she couldn't imagine one person having enough time to ever read. There was an abstract painting on the wall that looked like someone splattered black and red paint on a canvas and decided to call it art, and a rug that could have been designed by the same artist covered almost the entire office floor. Alberta didn't like the decor but figured she'd have to budget for a year in order to afford the cheapest item in the room.

When Giancarlo spoke he sounded more like a longshoreman than a lawyer, and it took her a few minutes to focus on what he was telling her. But when she did, she realized that her Aunt Carmela was a stranger to her.

"So, if I understand what you're telling me, *and* you're not BS'ing me," Alberta started. "My Aunt Carmela left me everything."

"That is correct."

Perplexed, Alberta replied, "Why would she leave everything to me?"

"I'ma so glad you asked that, Mrs. Scaglione," Giancarlo said.

"Please call me Alberta."

"Ofa course, Mrs. Alberta," Giancarlo said, not quite understanding the request. He then picked up a manila envelope that was lying on his desk and opened it up with a letter opener that was so sharp Alberta thought it could double as a carving knife.

"These are your aunt's own words that she wrote down justa before she went to live at Sisters of Mercy," he explained. "I, Carmela Rosanna Ferrara, am the black sheep of my family not because I ever did anything wrong, but because I was never married and don't have any children."

"That's very true," Alberta interjected. "My father could never understand that, it broke his heart that she was a spinster. And every time he said that word he whispered it like it was a venereal disease or something French, like he was embarrassed to say the word out loud."

"Ah yes, well," Giancarlo said. "May I . . . a . . . go on?"

"Please, nobody's stopping you."

Clearing his throat, Giancarlo continued reading the letter. "But after I die and everybody learns the truth of what I have, I know all my relatives are going to come crawling out of the woodwork to try to get a piece of my estate. Over my dead body! That's the last thing that I want to have happen. To prevent that, I am putting in writing that everything that I have goes to one person. Drumroll please."

Giancarlo stopped reading and looked up at Alberta. "I don't have-a any drums, sorry."

"Not a worry," Alberta replied. "The drums are rolling in my head."

"I leave all my worldly possessions and all my money to my niece, Alberta."

So that explains it. Sort of.

"But why? Why did she single me out?" Alberta asked. "Don't get me wrong, I loved my Aunt Carmela, but we all did—well, maybe not everybody, my brother Anthony didn't like her for some reason, something about her perfume smelling like Lysol— but nobody out-and-out *hated* her. Why would she just leave everything to me?"

At this question, Giancarlo's eyes widened and he threw his hands up in the air. "I asked her the same-a question when she told me of her decision," Giancarlo said. "I said to her, I said, Carmela, what makes thisa Alberta so *speciale*, I said."

"Really?" Alberta asked, suddenly insulted by this stranger. "You asked her that?"

"Yes, because as her lawyer, that'sa my job," he replied. "And all she woulda say is thata Alberta woulda understand why."

Wrong. Alberta didn't understand at all. But even though she didn't understand her aunt's motives, she did understand that she was now an incredibly wealthy woman.

"So, she left me all her money . . ."

"Almost three million dollars, plus her stock options."

"Oh, yes, of course, the stock options, wouldn't want to forget about those," Alberta quipped. "And her lake house that nobody ever knew she had."

"Oh, and there'sa one more thing," Giancarlo said.

"There's more?"

"You can't give away any of the money for at least two years," he instructed. "Carmela wanted that part in writing because she said your natural inclination woulda be to give the money away and not spend it on yourself."

Alberta laughed out loud. "My aunt knew me like the back of her wrinkled hand, and I didn't know a thing about her."

"Your aunt, she was a very private person."

"You're telling me! I didn't think she had a dime to her name!" Alberta cried. "Not for nothing but until she moved into the nursing home she lived with my father her whole life in an apartment in an old brownstone in Hoboken over a luncheonette, and she never told anybody she had a house of her own."

"She didn't want anyone to know," Giancarlo explained. "It was her own private . . . ah, how do you say? Refuge."

Alberta turned away from the lawyer because she had the sudden urge to cry and she didn't think it was proper to cry in such a masculine setting. She wasn't holding back tears because she thought it sad that her aunt kept such a huge secret or because she needed a home of her own to seek refuge and to escape her family, Alberta was holding back tears because she knew exactly how her aunt had felt.

"So where is this house?" Alberta asked.

"On Memory Lake."

"Where the hell is that?"

"In a little town in New Jersey called . . . uh . . . Tranquility. Such a pretty name for a town."

A very pretty name and, thankfully, to Alberta, a very memorable one. Located a little more than an hour northwest of Hoboken, which was where her ancestors emigrated to after leaving Sicily for a better life in America, Tranquility was the exact opposite of the Mile Square City. While Hoboken was a dirty, boisterous, crowded city, Tranquility was a clean, quiet, sparsely populated lakeside community. It was also where her entire family would spend two glorious weeks every summer.

"We used to vacation up there!" Alberta exclaimed. "The whole family and all our friends, two weeks every summer around the Fourth of July."

"Carmela told me . . . she didn't write this part down, but she told me . . . that it was her favorite place on earth."

"And that's the name of the lake?"

"Yes, Memory Lake," Giancarlo confirmed. "You don't remember that?"

"No," Alberta answered. "We always called it the Big Lake because, well it's huge. If your cabin was on the other side of the lake you might as well be living in New York."

Alberta shook her head in disbelief. Interesting that she couldn't remember the lake's name was

Memory Lake, and even more interesting that the memory of her Aunt Carmela would be forever changed thanks to this life-altering revelation. She was so lost in thought that she didn't hear what Giancarlo said to her, but only saw him waving a set of keys in front of her eyes.

"It'sa your new home."

And that's exactly where Alberta was when her life changed yet again.

Sitting outside the gray-shingled Cape Cod with the bright yellow front door on the banks of Memory Lake in one of the faded black Adirondack chairs, which perfectly matched the faded black window shutters, holding a hot cup of coffee in her hands, her black cat, Lola, snuggled cozily in her lap, Alberta still found it hard to imagine her aunt sitting here by herself without the rest of her family milling about all around her. How odd it must have been to be here without every member of the Ferrara family, young and old, talking, laughing, eating, arguing, fighting, *living* in the same overcrowded space. Odd and yet oddly splendid. Yes, absolutely splendid. Alberta imagined that her aunt must have sat here looking at the same sun as it rose over the same crystal blue lake, the smell of hydrangeas and honeysuckle from the cluster of bushes that hugged the house adding a sweet fragrance to the air, and understood for the first time in a very long time what it felt like to be at peace.

That peace, unfortunately, was interrupted when she saw something floating on top of the lake.

With all the changes in her life recently, Alberta sometimes questioned her judgment; things she had taken for granted turned out to be wrong and things she never believed in turned out to be true. It took her almost a lifetime to understand that *Finché c'è vita c'è speranza* could be more than an empty saying. Where there is life, maybe . . . just maybe there could be hope.

That might be true for Alberta, but for the dead body floating on top of Memory Lake, all hope had definitely run out.

# CHAPTER 2 – *Jinx*

### *In bocca al lupo.*

From the moment she was born, Gina Maldonado has had luck on her side. Most of it bad.

She wasn't supposed to enter this world for another three weeks, so when her parents got the urge to play the one-armed bandits and watch some dice spin round the roulette wheel in Atlantic City they didn't think twice about hopping into their used Ford Taurus to take the two-plus-hour drive in order to satisfy their craving. After all, in a few weeks, when the baby came, they wouldn't have time to take spontaneous trips, and they could definitely use some extra money to pay for the endless baby things they were going to have to buy. Play the slots, buy a stroller, that was their mind-set when they gambled on a road trip. Gina's grandmother just thought they were out of their minds.

"*Ah, Madon!*" Alberta shouted into the phone. "You two are crazy!"

"Why are we crazy?" Alberta's daughter shouted right back. "Because we want to have some fun?"

"If you want to have fun, come with me to St. Joseph's tonight for bingo," Alberta suggested. "They're having a progressive jackpot."

"I don't like to play bingo, Ma, you know that. I like to play the slots."

"But a casino is no place for a pregnant woman!"

"Oh, for Crise sake, Ma, this isn't 1950! It's not like there's gonna be a mob hit at Harrah's on a Thursday afternoon."

After a dramatic pause, Alberta replied, "You never know."

Lisa Marie Scaglione Maldonado was used to arguing with her mother. For as long as she could remember it's what they did. They argued about important things, inconsequential things. They argued on the phone, in private, in public, when they disagreed, even when they agreed. Lisa Marie didn't know why or how it really started, but at some point, very early on in her life, she became aware that arguing and shouting was their only means of communication. It was something she grew used to, like the small, dark birthmark next to her right eyebrow. No matter how hard she tried she couldn't fix it or make it look better. The birthmark always stood out, it was always going to be a flaw, and so she accepted it, just like she accepted her relationship with her mother. Normally it didn't bother her, but ever since she had become pregnant the novelty had worn off. Maybe it was the hormones or maybe she had just grown weary from the noise, but talking to her mother had become tiresome.

As always, she should've listened to her husband, Tommy, who told her to call her mother when they got to Atlantic City. But knowing that her mother would worry if she couldn't reach her all day long, she ignored his instructions and called before they left. Now she regretted her simple act of kindness.

Pressing the phone's receiver into her forehead, Lisa Marie leaned her back against the kitchen wall, closed her eyes, and took a few deep breaths. In and out, in and out, and with each breath she prayed her relationship with the child that was squirming inside her belly wouldn't be as combative as her relationship with her own mother. Or as loud.

Lowering her voice she restarted the conversation. "Tommy thought it would be nice to take advantage of his day off so he suggested . . ."

"He has the day off on a Thursday?" Alberta interrupted.

"Yes Ma, he has off on a Thursday," Lisa Marie replied. "He's scheduled to work the weekend so he has off today and tomorrow."

"I wish he had a real job," Alberta sighed. "It would be so much easier."

Again, Lisa Marie pressed the phone receiver against her forehead, but this time there was no attempt to de-stress, no deep breathing, she gripped the phone so hard her fingers almost melded into the plastic and she had to resist the urge to slam the phone into her face. Would physical pain drown out her mother's commentary?

"A stagehand at Radio City is a real job, Ma," Lisa Marie replied, the volume of her voice no longer quite so low, "And a good one too. It's just that he's the low man on the totem pole so he doesn't get to choose his hours, you know that."

"No, of course," Alberta said. "It's just, you know . . ."

Lisa Marie couldn't resist taking the bait. "No Ma, I don't know."

And Alberta couldn't be happier reeling her daughter in. "Well, it's always a new schedule every week with him, one week he's off Thursday, the next week it's Wednesday, and . . . well, with the baby coming, things are gonna get even more hectic and the one thing that makes a baby happy, Lisa Marie, the one thing . . . is a routine. That's all I'm trying to say. A baby likes a routine."

"I know that, Ma! Don't you think I know that? And guess what? I'm gonna be the baby's routine!"

"Well good . . . that's good then! I'm glad you do, 'cause that's very important to know. And I'll be here too, of course, the two of us together will make the baby very happy," Alberta declared. "Even if Tommy's never around."

As if on cue, Tommy appeared in front of his wife and tapped his watch, indicating that he wanted to leave. It was time to end things with her mother.

"We gotta go so we beat the traffic."

"I'll be waiting outside for you to pick me up."

Before Lisa Marie could tell her mother that she wasn't invited on their husband-wife-unborn-baby spontaneous getaway, Alberta hung up. And before Lisa Marie could tell her husband that their Taurus would be taking an extra passenger along for the ride, he already knew. Unlike his wife, however, Tommy understood the financial benefit of having Alberta in the backseat.

"Cool, now I won't have to pay for gas."

* * *

What started out as a bad road trip only got worse. And by the frequency with which Gina was kicking inside her mother's belly, it was obvious that she was just as unhappy as the rest of her family.

Three car accidents on the Garden State Parkway and Lisa Marie's uncooperative bladder meant they had to sit in traffic and pull into several rest stops, extending the already long drive by almost two hours. The bickering between Lisa Marie and Alberta that had started before they left home continued to ebb and flow for the whole ride except for the time they all stopped to sing along with Journey when Lisa Marie and Tommy's wedding song came on the radio.

"Don't ever stop believin', you two," Alberta commanded over the power ballad, her eyes suddenly filled with tears. Then she muttered under her breath so they couldn't hear, "Don't wind up like me."

When they finally got to the casino it was so crowded it wasn't until after they had dinner that Lisa Marie was able to get a seat in front of her favorite slot machine—*The Wheel of Fortune*. It took much less time for her to go through all her quarters.

"Here, I won my money back," Alberta said. "I popped three cherries on the Vegas Vixen."

She poured more than half the contents of her large plastic cup into her daughter's until it was filled with fresh, if far from virgin, tokens.

"Thanks Ma, I owe ya."

Those were the words Lisa Marie spoke just as she went into labor. She knew it could not be a good sign.

Neither Lisa Marie nor Alberta could ever agree on the sequence of events that followed, but the basic gist is that Lisa Marie's water broke just as Pat Sajak's recorded voice apologized because she landed on

Bankrupt and he had to deplete her accumulated savings. Then in response to his wife's screams, Tommy started running full speed and tripped over Alberta—who was on her knees drying the floor with some tissues—banged into the slot machine, and broke his arm.

"I never liked that Vanna White!" Alberta declared, throwing the wet tissues into her pocketbook.

They got directions to the nearest hospital and with Tommy and Lisa Marie now in the backseat both writhing in their individual pains, Alberta tried to start the Taurus, but neither the car nor the weather were cooperating. Alberta's attempts to revive the broken-down car were interrupted by an explosive thunderclap followed by a torrential downpour that made it sound as if a really loud, but really bad, symphony was blasting from the radio. There were shrieks of agony from the backseat, curses of frustration from the front, and the sound of the rainstorm assaulting the exterior of the car like rapid machine-gun fire tearing through an enemy camp. They were under siege and ready to admit defeat until Lisa Marie screamed the words that reminded them of why they were there in the first place—the words you only want to hear when there is an obstetrician present: "This baby is coming!"

The Taurus might be dead, but Lisa Marie was bursting with life.

After a struggle, Alberta and her son-in-law, right arm dangling uselessly by his side, got Lisa Marie back into Harrah's while outside the downpour quickly escalated into a Nor'easter. Waterlogged, but laser focused, Alberta instructed a cocktail waitress to get some help, and a few minutes later the frazzled employee returned with the house manager and a doctor. The two men took one look at the motley crew, heard Lisa Marie's guttural cry, and knew exactly what was going on.

On the way to a back room where she could presumably give birth in private and not among the gamblers, underneath a cloud of stagnant cigarette smoke, and out of earshot of the nonstop whirl and buzz of casino sounds, Lisa Marie fell to her knees and rolled onto her back.

"It's coming! Now!"

So right there in between two rows of slot machines at thirteen minutes after midnight on Friday the thirteenth, Alberta's granddaughter was born. Despite the unorthodox setting and being three weeks premature, the doctor proclaimed that Gina was healthy and robust, and her loud cries proved his point. Staring at the newest member of their family, both parents and grandmother felt like the luckiest people in the world, as if they truly did hit the jackpot.

"Have you decided on a name?" Alberta asked.

Lisa Marie and Tommy replied at the same time, "Gina."

Hearing her granddaughter's name for the first time, Alberta kissed the gold crucifix she always wore around her neck and started to cry. "That's the most perfect name in the world."

The elderly woman at the end of the row, who saw three lemons pop up on her screen for the fourth consecutive time, didn't share that opinion.

"You shouldn't call her Gina, you should call her Jinx!" the old crone spat. "I've had nothing but bad luck since she showed up!"

Lying on the soiled carpet that was the casino floor, Lisa Marie clutched her daughter closer to her breast and started to laugh hysterically. Understanding that she wasn't having an emotional breakdown, but rather acknowledging the absurdity of the situation, Tommy and Alberta joined in. Over their raucous laughter, Lisa Marie told the crotchety old gambler that she agreed with her. "Now *that's* the most perfect name in the world!"

And that's how a stranger's random, rude comment, coupled with the specific and unfortunate timing of her birth, transformed Gina into Jinx.

Despite her nickname, it wasn't like Jinx traveled through life with a dark cloud over her head. She did, however, carry with her the memory of her birth. As a result, Alberta's favorite phrase where her granddaughter was concerned became "*In bocca al lupo!*" which literally means "into the mouth of the wolf," but is the Italian way to say "good luck." The wolf could be a difficult situation or a relentless boss, and the saying means to give strength when facing such an adversary or crisis. Jinx had learned to reply, *Crepi il lupo*—"May the wolf croak." Maybe it was because Alberta and Jinx had made this their own private saying or because it suggested bad luck would always be nipping at her daughter's heels, but Lisa Marie hated the phrase. Each time she heard it, she would scold Alberta, but like most things said by daughter to mother, it went ignored. Or overruled.

"If you would've just listened to me and stayed home that day, Jinx would've been born in a nice, clean hospital like everybody else," Alberta reminded her daughter, "But no, you had to traipse all the way down to Atlantic City to go . . . *gambling*!"

"And if only you would drop dead and leave me alone I would be a lot better off!"

The verbal sparring between Alberta and Lisa Marie that relaxed a bit after Jinx's birth, quickly resumed its ugly nature and seemed to intensify with each passing year. Jinx couldn't remember a time her mother and grandmother were in the same room together that didn't end up with both of them shouting and one of them walking out to the echo of a slammed door. No one could explain or rationalize it, but the two women just didn't get along and brought out the worst in each other. The summer before Jinx was about to start ninth grade things got much worse, and the animosity that was bubbling underneath both women rose to the surface in a heated argument that became known by the Ferrara clan and their close friends as The Fight.

There are many versions as to how The Fight started, but everyone agreed that it ended when Lisa Marie told Alberta to go to hell. On its own, the comment wasn't terribly shocking—the words themselves had been uttered by both women many times before— but there was something in Lisa Marie's eyes and something about her demeanor that gave new weight to the volatile phrase. Had Alberta remained silent or stormed out of the house, perhaps nothing would have changed, but she didn't. Almost sensing that Lisa Marie had raised the bar on their ongoing feud, Alberta instinctively upped the ante. When she responded in a calm voice and with a steely glare, it was a combination that, as far as Lisa Marie was concerned, put an end to their relationship.

"Where do you think I've lived my entire life?"

Shortly thereafter, Jinx found herself reluctantly moving with her parents and younger brother, Sergio, to Florida. And not the fun part of Florida near the ocean or Disney World, but a town named Eufala in the landlocked portion of the state that's geographically closer to Alabama than to real Florida. She hated everything about it except its name, which she thought sounded ironically and appropriately like an Italian curse word. But it was nothing like New Jersey and nothing like where Jinx dreamed she would grow up. She felt as if her life was finally living up to her nickname.

Distance helped her mother stay true to her conviction, and soon it was as if Grandma Alberta never existed. She wasn't mentioned in conversation and her photos were mysteriously absent from the rest of the family pictures that were scattered around their new home. Eeriest of all, her mother grew quieter. Without Alberta to battle, Lisa Marie no longer had a reason to shout. Jinx was certain her mother would miss their squabbling, not to mention the volume of her own voice, and cart the family back to Jersey, but that never happened.

When Jinx was applying to college she specifically chose a few Northeastern schools hoping to get back to the life and grandmother that she missed, but her mother, sensing her daughter's true motives, put the kibosh on that possibility and told her that they couldn't afford anything more than a local community college. Not wanting to wind up with a relationship that mirrored the fractured connection between her mother and grandmother, Jinx didn't fight what she knew was a lie. She agreed to attend nearby Chipola

College, and four years later graduated summa cum laude with a journalism degree.

But the moment she had her diploma, she knew her time as a Floridian and a dutiful daughter had come to an end. Yearlong sunshine was nice, but so was home, and that's where Jinx wanted to return.

*"In bocca al lupo."*

Jinx was surprised to hear her mother use that phrase when she told her she was moving back to New Jersey, but Lisa Marie simply said, "That's where you're going, isn't it? Right into the mouth of the wolf?"

Ignoring her mother largely because she knew she was never going to change her mind where her grandmother was concerned, Jinx just hugged her tightly and told her that it would be wonderful if she came up for a visit. She expected her mother to scream at her for daring to make such a comment, but she was pleasantly surprised when all she received was silence and a raised eyebrow. Maybe her luck was changing after all.

And it did begin to change and all for the better.

In short order, Jinx found an apartment, a room-mate, and a job as a reporter for *The Upper Sussex Herald*, the paper that covered the news for all the towns in Sussex County. She knew it was fate when she found out that her grandmother was living in one of those towns—Tranquility—the same lakeside com-munity where she vacationed as a young girl and still had such wonderful memories. She hadn't embarked on a foolish journey. She was meant to reestablish a relationship with her grandmother, one of the people who had witnessed her auspicious entrance into this world. Nothing could possibly go wrong now.

When she saw two police cars parked in her grandmother's driveway, she feared something had, in fact, gone horribly wrong. When she saw her grandmother was fine and standing next to a cop, she was greatly relieved. But when she saw the wet dead body of the woman on the ground at their feet, she knew that her luck had given out. The wolf had followed her back home.

# CHAPTER 3–
## *Alberta & Jinx*

**Loda il mare e tienti alla terra.**

"Oh my God! Everybody was right!" Jinx screamed. "I really am a jinx!"

Startled by the outburst, Alberta and the young cop both turned around and were surprised to see Alberta's granddaughter staring back at them. They were both not only startled, but unhappy. Alberta because she didn't want Jinx to be so close to death, and the cop because he knew he was going to get into trouble for allowing someone to stumble onto the crime scene.

"Jinx!" Alberta shouted. "Oh honey, no, don't look!"

Too late. The image of the dead woman's soaking wet body had already seared itself into Jinx's brain. Lying on the grass without one of those police-issued body bags covering her up, the dead woman was fully exposed, and Jinx's impulse to look away was thwarted by curiosity.

The only dead bodies she'd ever seen before were in caskets, and thanks to embalming fluid and strategic posing they always looked artificial and often bore little resemblance to how they looked when they were alive. This body was an example of death untouched, and Jinx couldn't help but think it was beautiful, that she was bearing witness to the true essence of Nature without human interference.

The woman's hands weren't unnaturally crossed in front of her chest clutching a rosary, her eyelids weren't glued shut, her face wasn't spread wide making the skin look as if it was being pulled down by some carefully hidden industrial-strength tape. This woman, despite being dead, looked more alive than any coffin-confined corpse Jinx had ever seen.

Her eyes were open and staring directly into the morning sunshine, her hair splayed out around her head like a tangled mass of black and gray as if she just stepped out of the shower. Her skin, lined and creased with age, didn't resemble a solid rock carved with facial features, and hung loose around her neck. Most interesting, however, were her arms and hands.

Instead of being forced into the prayer position in an attempt to convince Saint Peter that she was willing to accept her fate, her arms fell at her side and her fingers curved slightly downward so it looked like her hands were digging into the grass. It was probably rigor mortis settling in, but she seemed to be clutching the earth, and Jinx got the distinct impression that this woman did not want to leave the world of the living just yet. Jinx had never considered herself to be morbid, but staring into the face of uncensored death for the first time, she couldn't help but find the unexpected turn of events fascinating.

The cop, playing bodyguard to the dead woman, merely found Jinx's presence to be a nuisance.

"I'm sorry, Miss, but I have to ask you to leave," Detective Miyahara commanded in a voice too high-pitched to be commanding. "This is an active police investigation and you're trespassing."

As if working in tandem, Alberta, holding an unfazed Lola in her arms, and the detective shifted their positions to stand in front of the dead body to block Jinx's view. *How cute,* Jinx thought, *they feel as if they need to protect me, but how wrong.*

"I'm not trespassing," she stated. "This is my grandmother, and we have a standing date for breakfast every Wednesday morning." To illustrate her point, she held up the paper bag she was carrying. "In here is her favorite breakfast treat. Tell 'em, Gram, tell 'em what's in here."

Alberta's eyes lit up with anticipation. "You got one?"

"Of course I did," Jinx replied. "I made sure I got to Vitalano's early because they always sell out."

"Oh, you're such a good girl," Alberta gushed.

"I keep telling Joey that he has to make more, meet demand with supply, but he keeps saying that if he makes more they'll no longer be special," Jinx said. "Which makes sense from a purely creative standpoint, though not a financial one."

"Such a good girl," Alberta repeated, then turned to Detective Miyahara and asked rhetorically, "Isn't she such a good girl?"

Clinging to the last ounce of his patience, the detective answered, "Honestly, I have no idea if she's good or not, all I know is that she's trespassing."

"I already told you I'm not trespassing. Are you deaf?" Jinx asked. "She's my grandmother, and I practically live here, so if anybody's trespassing it's you."

"Me?"

"Yes, you," Jinx answered. "I only have *two* Nutella-filled croissants . . ."

"My favorite! It reminds me of my childhood," Alberta interrupted, reveling in the memory. "I used to watch my Grandma Marie make them fresh. I've tried, but I just can't make them like her. I'm good in the kitchen, but . . ."

"She's *very* good in the kitchen," Jinx corrected.

"Thank you, lovey," Alberta said. "With regular food I'm good . . . lasagna, ravioli, *giambotta*, even a meatloaf . . . but baking and desserts, no, I could never master that like my grandmother, she was the best."

"Oh come on, Gram, you're being modest, your anisette cookies with the rainbow sprinkles are delicious."

"Because you never tasted Grandma Marie's!"

"True, but I can't imagine they're any better than Grandma Alberta's."

Alberta beamed. She didn't care about the compliment, she only cared that she was sharing the morning with her granddaughter after so many years of separation. Even if their weekly morning ritual was being interrupted by a detective and a dead woman. The detective, on the other hand, wanted his crime scene to have one less intruder.

"Now look, I'm not going to ask you again," he started, his voice reaching an even higher pitch. "You need to leave."

"And I'm not going to tell you again that I have more right to be on this property than you," Jinx replied. "I only have two croissants, one for me and one for my grandma, which leaves none for you, so there's no need for you to stay."

The detective looked at Alberta for help, but she just smiled and readjusted Lola in her arms, cradling her like a newborn. It wasn't a ladylike position, but Lola hardly had the temperament of a lady. The detective realized it was two against one. He tried to remember his training, which was to remain calm and in control no matter how uncooperative civilians might get during an investigation. But the problem with Detective Kichiro Miyahara was that despite all the sensitivity training he'd had to endure throughout the course of his career, one simple fact always got in the way: He much preferred dead people than the living.

"If you don't leave now, I'm going to have you arrested!"

In his frustrated fury, Kichiro's voice reached such a high pitch that he sounded like a soprano at the end of a particularly trying aria. It was a sound that Lola found so delightful she tried to mimic it with her own high-pitched meow. Jinx thought the whole situation was so funny she almost laughed in Kichiro's face until she remembered she really did have the right to stay.

"Wait a second, you can't arrest me!" Jinx shouted, then proudly declared, "I'm a journalist."

"That's right, you are," Alberta confirmed. "I keep forgetting that."

Kichiro examined Jinx thoroughly and thought the reason Alberta kept forgetting her granddaughter was a journalist was because her granddaughter looked nothing like a journalist, at least none that he had ever met. Her long, jet-black hair fell in waves around her face and extended well below her shoulders. There was no way it looked like that first thing in the morning after a night's sleep. She must've spent hours blow-drying it to get it to look so perfect. Her makeup was soft and minimal, but he knew from watching his own girlfriend get ready for a date that it took longer to achieve the I'm-hardly-wearing-any-makeup-look than it did to pile on the cosmetics.

And while her clothes were appropriate for mid-July, they were all wrong for a reporter. She wore a green sleeveless cotton top, trimmed in eyelet lace that skimmed the top of her formfitting jeans, which were cuffed up to show her ankle and make her three-inch-heel brown leather sandals stand out even more. The detective was convinced she was lying because there was no way a journalist would wear such high heels. What if she had to run somewhere to catch a scoop? No, this woman was far too pretty and far too pre-occupied with how she looked to be a real journalist.

"You don't look like a journalist," the detective announced.

"You don't sound like a detective," the journalist replied.

"Well, I am."

"I am too. So there."

Alberta shook her head, a little amused but also a little disgusted. All three of them had been ignoring what was right in front of them. Or in this case, what was right at their feet.

"Now that that's settled," Alberta said. "Could we please deal with Lucy?"

"Who's Lucy?" the detective and the journalist jointly asked.

"Lucy Agostino!" Alberta told them. "The dead lady on my lawn!"

Jinx and Kichiro were both stunned to find out that the corpse had a name, and one that Alberta knew.

"You know her?" the detective and Jinx asked, again in unison.

"Of course I know her," Alberta replied. "I never liked her, but I knew her all the same."

There was no reason that Jinx should be surprised by this revelation since there were decades of her grandmother's life that were a mystery to her. She hardly knew anything about her childhood, her early married life, and nothing at all during the years she was involuntarily sequestered in Florida. Still, this announcement that her grandmother and the dead woman were somehow linked was spooky. Journalistic instinct faded and Jinx was overwhelmed with the feeling that she would rather be sitting at the kitchen table with her grandmother eating Nutella-filled croissants, petting Lola, and gossiping rather than standing outside in the morning sunshine discussing her grandmother's relationship with the recently deceased Lucy Agostino. Contrary to her pronouncement, Jinx was still more granddaughter than reporter.

"Seriously, Gram," Jinx began. "You know . . . I mean, you *knew* this woman?"

Glancing at Lucy's inanimate body, Alberta was overcome with a flood of memories. And even though she was deeply saddened to see someone she once knew dead, none of the memories were pleasant.

There was a memory of Lucy pushing seven-year-old Alberta off the seesaw on the playground at St. Ann's elementary school and Alberta screaming when she broke her arm. Then Lucy pointing her finger at Alberta, laughing wildly and encouraging a group of girls to do the same because Alberta had been unlucky enough to wake up with a cluster of ugly pimples on her nose the day of the Immaculate Conception High School Junior Prom. And the flashbacks concluded with a final picture of Lucy standing in front of Alberta and her husband, Sammy, telling them both that she was sorry their picture in the local paper announcing their wedding made Alberta look so fat. No one would argue that Lucy Agostino had been a thorn in Alberta's side her entire life, especially not Alberta. And no one, especially Alberta, would also argue that after all the years of being her nemesis it wasn't ironic she should wind up dead on Alberta's property. Karma, like Lucy, really was a bitch.

"I knew Lucy almost my whole life," Alberta confirmed. Then she pointed at the man walking toward them and said, "And *Dio mio!* So did he."

"Chief!" Kichiro cried. "Thank God."

"Looks like we got ourselves a little reunion," Vinny announced.

"Vinny D'Angelo?" Alberta said, dumbfounded. "What in the world are you doing here?"

"Alberta Scaglione, I'm disappointed in you," he said. "Don't you recognize your own chief of police?"

"Chief of police?" Alberta questioned. "You?"

"Don't act so surprised," he said. "People change."

Still confused, Alberta replied, "True, but I never imagined you would follow in your father's footsteps."

Smiling wistfully, Vinny said, "Sometimes a kid doesn't have a choice."

Although Vinny D'Angelo came from a long line of blue bloods and was Tranquility's chief of police, whose jurisdiction included several of the neighboring small towns in the county, it was not his first career choice. It unfortunately was the only realistic one.

At six feet four and built like a linebacker, Vinny looked like someone who would be a natural-born protector, but he was actually a natural-born voyeur and preferred to hang out in the shadows. He was more adept at watching events unfold than participating in them, and as a young man had wanted to become a writer. Unable to afford the college tuition needed to fulfill his dream, Vinny reluctantly accepted the path his father, his grandfather, two of his uncles, and even a female cousin had taken before him, and became a cop. Surprisingly, it was a decent fit.

As a cop in a small town, most of the time he and his small ten-person police force simply watched what was going on around them or listened to eyewitness accounts of petty wrongdoings and misdemeanors. Rarely did Vinny have to participate in the action, and that suited him just fine. Less real police interaction gave him more time to reflect.

Early on as a rookie cop he started to keep a journal, which he still maintained on a daily basis. Some entries were a mere cataloging of events, others were his personal reflections on crimes and criminals, both the interesting and the mundane, that went well beyond the department-sanctioned accounts he'd been required to submit. It had always been his hope that he would turn the long-running record of what he'd witnessed over the course of nearly four decades on the force into a novel when he retired. Until then he would continue to deal with the current police matters, and the first on the list involved Tranquility's newest resident.

"I heard you moved into Carmela's old place," Vinny stated. "Such a beautiful house."

"I guess I shouldn't be surprised that you knew my aunt owned all this, being the man in charge and all," Alberta said. "But I'm still in a bit of shock that it's mine now. Or that you're standing in my backyard."

"I've been meaning to come over and say hello, but . . . well, you know how it is," Vinny replied apologetically. "Sorry it took police business to get me to visit."

"Regardless of the circumstances, it's wonderful to see an old friend."

"Grandma," Jinx started. "Seriously . . . you know the chief of police too?"

"Know him?" Alberta replied, letting out a huge laugh. "I babysat him and his little brat of a sister."

"Correction," Vinny said. "You babysat my bratty sister, Frannie, and I just happened to be in the house at the same time."

"That's true, you were the good one," Alberta confessed. "Francesca was such an *istigatore* . . . a troublemaker! The second I turned my head she was trying to burn down the house."

"She wanted to cook like you?" Jinx asked.

"No! She liked to play with matches," Alberta replied.

"My sister had a thing about fire," Vinny added. "Luckily she grew out of that phase once she discovered boys."

Vinny took a moment to rediscover Alberta and smiled. "It's good to see you again."

Alberta smiled back. "It's good to see you, too, Vinny. Even if this is an official visit."

At the same time all four of their heads snapped to look at Lucy, who of course was still sprawled out on the grass, awaiting the arrival of some other members of the Tranquility police force to escort her to the morgue.

*"Loda il mare e tienti alla terra,"* Vinny whispered.

"What was that, Chief?" Kichiro asked.

Nodding her head, Alberta answered, "A little Italian saying. It means, 'Praise the sea, but keep on land.'"

Vinny bent down closer to Lucy, and the shadow of his hulking frame seemed to swallow up her lifeless body. Although his career was spent mostly giving tickets to speeding drivers and hunters trying to get a jumpstart on deer season, he, of course, had seen a few dead bodies up close and personal. He was grateful that it never got easier, he didn't want to lose that part of himself to the job that had already taken so much of his life.

He wanted to close Lucy's eyes so she would look as if she was sleeping, but he wasn't wearing gloves and didn't want to tamper with the body. He doubted it would make any difference to the medical examiner, but he was a cop, after all, and cops had to follow the rules. "No matter how beautiful a body of water looks, the sea, the ocean, a lake, it's still a dangerous place," Vinny muttered almost to Lucy's spirit, "Better to keep your feet planted firmly on the ground."

"I couldn't agree more," Alberta said, holding Lola closer to her chest.

Standing up, Vinny turned to the others to announce, "Looks like a pretty simple case of drowning to me." Looking at his detective, he asked, "But any witnesses, Kich?"

"Just Mrs. Scaglione," the detective answered. "She called 911 when she saw the body floating in the lake."

"Mrs. Scaglione," Vinny scoffed good-naturedly. "Not for nothing, but you'll always be Alfie to me."

"And you, Vinny D'Angelo, will always be wrong."

"Wait a minute . . . *Alfie?*" Jinx asked.

"Vinny thinks he and everything he says is clever," Alberta said. "Always has."

"It *is* clever and so am I," Vinny replied, laughing. "The first two letters of your grandma's first and last names, *A, l, f, e* . . . add it up, it's Alfie."

"That's such a cool nickname, Gram," Jinx declared. "I love it!"

Still laughing, Vinny admitted, "Alfie doesn't share your opinion."

"Please, I don't care what you call me," Alberta said waving a hand in front of her face. "I meant you're wrong about Lucy."

Confused, Vinny lifted his chin and scrunched up his forehead. "What are you talking about Alfie?"

"Just what I said, you're wrong about Lucy."

"I am not wrong about Lucy."

"Yes, you are!" Alberta implored. "Just like you were

wrong when you said Peter Lemongello was gonna be the next Sinatra."

"Peter fooled a lot of us, Alfie," Vinny said. "He had an amazing voice."

"That might be true, but you want to know what else is true?"

"What?"

"Lucy didn't drown, she was murdered," Alberta announced. "And not for nothing, I can prove it."

# CHAPTER 4

*Il cuor non spaglia.*

Alberta was not a violent person. Loud, argumentative, disagreeable, and frustrating, but never violent. It's just not what good little Italian girls did. And Alberta was a good little Italian girl who had grown up to become a good little Italian woman. Violence was a man's territory. Whether that be joining the mafia or manhandling a woman, Alberta detested such glorifications of violence and, luckily, physical brutality had never been a part of her life. Explosions of emotional strife and struggle were like landmines in her world, inescapable and never where you'd expect to find them, but she considered that to be normal. Families fight, but people shouldn't kill, that could be Alberta's motto.

And yet standing over Lucy's dead body forced Alberta to face violence head-on as she was certain that Lucy's body was lifeless for only one reason: murder.

Alberta shivered and let her cheek press against the warmth of Lola's fur. She had been living here for less than a month and already brutality had visited her doorstep. Was it an omen? Did Carmela's unexpected gift carry with it some curse like King Tut's tomb and was Alberta destined to find herself in the eye of some violent storm for the rest of her life just because her aunt showered her with such wealth? If this was going to be the price she'd have to pay, Alberta was ready to give it all up. First, however, she needed to answer one very important question.

"What do you mean you can prove that Lucy was murdered?" Vinny asked.

Startled back to reality, Alberta handed Lola off to Jinx so she could speak with her hands as well as her mouth. "Just look at her," she answered, spreading her hands wide apart and gesturing at Lucy's unmoving body. "It can't be any clearer than if she had a sign pinned to her forehead that said, 'I'm a Murder Victim' written in her own blood."

Vinny placed his hands on his hips and puffed up his chest so his upper body looked even broader and more powerful than it actually was. It was one of the pieces of body language that he had perfected over the years to intimidate suspects and untrustworthy witnesses. Since Tranquility wasn't a hotbed of crime, he didn't get to use it very often, but he was happy to know that this particular physicality was still part of his bag of cop tricks. Towering over Alberta's five-foot-five frame, he could see the gray roots on top of her head refuse to disappear completely underneath her dyed black hair. He didn't want Alberta to cower in his presence, but he did want to remind her that he was in charge.

"Alfie, I think you've watched one too many episodes of *Law & Order*," Vinny said dismissively. "I can't believe you think this is a murder scene."

Even though it had been many years since they were

last in each other's company and to the untrained eye Vinny did look borderline menacing, she knew the man far too well and for far too long for familiarity to be replaced with fear. "And I can't believe you can't see the truth, Vinny," she continued. "This is the corpse of a murdered woman."

Vinny and his detective shared a look of frustration that neither one of them tried to conceal.

"How can you tell that just by looking at her?" Kichiro asked.

"*Madonna mia!*" Alberta exclaimed. "Because she's wearing a navy blue suit, that's why!"

Frustration was quickly replaced by bewilderment. And the feeling wasn't exclusive to Vinny and Kichiro, Jinx shared it as well.

"Gram, it's a nice suit and all," Jinx said in a placating tone, "but I hardly doubt someone would kill her for it."

Alberta sighed and realized that her granddaughter as well as the two men in the blue uniforms looked at life primarily with their eyes and not with their minds. For a moment she was reminded of her husband and she felt her chest tighten. She had spent her entire married life with a man who could only see with his eyes, and it was not always a pleasant experience. Smiling, but shaking her head dismissively, she tried to explain. "*Il cuor non spaglia.*" It was not a very well-received explanation.

"Again with the Italian!" Kichiro shouted, raising his arms in the air so he looked very Italian himself. "Is it too much to ask you to keep confusing us in only one language?"

"Trust your instincts," Alberta translated. "Don't they teach you that at the police academy?"

"They teach us to trust evidence and the facts," Vinny said, trying not to make the tone of his voice sound as condescending as he knew it did. Alberta might be trying his patience, but she was still an old friend and deserved his respect. Alberta didn't feel quite the same way.

"Well they're teaching you how to be *tonto* . . . stupid is what they're doing," she replied.

Just as Kichiro was about to say something that was definitely going to be interpreted as disrespectful in more than one language, Vinny held up his hand to silence him. Part of being a cop meant listening to comments from the public, even if those comments weren't necessarily positive or constructive. But regardless of how strongly he believed in the value of the police–citizen relationship, even he was beginning to lose his calm demeanor.

"Alfie, if you have something to say, will you just please say it?" Vinny demanded.

"From the time we started kindergarten at St. Ann's until the day we graduated from Immaculate Conception High School, Lucy and I wore the same uniforms. They were practically identical . . . white shirts with navy blue crisscross ties, navy blue vests, navy blue skirts, and navy blue socks. The only other color was a little gold patch on the vest," Alberta finished by throwing her hands into the air like an animated maestro. "*Capisce?*"

No *capisce*, only crickets. Alberta paused, confident that once this information sunk in, she would be applauded for her clever deduction. But when she saw the baffled looks on the faces of her three audience members, she knew she would have to resume her performance.

"Lucy hated navy blue, hated it with a passion!" Alberta exclaimed. "I remember her telling me once in twelfth grade that after she graduated she was never, *ever* going to wear navy blue again. Then of course she had to tell me that I shouldn't wear it either because it didn't go with my olive complexion . . . which is a complete lie because I look very good in navy blue, thank you very much, but Lucy hated the color."

Once again Alberta's reasoning was met with silence and bewilderment and not the path to understanding she had hoped it would. Vinny didn't have to confer with the group to take on the role of their spokesperson.

"So help us understand, Alfie, just how do you go from Lucy hating navy blue to Lucy being murdered?"

Once again Alberta was reminded of her husband. How many times had he stared at her with a blank face, unable to figure out what she was talking about even when she was speaking in plain English? Or plain Italian, which was Sammy's native tongue. It was frustrating then and it was frustrating now, the only difference being that then she had to keep her mouth shut in order to maintain order in her marriage; widowhood had helped her find her voice.

"Lucy never wore navy blue, for Crise sake!" she shouted. "So if Lucy committed suicide or had an accident, she changed her clothes *after* she died because there's no way she'd be caught dead in that outfit she has on right there."

They all looked at Lucy dressed in her navy blue business suit and the irony of Alberta's words was not lost on any of them, even Alberta. However Lucy died, she was indeed caught dead wearing the color she loathed. But could that fashion faux pas possibly have been fatal? Could the color of her outfit be a clue to how she really died? Or could Alberta simply be projecting her own personal and vicious desires as to how the deceased became deceased?

"Maybe it just makes you happier to think that Lucy was brutally murdered."

"Like I said, Vinny, I never liked Lucy Agostino," Alberta admitted. "But that doesn't mean I wanted to see her dead by accident or by murder."

Backtracking a little from his rather blunt comment, Vinny replied, "Well I'm not saying you had anything to do with it . . ."

"You better not be accusing my grandmother of anything like that," Jinx interrupted.

It was wonderful to be protected even if it was unnecessary. Alberta wrapped her arm around Jinx's waist and felt her warm skin next to hers. "He wasn't implying anything, lovey, he's just trying to assert his power. But he forgets that I could rattle off several examples that would prove that Vinny wasn't Lucy's biggest fan either."

Embarrassed, Vinny forgot about trying to look intimidating and tilted his head to the side, putting his hands on his hips like an overgrown boy and pouting because he wasn't allowed to stay up past his bedtime. "Now come on, Alfie, that's not true and you know it."

"Class field trip to Philadelphia in 1970," Alberta said, raising her eyebrows suggestively. "Ring a bell?"

"What happened in Philly in 1970?" Kichiro asked, more than a little interested. "And just what kind of bells did you ring?"

"None of your business," Vinny barked. "And if you open your mouth any further Alfie, I swear to God . . ."

"I'm not going to say a word," she replied, relishing her ability to make an old friend squirm. "All's I'm gonna say is that by the time we got back on the school bus to come home, you wanted to see Lucy dead too."

It was Kichiro's turn to whine. "That's not fair! Tell us what happened."

"Go see what's taking so long," Vinny instructed. "It's time to get Lucy to the morgue."

Once again Alberta was ripped from the past and planted right smack-dab in the present. Lucy Agostino was dead, and she somehow died in Alberta's lake, the lake she looked at every night before going to bed and every morning when she got up. The expansive Memory Lake was more than just a body of water to Alberta, it was a symbol of how peaceful and bountiful her life could be. After years of stagnating and moving through life as if she were wearing cement blocks for shoes, she had now been given the opportunity to float and glide through life, like a lightweight boat skimming over the water's surface. But thanks to Lucy, that image was marred. Now when Alberta looked out at the lake the first thing she'd see wouldn't be promise and hope, but the floating dead body of a longtime nemesis. She had to hand it to Lucy, she got the last laugh. She was able to annoy Alberta throughout her life, and found a way to do so even after death.

The next day after the medical examiner performed the autopsy on Lucy, Vinny was forced to use the same accolade about Alberta.

"You were right, Alfie," Vinny said on the phone. "You're a very clever girl."

Since Alberta was cooking dinner, her focus was on her recipe, so Vinny's words didn't make much sense, as she didn't know what he was referring to. "What are you talking about? I'm in the middle of making gravy, there's nothing clever about that."

"You were right about Lucy."

Few things could distract Alberta from her cooking, Vinny's comment turned out to be one of them.

"What did you find out?"

"Well the first thing I learned was *Il cuor non spaglia*," he replied. "Trust your instincts."

Letting out a deep breath, Alberta looked out the window over the kitchen sink. A soft breeze filtered into the room making the yellow and white gingham curtains flutter. In the distance was Memory Lake, the lake that just yesterday had a dead body floating on top of it. The body was no longer there, but the lake contained its stain, was contaminated by it, and would be for a long time to come. Suddenly Alberta became very nervous and wasn't sure she wanted to ask what else Vinny had found out, because once you hear something you can't unhear it, you can't forget about the truth no matter how hard you try, but she knew she had to ask.

"And what's the second thing you learned?"

"Lucy didn't commit suicide, nor did she die from an accidental drowning," Vinny announced. "She was stabbed once right through the heart."

"*Dio mio,*" Alberta said softly.

"Lucy Agostino was definitely murdered."

# CHAPTER 5

*Il frutto cade non lontano dall'albero.*

"Should we really be eating at a time like this?" Jinx asked, her mouth full of chicken cacciatore.

"Just because somebody's dead, we're not supposed to eat?" Alberta asked rhetorically. "*Mangia!* And that goes double for you, Lola, you're getting too skinny."

Whether Lola purred in defiance or agreement no one knew, but at least she didn't turn her nose up at her meal like she normally did. One whiff of the cut-up chicken Alberta prepared and the cat started to devour her plate. Jinx, however, was proving to be a much more finicky eater.

"Well, Gram, somebody didn't just die, somebody was, you know, murdered."

Alberta still couldn't believe that a woman she'd known since childhood, her longtime nemesis, the one and only Lucy Agostino had actually been murdered. People die all the time, it's a natural course of life that nobody can escape regardless of how hard they try, because in the end death always wins, whether it be from disease or an accident, but murder? That's just not how it's supposed to be, especially in an idyllic lakeside community like Tranquility.

It would've shocked Alberta had she only read about Lucy's death in the newspaper or overheard it as a piece of local gossip on the checkout line at the ShopRite, but she had been a witness to Lucy's death. No, she didn't see the murder itself take place, but she was presumably the first person, after whoever killed Lucy of course, to see her dead body, and that was close enough to have rattled her nerves.

God must really be a comedian, Alberta thought, a regular Don Rickles, because no one else in the world would've brought these two women together in such an everlasting way. Before yesterday, Alberta didn't care if she ever saw Lucy again, not since the last time their paths crossed, which ironically was at the wake of a mutual relative—Alberta's sister-in-law's cousin's husband's grandfather and Lucy's uncle's brother-in-law's cousin's father—but now they were eternally intertwined, forever linked like Lucy and Ethel or Lucy and Charlie Brown, and now, ladies and gentle-men, Lucy and Alberta. It just wasn't fair.

Why couldn't Lucy—the Italian, not the redhead or the cartoon character—have been found dead in somebody else's lake, on somebody else's property? Why did she have to end her time on this earth in the one place that Alberta expected would bring her peace and comfort for the rest of her life, the one place she could finally call her own? Why did Lucy have to show up *not breathing* in Alberta's own backyard? She really didn't have to ponder those questions for too long before she knew the answer: Lucy Agostino was a ballbuster.

Alberta didn't know if Lucy had a say in the matter, but it was as if God asked her to pick the last place on the planet where she'd like her body to be found and he put her there. Because as much as Alberta didn't like Lucy, Lucy liked Alberta even less. Why? Alberta had no idea. All she knew was from the moment Lucy laid eyes on Alberta in grammar school, Lucy decided she didn't like her. It wasn't a passing phase, it was a lifelong grudge. And no matter what Alberta did, she was never able to change Lucy's mind.

In the beginning she tried to ignore her, but that only got Lucy angrier. Then she tried to fight back, but Lucy only fought back harder. As they grew older Alberta tried to appease her and do what her mother always did with her father, *calmare la acque*—keep the peace—but that only resulted in Lucy calling Alberta weak, *donna debole*, and, of course, many less respectful names. And while it wasn't as if Lucy bullied Alberta every single day of her life, it was still a well-known fact to everyone who knew them both that the two just didn't get along for reasons that were unknown to everyone. It was just accepted that Lucy was oil, Alberta was water, and never the twain should mix. Until now.

Try as she might to have a nice dinner with her granddaughter, Alberta couldn't get Lucy's dead body out of her mind no matter how delicious her chicken cacciatore tasted. And it made sense because she had watched two men place Lucy's corpse in a body bag, zip it up, and carry it away. Even though she hadn't seen or sparred with that body in years, it was as if they had carted off a piece of Alberta too. While Alberta sat on a chair at the round, wooden kitchen table that her father had built—one of the few pieces of furniture she brought with her when she moved in—a tiny piece of her was miles away, cuddling up next to Lucy on the metal slab at the morgue that was Lucy's temporary home. The thought of it made Alberta shudder. Maybe it was because of her age and the fact that she was technically in the final stage of her own life, but as much as Alberta didn't like Lucy, she hated to think of her all alone in that little compartment. Alberta chuckled to herself. Of course God had a role in all this, how else would He have gotten Alberta to have sympathy for Lucy, if not to make her the one to find the body. Then again, maybe God had nothing to do with it.

"I bet this is all because Lucy's still giving me the *malocchio*!" Alberta declared.

"The *what*?"

"The *malocchio* . . . the evil eye," Alberta explained.

"Oh my God," Jinx exclaimed with a mouthful of chicken. "I haven't heard that word in years."

"Well it's always there, the *malocchio*, and now it all makes sense," Alberta said. "That's why I was the one who found Lucy outside my back door. She put the evil eye on my head when she was alive, why not put the *malocchio* on me from beyond the grave? Destroy my peace and make me be a part of her death for the rest of my life." Shaking her head, Alberta started to laugh, "*Dio mio*, that's just like Lucy."

"If you say so, Gram, but I still wonder who killed her," Jinx mused, then added, "Could you pass the cheese?"

Startled, Alberta hesitated before handing the bowl of Parmesan to her granddaughter. She wasn't startled because she found Jinx's comment inappropriate dinner chatter—coming from a large Italian family she knew that very few topics fell under such a category—she was startled because that thought hadn't yet popped into her head. She was so consumed with the fact that someone she knew for decades was murdered she never took a second to consider that someone else had to have committed the murder. Because where there's a murder, there has to be a murderer, and if Alberta knew the murder victim, maybe she also knew the murder suspect? Unfortunately, since Lucy was not a very likable person, the list of suspects could be quite long.

"It could be anybody, I guess," Alberta inferred. "I lost track of her these past years, but she didn't have a lot of friends when we were younger."

Scooping up some gravy with a piece of crunchy semolina bread, Jinx said, "Just because you don't have a lot of friends, doesn't mean you have a lot of enemies. Or, you know, just one who hates you enough to kill you."

Jinx swallowed and Alberta noticed that her expression had changed. She looked more like the confused teenager who was forced to move to Florida than the confident young woman who had returned to her doorstep. "Grandma, do you really think someone hated her enough to kill her?"

Clearly the short answer was yes, but Alberta was unwilling to destroy her granddaughter's innocence. Jinx was no longer a child, but in Alberta's eyes she would always be a little girl. "I don't know, lovey," she hedged. "Let's leave questions like those for the police to answer."

\* \* \*

"Jinx, I don't care how many times you ask me, the answer is still going to be no!"

"Why?"

"Because I said so, that's why!"

Jinx wasn't having a conversation with her grandmother or her mother or any member of her family for that matter, she was talking to her boss, Troy Wycknowski, who, like Jinx, had had his very own nickname since the day he was born—Wyck. It was the main reason Wyck hired Jinx on the spot when she interviewed to be a reporter for *The Upper Sussex Herald,* the county paper for which he served as editor-in-chief. Since they shared a common denominator, having been given nicknames for reasons that were beyond their control, Jinx's birth and Wyck's surname, Wyck held a special fondness for Jinx. Even though they had only known each other for a short time, as the father of three boys, he had quickly begun to think of Jinx as the daughter he never had. At the moment, he acknowledged that his adopted daughter was entering her rebellious stage.

"Come on, Wyck!" Jinx pressed. "This is a no-brainer! There's been a murder, there's going to be a murder investigation, and I'm related to an eyewitness."

Wyck kept his eyes on his computer screen to maintain an air of indifference, but Jinx knew she was starting to make a dent in his steely demeanor, because his cheeks were getting almost as red as the unruly mop of hair on top of his head. And that only happened when he got excited about a hot story. "Your grandmother actually witnessed the murder?" Wyck asked, a bit more intrigued.

"Well, no, she didn't exactly, you know, *witness* the

incident," Jinx hedged. "But she reported the crime and she knew the victim her entire life."

The redness in his cheeks faded and with them, Jinx felt, were her chances to get a byline on a story that was a bit more serious than covering a holiday tree lighting or the local school play. He just had to give her this assignment so she could stop wasting her talents reporting on such lightweight fare, didn't he? Hadn't Wyck said that she possessed the qualities necessary to become a savvy investigative reporter? And hadn't she proven herself to be a quick learner and dedicated employee these past two months on the job?

"You've only been here two months, Jinx! Hell, this is the first real job you've ever had," Wyck said while continuing to type furiously. "I just can't hand over a story like this to a neophyte. It isn't fair to the rest of the team."

"But the rest of the team doesn't have a connection to Lucy like I do!"

Jinx was completely aware that she had crossed the line from eager cub reporter to petulant child, but she couldn't stop herself. Ever since she got the idea the other night during dinner with her grandmother—that she could use Lucy's death to her advantage, to climb the ladder of professional success at work—she had become obsessed. She wasn't entirely proud of it, but there was nothing else she could think of except working on this case, cracking it, and bringing whoever killed Lucy to justice. And, of course, being awarded some prestigious journalism prize for her objective, yet personal, reporting as a nice bonus.

Closing his eyes, Wyck breathed deeply through his nose, letting his chest and shoulders fill up with air and rise, then after a few seconds he let them both deflate with the exhale. Wyck went through his routine twice more, then opened his eyes refreshed and ready to end this battle.

"My final answer is no," he proclaimed. "I understand that you're disappointed, but I promise that you will get your chance to shine. For right now, however, I need your spotlight to be focused on other stories . . . like the Tranquility Waterfest."

Jinx didn't need any deep-breathing exercises to help her deflate. Those two words took care of it by themselves. The Tranquility Waterfest was the annual celebration of the lakeside community, and in honor of the town's centennial this year, the town council was pulling out all the stops to turn this into a real extravaganza. The jaw-dropping activities would include swim races in several categories from beginner to senior citizen, a remote-controlled speedboat obstacle course, scuba-diving lessons, and an exhibition from the state's one and only professional synchronized swimming team, the Droplettes. However, as far as Jinx was concerned, none of these attractions were nearly as fascinating as the mystery of why Lucy Agostino's dead body was found floating in Memory Lake.

Jinx opened her mouth to rebut, but before any words could come out, Wyck spoke first. "And please note that I used the word 'final.'"

Case closed, Jinx thought, and so was her career as a real reporter. Hardly the truth, but in that moment it's how Jinx felt, so she decided to honor it. Later that afternoon, Alberta dragged her off to the morgue to honor another moment—the moment Lucy would be entered into the state's official registry of deceased persons.

"Why do you have to identify the body, Gram?" Jinx asked before Alberta had time to buckle up her seatbelt.

"Because Vinny asked me," Alberta replied.

"I know that he asked you, but you're not the next of kin, you're just . . . I'm not even sure what you are . . . frenemy?"

"I think 'old friend' sounds nicer," Alberta said. Jinx recognized the same finality in her tone that Wyck had used earlier, so she didn't contradict her grandmother. Of course, she had more questions that she asked nonstop on the drive to Saint Clare's Hospital.

"So, Lucy's only daughter lives in California?"

"Yes, Enza moved to San Francisco, no San Diego, no . . . well she moved someplace that has a San in front of it before she got married," Alberta remembered. "So she's been there for almost twenty years, I guess."

"And she's never come back?" Jinx asked.

"No," Alberta replied quietly. "Never."

Alberta gazed out the car window not really taking in the low-rolling hills that made up a large portion of Tranquility Park, but thinking about her own estranged daughter, Lisa Marie, and that she had more in common with Lucy than just upbringing and nationality. They shared the pain of losing a child.

"Lucy and Enza had a falling-out, nothing specific that I know of, just a series of things that they couldn't resolve and so . . ."

Alberta's voice trailed off and Jinx, knowing all too well the complicated relationship between her own mother and grandmother, didn't force the issue, but allowed Alberta to sit in silence next to her all the while incredibly grateful that she didn't follow the same road her mother took. Where her mother kept her hands firmly in her pockets, Jinx reached out to grab hold of Alberta, and she wasn't about to let go.

When she pulled her bright red Chevy Cruze into a spot in the parking lot of Saint Clare's Hospital, she finally broke the silence, albeit with an all-too-cheery, "We're here."

Vinny was sitting on a bench in front of the hospital waiting for them. He was deep in thought, staring at the ground and holding his policeman's cap gingerly with two fingers so it swayed slightly in between his knees. With his jet-black hair slicked back to show off his Roman nose, smooth broad face, and square jawline, he looked more like an aging movie star than a soon-to-be-retired chief of police.

"Sorry to ask you to do this, Alfie, but Enza isn't going to be able to get to town 'til next week," Vinny said as the two women approached. "And I didn't want Lucy to have to wait that long."

"I'm sure she appreciates it," Alberta replied.

When Vinny finally stood up, Jinx couldn't help but feel some butterflies in her stomach, because despite his age he really was quite a handsome and very well-preserved hunk of man. She then immediately and silently chastised herself for having carnal thoughts en route to a morgue. Alberta must've caught the lecherous look in her granddaughter's eye, because when she hooked her arm in hers, she leaned over and whispered, "The girls were always crazy about him."

But once they entered the ground floor of the hospital, all thoughts about handsome men and schoolgirl crushes were obliterated by the uninviting setting. Inside the morgue they were surrounded by nothing but cold, gray steel. The entire room smelled like it was drenched in bleach-scented sanitizing cleanser that disinfected any romantic scent that may have lingered in the air.

In one end of the room was an orderly doing double duty as the morgue attendant who had clearly adapted to the environment. He didn't flinch when they walked into the room because he was wearing old-school earphones, the big and clunky kind sported by disc jockeys in the seventies that had recently made a comeback, and the music he was listening to must have been loud enough to drown out any other sound. He was also glancing at some documents and typing on his computer keyboard so he didn't notice anyone else was in the room until Vinny tapped him on the shoulder.

"Luke," Vinny said loud enough so he could be heard over the music blasting into the orderly's ears. "You have some company."

"Hey Chief, welcome to the Dead Zone."

When the orderly looked past Vinny and saw Alberta and Jinx standing behind him, his face grew so pale it looked as if he was about to become the newest resident of the morgue instead of its gatekeeper.

"Oh my . . . I'm so, so, so, so . . ."

"We get it, honey, you're sorry," Alberta said, trying to help him out.

"Really, really sorry."

"Easy, Luke," Vinny said. "But seriously, you need to

knock it off with that joke before it gets you into real trouble."

"Will do, Chief," Luke said. "Who're you looking for?"

"Lucy Agostino."

Luke consulted a chart on his desk and replied, "She's number thirty-two."

Without asking for direction, Vinny walked over to the fourth drawer in the center row of the wall on the left side of the room. With his hand on the handle, he turned to Alberta, "Are you ready?"

"Vinny, I've already seen her, this is just a formality."

"I know, but . . ."

"No buts, will you just open it up so we can get this over with?"

Slowly, Vinny pulled open the drawer to reveal a body covered in a white sheet. All that could be seen were bare feet, the toenails painted with red nail polish that had begun to chip and smear. A tag was tied around the big toe on the right foot that presumably had Lucy's name written on it. Without saying another word, Vinny pulled back the sheet to reveal Lucy's face, and both Alberta and Jinx immediately understood why Vinny had tried to prepare them.

"Oh, Lucy," Alberta gasped, making the sign of the cross and then bringing her gold crucifix to her lips to kiss it.

The woman on the metal slab resembled the woman they had seen on the banks of the lake, but with her dignity stripped. Her face had gotten puffier and her features slightly overexaggerated, so while her face didn't look disfigured, it had definitely changed. Her hair, now dry and unstyled, framed her face like a cloud of black smoke highlighted with shards of gray. And most striking of all, the navy blue business suit was gone and there was nothing left to cover up the pale, freckled skin around Lucy's neck and shoulders. Even if she hated the color, it was better for her to be covered in that than naked with just a thin sheet to cover her body.

"So just for the record, you can identify this woman?" Vinny asked.

"Yes, yes, this is Lucy Agostino, I'm sure of it," Alberta said, nodding her head. She then looked away and waved her hand in front of the drawer, indicating to Vinny that showtime was over.

"Thank you," he said, pushing the drawer closed.

When they walked out, Jinx held onto her grandmother's arm and Vinny put his hand underneath Alberta's elbow. They all felt the same instinctive need to make some kind of connection.

Later that night sitting outside on the Adirondack chairs, drinking herbal tea underneath the glow of the moonlight, Alberta and Jinx were about to make an even deeper connection than the one they already shared.

"Lovey, I know you want to say something," Alberta said breaking the silence. "So why don't you just spit it out?"

"You really do know me so well, don't you?"

"What kind of question is that, you're my granddaughter."

Almost blushing, Jinx could feel the love stretch from Alberta's heart and penetrate her own. "We make a great team, don't we, Gram?"

"Yes, we do," Alberta said, reaching out to hold Jinx's hand.

"Then let's make it official."

Confused, Alberta thought the stressful events may have finally gotten to Jinx. Or could Lisa Marie have done something despicable and told Jinx that she was adopted and not biologically connected to the Ferrara family? "Honey, what are you talking about? It is official, we're blood."

"I don't mean personally, I'm talking professionally," Jinx clarified. "Well maybe not super professionally like with an office and a shingle with our names on it, but sorta, kinda professionally."

Now Alberta was thoroughly and officially confused. "Jinx, I love you, but are you all right? I have no idea what in heaven's name you're talking about."

Placing her cup of tea on the black plastic table between them, Jinx shifted her chair so she was directly facing Alberta. "I'm sorry, I know I'm not being clear, it's just that I have an idea, and it involves you."

"Whatever you want me to do, I'll do, you know that."

"Well, let me tell you what my idea is before you commit to something you might regret."

Surprisingly, Alberta didn't get nervous because of Jinx's warning, but rather excited. She had no idea what her granddaughter was going to say, but she had an inkling that it was going to shake up her life even more than it had already been shaken up. And despite having lived a traditional life for her first six decades, she was eager to make up for lost time and embrace unconventionality.

"Ever since Wyck, my editor, told me I couldn't investigate Lucy's murder, I've been doing some thinking," Jinx started. "And I keep thinking, why do I need his permission to investigate? If I do it on my own time, there's nothing he can say about it. And if I uncover some facts and details that I can use as a reporter, well, I'll have no choice but to use them, right?"

Unsure where Jinx's rationale was leading, Alberta answered warily, "Sure, honey, I guess that's right."

"And then after seeing poor Lucy in the morgue, well I just thought I have to do something, I mean, we can't just stand by and do nothing, right?" she asked. "So I've been thinking . . . with my reporting skills and your knowledge of the murder victim, who better to work together to solve this crime, but me and you!"

Alberta let Jinx's statement sink in and her immediate response was to smile. Jinx reminded Alberta of herself when she was a young woman—she had moxie. But instead of burying it to follow tradition and become a wife and mother, Jinx was creating her own life for herself. Alberta couldn't be prouder of her granddaughter or more excited to join forces with her.

"I'll do it."

Ignoring her grandmother, Jinx continued, "It'll give me the chance to prove to Wyck that I'm a good crime reporter, and it'll give you the chance to avenge your friend's death. Even though, you know, Lucy wasn't really your friend. But just think how she'll react if you uncover who killed her, she'll be royally pissed off if she has to be eternally grateful to you from beyond the grave!"

"I said I'll do it."

"And if that isn't enough of a reason to convince you, it'll give us a chance to really get to know each other, more than just grandmother and granddaughter, but as two independent women."

"Jinx, *basta,* enough already! If you would just shut up for a second, you'd hear me, I'll do it!" Alberta said laughing. "I'll team up with you to find out who killed Lucy."

"Oh my God!" Jinx shouted. "Seriously? You mean it? That's wonderful!"

As they hugged each other, Alberta looked up at the oak tree, shining magnificently in the purple sky. "*Il frutto cade non lontano dall'albero.*"

"What in the world does that mean?"

"The apple doesn't fall very far from the tree," Alberta said. "You and me, lovey, we're very much the same. We're both looking for a challenge, to find out what breathes life into our soul. I'm just so happy you started your journey much earlier than I did."

Looking into her grandmother's eyes, which were accented by age with crow's-feet but were the same shade of green as her own, Jinx smiled because she felt exactly the same way.

# CHAPTER 6

*Non tutte le ciambelle riescono col buco.*

Nothing brings a family together like death. Someone dies and families gather. It's a timeless tradition and when the dead person is a long-lost acquaintance like Lucy, attendance at the wake is more obligatory than mandatory. Such an event feels more like a social gathering than somber affair, which would explain why Alberta was sitting at her kitchen table applying her makeup while the rest of her family was milling about in various stages of undress before they had to leave to pay their final respects.

Jinx was standing by the sink fully clothed, but only from the waist down, blow-drying her hair. Alberta didn't care that she was matching her black and gray herringbone just-above-the-knee pencil skirt, stockings, and black slingback pumps with only a bra, she was concerned that she was going to kill herself.

"Jinx, be careful not to get that thing wet," Alberta cautioned. "Or else Lucy'll have company in her casket."

"Don't worry, I do this all the time at home," Jinx

shouted over the noise of the dryer. "The electrical outlet in my bathroom doesn't work."

"*Ah, Madon,* 'don't worry,'" Alberta cursed. "Famous last words."

Alberta tilted the mirror on the kitchen table so she could keep a watchful eye on her granddaughter behind her, and took one last look at her makeup. She was disappointed in herself that she was vain enough to care about how she looked for a memorial service, but this one was for Lucy and she had always tried to outdo her nemesis when it came to looks. Old habits die hard.

Her lipstick was Estée Lauder's Pink Parfait, which despite its festive name, looked sophisticated and restrained. She only put on a touch of mascara and eyeliner, and her Lancôme eye shadow had the fancy name of Cashmere, but was really just a shade darker than her olive complexion. Alberta ran her fingers through her hair to fluff up her pageboy and was grateful that she still had a thick head of hair, artificially colored of course, but still her own and not a Tova Borgnine wig. She did notice some of the roots turning gray where she parted her hair on the left and made a mental note to make an appointment with Adrianna, the girl at A Cut Above, but overall she was pleased with the sight.

"Not bad for an old broad," she said.

"What?" Jinx shouted as she turned off the dryer.

"Nothing."

Just as Jinx grabbed her freshly ironed black silk blouse from the back of one of the kitchen chairs, the bathroom door opened, and Alberta's older sister, Helen, emerged. Unlike Alberta, Helen was not happy with Jinx's outfit.

"You cannot wear that to a wake!" she declared.

"Of course not, Aunt Helen," Jinx agreed. "I'm putting this on."

"I don't care what you put on, underneath you'll still look like a *putan*."

"Leave her alone, Helen," Alberta said, screwing the back of her diamond stud earring in place, "It's a pretty bra."

"It's red! And lacy!" Helen shouted. "And red and lacy have no place in a church."

While Jinx finished getting dressed, Alberta finished yelling at her sister.

"First of all, we're not going to a church, we're going to Ippolito's Funeral Parlor," Alberta started. "Second, she's wearing a black blouse, so no one's gonna know what kind of bra she has on. And third, you of all people should know that God likes fancy things. Have you seen how ornate the priest's robes are these days? If you squint it's like Liberace's delivering mass."

"If only Jesus could pack a house like Liberace used to," Helen mused.

Helen knew all about priests and mass and churches, because for most of her life she was known as Sister Helen and was a Franciscan nun, until she recently decided she wanted a career change after forty-one years and left the convent. She had yet to give an explanation as to why and had only told her Mother Superior that her conviction to leave was as strong as it had been to become a Bride of Christ, and she now wanted a divorce. When Alberta pressed her for a more detailed answer, Helen would only say that it was time for her to move on. Alberta desperately wanted to know the truth behind her sister's startling decision so she could help her transition back to civilian life, but she knew how stubborn Helen could be and didn't push the subject.

Alberta did offer to share the lake house with Helen, but Helen said she had spent her entire adult life bunking with other single women and wanted to experience what it was like to live on her own. Secretly, Alberta was relieved because she wanted that experience as well. She also knew from previous experience that living under the same roof with her sister was not easy. Helen was demanding, outspoken, blunt, and critical, and Alberta figured the only reason the other nuns didn't throw Helen out of the convent long ago was because they all had the patience of saints.

"You two know we're not going to one of those singles bars, right?" Helen asked rhetorically.

"We know where we're going, Aunt Helen," Jinx replied. "But it isn't a sin to want to look nice."

"Actually it is," Helen corrected. "But I'll let it slide because you do look very nice in that getup. What about me? Do I look presentable?"

Jinx smiled at her aunt. Despite Helen's bristly nature, she loved her. More than that she admired her. Even though she was raised by a lapsed Catholic and didn't have a strong connection to religion, Jinx knew how hard a nun's life could be and that it demanded not only devotion but discipline. She also knew that to leave your home, whether it be Eufala, Florida, or a convent, demanded the same amount of courage. Deep down, Helen and Jinx had a lot in common. The surface told another story.

Helen's hair was all gray and cut short so she looked like Audrey Hepburn's grandmother, without any of the movie icon's fashion sense. She was wearing a black cotton V-neck sweater, a black skirt that fell somewhere between her shins and her ankles, and what could only be described as sensible shoes. The only accessories were the gold crucifix necklace that her parents gave her the day she became a novitiate and her glasses.

"You look beautiful, Aunt Helen, as always," Jinx said. "And I love the glasses, are they new?"

"Yes, I needed a new prescription and I decided to jazz things up a bit," she replied. "Do you like the color? I call it Blessed Mother Blue."

"And I'm sure that makes her very happy," Jinx said smiling and meaning every word of it.

Helen grabbed her black leather shoulder bag, put her head through the long strap, and impatiently tapped the bag that hung at her hip. "Can we go now?"

"We're just waiting for Joyce," Alberta said.

Plopping down on a chair opposite her sister, Helen rolled her eyes and huffed, "When are we not waiting for Joyce?"

Joyce Perkins Ferrara was the final member of Alberta's family now residing in Tranquility. Alberta and Helen's sister-in-law Joyce was separated from their younger brother Anthony and now lived on the opposite side of the lake from Alberta, while Anthony—or Ant as he was more commonly referred to—had lived in Florida for the last several years. Not anywhere near where Jinx grew up, but in fancier Clearwater, off the Gulf of Mexico.

The rest of the family took their separation much harder than Joyce and Ant did. Each and every Ferrara knew the couple had broken so many conventions and fought so many obstacles just to marry in the first place that it was a devastating blow when they announced that they were essentially calling it quits. It wasn't a common occurrence to see an African American bride walk down the aisle to be greeted by her Italian American groom, and it had taken a long time for the families on both sides to embrace the idea with the same love that the couple shared for one another. Unfortunately, their love wasn't strong enough for their marriage to last.

"I love your brother, I always will, and he loves me," Joyce had announced. "But we just can't live together anymore."

Neither one of them felt the need to get divorced, not out of any religious observance, but because they had no desire to marry other people. They just knew that they didn't want to live with each other, so they lived apart.

Ant moved to Clearwater to live near his cousin Ralphie, working part-time as a plumber and spending his free time fishing, while Joyce moved from their Victorian house in Rutherford, New Jersey, to a lakeside cottage in Tranquility and retired. She had spent decades working as an investment banker, made a ton of money, and just like Helen, one day decided that she had had enough. Since then she's spent most of her time fulfilling her lifelong dream of becoming a painter.

"When the sun sets over Memory Lake," she'd said, "the colors are so beautiful it's like the paintings just paint themselves."

Alberta was quite upset when Joyce and Ant announced their separation because she always thought they had a perfect marriage. However, she was thrilled when her brother announced that he was the one who was moving away because she always liked her sister-in-law better and would have missed having her so close.

"Here she is now," Alberta announced.

Rising from the table, Helen said, "It's about time."

"Sorry I'm late, girls," Joyce said, bursting into the house. "I just washed my hair and I couldn't do a thing with it."

Alberta and Jinx laughed because Joyce's hair was a close-cropped Afro that required absolutely no maintenance. Helen failed, or more likely, refused to get the joke.

"What's there to do?" she asked. "You have less than an inch of hair on your head."

Ignoring her sister-in-law's barb, Joyce cried, "I love your glasses, Helen! The blue matches your eyes!"

"Thanks," Helen replied begrudgingly, then after a pause, she added, "Nice earrings."

"You know I love my gold hoops," Joyce replied. "Reminds me that I had to jump through hoops all my life working with those bastards on Wall Street!"

Joyce, Alberta, and Jinx laughed, and even Helen allowed herself a smile. They were four very different women, but they had one thing in common, they were family. A family with a mission to fulfill.

"C'mon, ladies," Alberta announced. "Lucy needs us."


Ippolito's Funeral Home was packed, and Alberta was not happy.

"Did she pay all these people to come?" she quipped.

"Alberta, be nice," Joyce admonished. "I'm sure you'll have twice as many at your wake when your time comes."

"Thank you," Alberta said. "You always know the right thing to say."

Unfortunately, Helen didn't.

"Looks like Lucy's daughter and Jinx shop at the same store."

While it was rude to comment negatively about the deceased's only child, Helen had a point. Enza Saulino, Lucy's daughter, looked like she really was going to spend the night at one of those singles bars receiving welcomed advances instead of welcoming mourners at her mother's memorial service. Stiletto heels, bare legs, black sleeveless cocktail dress that stopped mid-thigh, unnaturally black hair pulled back into a ponytail, sparkling jewelry adorning her wrists, ears, and neck, and a face that was shimmering in cosmetics and Botox.

"*Maria Santissima!* I'm glad Lucy can't see this," Alberta said. "It's disgraceful."

"*Non tutte le ciambelle riescono col buco,*" Helen added.

"What's that mean, Aunt Helen?" Jinx asked.

"It means not every doughnut comes out with a hole," she explained.

"Oh, of course . . . 'cause that makes perfect sense," Jinx said.

"It means things don't always turn out as planned," Alberta translated further. "A daughter doesn't always turn out exactly as her mother had hoped."

Jinx knew that her grandmother wasn't only talking about Enza, but about her own mother as well, and once again she felt conflicted. She was thrilled that she and her grandmother were building a strong relationship, but was sad that her mother's relationship with Alberta had disintegrated. Maybe someday she could help bring those two together, but right now she was more interested in why it seemed like a bejeweled Enza was holding court all by herself when she should have been surrounded by her family.

When they got to the front of the receiving line, after exchanging the usual pleasantries and condolences, Helen's blunt approach brought forth some answers.

"It must be hard for you, staying at your mother's place all by yourself," Helen said. "Where's your husband?"

"Tito is home sick with an ear infection," Enza replied, her accent still New Jersey thick even though she'd spent years living thousands of miles away on the west coast. "He couldn't make the flight."

"And Tito, Jr.? Is he sick too?"

This time, Enza didn't reply as quickly. "No, no, TJ's in college . . . exams . . . he wanted to come, he really did, but I told him that Grandma wouldn't want him to endanger his studies, so I came by myself."

"You're such a good daughter," Joyce lied. "Lucy always said that."

"What else could I do?" Enza replied, squinting hard, but failing to produce any tears. "I'm all she had."

"And it looks like you now have everything she ever had," Helen commented. "Take good care of that diamond necklace, it was your mother's favorite."

No amount of Botox could prevent Enza's face from showing her inner rage. Her eyes glared, her silicone-injected lips snarled, and her chemically enhanced mask of a face shifted just enough to let her anger shine through. Luckily, one of the funeral home's staff came up to Enza at that moment and whispered something in her ear.

"Excuse me," Enza said through clenched teeth.

"Of course," Helen replied as spokesperson for the group. "Don't let us keep you."

When Enza was out of earshot, Jinx proclaimed, "Oh my God, Aunt Helen, Aunt Joyce, you two are born detectives! You're really going to be able to help me and Grandma."

"What are you talking about?" Helen asked.

"Jinx and I have decided that we're going to find out who murdered Lucy," Alberta answered. "And the two of you are going to help."

Standing in front of Lucy's casket, Helen and Joyce exchanged quizzical looks. After a moment they shrugged their shoulders at the very same time.

"Sounds like fun, if you ask me," Joyce declared.

"Just remember that I volunteer at the animal shelter on Tuesdays and Thursdays," Helen said. "So you'll have to work around my schedule."

"Then it's official," Jinx announced. "The Ferrara Family Detective Agency is now open for business."

After they finished saying their prayers, Alberta lingered next to the coffin by herself. She stared at the woman she had known almost her entire life for what would be the last time. Alberta had buried many people in her life—her husband, her parents, very close friends—and she knew the suffocating weight grief could have on a heart. She wasn't feeling that now. What she was feeling was different, but just as unwelcome because it was the presence of her own mortality. She was basically the same age as Lucy. They had lived very similar lives, their journeys were almost identical, so Lucy could easily be standing over Alberta's dead body. The thought was both sobering and humbling. Who could have done such a thing to her? Alberta tried to think if there was anyone in her life who hated her so much that they would stab her in the heart, and she came up empty. What could Lucy have done to wind up in a state of eternal slumber? Who did she cross or what did she know that had gotten her murdered? Alberta would start to get answers sooner than she thought.

"Gram, I just found out something exciting," Jinx whispered as she pulled Alberta away from the white marble casket and next to a beautiful display of yellow and pink flowers.

"What, lovey?"

"I was walking by the funeral director's office and I overheard him talking to Enza," Jinx explained.

"You mean you eavesdropped."

"Only if you choose to look at it that way," Jinx admitted.

"Well, eavesdropper, what did you hear?"

Jinx leaned in to sniff one of the flowers and motioned for Alberta to do the same. They looked like they were two women remarking on the bouquet's beauty and not amateur detectives getting their first break.

"Enza is going to be tied up tomorrow morning at the bank closing out her mother's accounts and dealing with all the financial stuff," Jinx whispered.

"Why is that exciting?" Alberta asked, just as quietly.

"Because while Enza's away, we'll be able to break into Lucy's condo and do some investigating."

Alberta jerked her head away as if the flowers had suddenly become a target for a hungry bumblebee. "You're *pozzo*! That's crazy, we can't do that."

"Of course we can," Jinx corrected, grabbing her grandmother's hand and leading her over to the next floral display, a huge heart made out of red carnations with a sash across it that read "Beloved Grandmother." Once again, Alberta was reminded that she could easily be the one laying inside the white satin-lined coffin instead of Lucy.

"But that would be breaking and entering," Alberta stated. "That's illegal."

"Gram, if we have to become criminals to solve this crime, that's what we'll have to do," Jinx replied. "I'll pick you up at eight. Wear rubber-soled shoes so you don't make any noise."

Alberta knew she should refuse to participate in Jinx's plan, but she didn't want to disappoint her or herself. She couldn't really explain it, but she felt as if she had no other choice. "*Bene*," Alberta said, "And don't forget to wear gloves so we don't leave any fingerprints."

Jinx positively beamed. "Sounds like this won't be your first time at the rodeo, Gram."

Alberta tried to hide her smile, but Jinx's enthusiasm was infectious. "I'll see you at eight, partner."

# CHAPTER 7

*Cattivo tre fa frutti cattivi.*

When Alberta crawled through the back window over the garage that was attached to Lucy's condo, she wasn't thinking that she could be arrested for breaking and entering. She wasn't thinking that she was desecrating a dead woman's home. Her only thought was that she had to go on a diet.

"Push harder, Jinx!" Alberta yelled. "My fat ass needs some help."

"I'm pushing as hard as I can," Jinx grunted, her shoulder strategically placed underneath Alberta's buttocks. "You really carry your weight well, Gram, I never would have thought you weighed so much."

"Thanks, lovey," Alberta replied. "I think."

Wedged in between the open window frame, Alberta grabbed onto the inside windowsill for leverage as she tried to hoist the rest of her body through. Witness to her struggle, Jinx squatted, then rose up with all her strength. Alberta finally tumbled through the window and landed on the carpeted floor with a thud.

"Ah, *mannaggia!*" Alberta cursed under her breath.

Jinx grabbed hold of the windowsill, pulled herself

up, and with a contortionist's dexterity made it through the window to land on both feet next to Alberta's unmoving and slightly twisted body.

"Show-off," Alberta teased.

"Are you all right?" Jinx asked as she helped Alberta get back up on her feet.

"I'm fine," Alberta replied, grimacing and rubbing her hip. "I just have to cut back on the pasta."

She looked around the room that was filled with boxes from QVC, mismatched pieces of furniture, and even a refrigerator that looked like it came from the year of the Flood and felt like she was having a senior moment. "Jinx, where the hell are we?"

"Unless Lucy was a major hoarder, I'd say this is the spare room."

Jinx opened the door slowly and listened to make sure they were alone. When she was satisfied that they were the only ones in the condo, she motioned for Alberta to follow down the flight of stairs that led into the living room. Lucy's condo was actually a townhouse situated on a hill so the garage behind the building was actually a flight above the entrance in the front. Upstairs was the spare room, the garage that also doubled as a laundry room, and a small sitting area. Downstairs was the living room, kitchen, bedroom, and bathroom. None of the architecture was high-end and the furnishings were modest, but it was a nice, spacious condo and exactly the type of home Alberta considered buying before she became the recipient of Aunt Carmela's final wishes.

Instinctively Alberta and Jinx split up, with Alberta taking the living room and Jinx going into the bedroom. Alberta rummaged through a pile of magazines on the glass-topped coffee table and then pulled out a wicker basket underneath one of the end tables that was filled with paperbacks when it suddenly dawned on her that she had no idea what she was looking for.

"Jinx!" she cried. "What the hell are we looking for?"

"Evidence," Jinx cried back.

"What kind of evidence?"

"I don't know, Gram, I guess it's like pornography, we'll recognize it when we see it."

"Oh, okay."

Alberta resumed her search and opened a drawer in the media console that housed Lucy's flat-screen television when Jinx's comment finally resonated. "I don't think Lucy would have any girlie magazines lying around."

"No, not real pornography, it's just a phrase," Jinx shouted. "Look around for anything suspicious, anything that looks like it doesn't belong here."

Once again rummaging through the drawers of the console, Alberta was overcome with such strong emotion she almost fell over. She wasn't sure if what she and Jinx were doing was wrong or right, but she knew that it was exciting. And she hadn't felt excited in years. When she heard voices on the other side of the front door, her excitement swiftly shifted into fear.

She ran into the bedroom on tiptoe so she wouldn't make any noise even though, as instructed, she was wearing her rubber-soled, Easy Spirit casual wedges, grabbed Jinx's arm, and fought the urge to scream. "Somebody's trying to get in."

"That's impossible," Jinx said. "Enza told the funeral director she wouldn't be free until late this afternoon."

They both heard two voices having a conversation

outside the front door followed by the telltale sound
of a key entering the keyhole.

"She lied," Alberta announced.

Knowing that they wouldn't have enough time or
be able to be quiet enough to race up the stairs and
crawl back out the garage window, Jinx pulled Alberta
back into the bedroom and into the large closet. Jinx
slid the sliding door closed and they camouflaged
themselves the best they could behind the rows of
Lucy's clothes.

Alberta breathed in deeply and felt as if Lucy was
in the closet with her. The faint scent of Shalimar,
Lucy's signature fragrance since she was old enough
to be allowed to wear perfume, still lingered in the
air. She closed her eyes and imagined the woman
standing next to her ready to hurl yet another insult
her way. Alberta shook her head and opened her eyes,
determined to stay alert and not reminisce.

For a few moments all they heard was muffled
sounds and footsteps, until Enza and her guest entered the bedroom. It was as if Alberta and Jinx had
a front-row seat at a performance neither they, nor
anyone else, was invited to.

"I swear to God, Donny, I could just kill my mother!"
Enza shouted as she entered the bedroom.

"Looks like somebody beat you to it, babe," Donny,
whoever he was, replied.

Alberta and Jinx looked at each other, their eyebrows raised as a silent signal that they were both
surprised to hear a man who wasn't Enza's husband
call her "babe."

"Well, I can't wait to find out who did it, so I can

kill them for denying me my right as my mother's daughter!"

There was a creaking sound as someone jumped on the bed.

"You might not have the collection, but you can have all of this."

The voice belonged to Donny and clearly he was sprawled out on Lucy's bed inviting Lucy's daughter to join him.

"Oh please, I can have you anytime I want," Enza said dismissively. "But right now what I want is that collection."

Alberta was shocked, not by the brazenness of Enza's comment, but by how much she sounded like her mother. *Cattivo tre fa frutti cattivi,* she thought to herself—bad fruit falls from bad trees. She didn't like to harbor such ill will toward the dead, but Lucy had not been a very nice person while she was alive, and it appeared by what Alberta was overhearing that her daughter had inherited that trait.

"Donny first, the friggin' collection later."

They could hear Enza walking around the room, pulling open the drawers of Lucy's bedroom chest. "You lasted about three minutes this morning, what makes you think I want to go for seconds?"

Ignoring the insult or just immune to it, Donny replied, "I was just getting warmed up this morning, you know I like to start my day with a quickie."

Alberta and Jinx heard the sound of a belt buckle being undone and then the sound of their own hearts starting to beat more rapidly. They both wanted to slide open the closet doors and run from their hiding space before Donny could undress any further when they heard another creaking, this time when Enza started to slide back the closet door on her own.

Jinx held Alberta's gloved hand and squeezed it tight as light from the bedroom sprayed into the closet. Together, they leaned to the left to get as far away from the sudden illumination as possible without taking a step or making any noise, but they both knew that they were seconds from being exposed and there was absolutely no way for them to escape. In that fearful moment they both learned a detective's most valuable lesson: The importance of having an exit strategy. In the next moment they learned the second most important lesson for anyone considering a career in undercover detective work: Sometimes it's all about luck.

Just as Enza started to slide the closet door open even farther, her cell phone rang. "Oh for God's sake!" she exclaimed. "It's Vinny."

Alberta was conflicted. She was thrilled for the interruption, but disappointed to hear that Enza, like herself, took the Lord's name in vain.

"Hi, Vinny, how are you?" Enza said, her voice suddenly a combination of distraught and demure. After a pause, she continued, "Of course, that's no problem, I'll be right there."

When she spoke again it was obvious that Vinny was no longer on the receiving end. "I have to go to the friggin' police station to sign some papers."

"Cool beans, babe," Donny sighed. "I'll wait for you here. The food in the fridge is still good right? Your mother hasn't been dead that long?"

"You can't stay here, you idiot! You're posing as one of my mother's lawyers!" Enza yelled. "If somebody finds you here alone, they'll figure out I'm not happily married with a sick husband and a kid in college, but saddled with a deadbeat loser and a college dropout."

Alberta and Jinx looked at each other and at the same time mouthed, "Oh my God."

"Your husband's gotta be sick if he thinks you're happily married," Donny replied.

Furious, Enza slammed the closet door shut and told Donny to put his pants on. "I'm taking you back to the hotel and I'll pick you up later."

"Whatever you say, boss lady," Donny replied, slapping his belt buckle back into place.

Alberta and Jinx waited a full minute after they heard the front door slam shut before emerging from behind Lucy's clothes and the closet door. The bedroom looked exactly the same except for the rumpled comforter on the bed, but somehow the room was tarnished. The exotic scent of Shalimar replaced by the crass innuendo of Enza's and Donny's words.

"I can't believe the things that came out of their mouths," Alberta remarked.

"I know!" Jinx replied. "We have to find out what kind of collection Lucy had."

Clearly, Alberta and Jinx interpreted those words very differently. Alberta was upset by the way that Enza spoke of her recently deceased mother and wondered if her own daughter, Lisa Marie, would carry the same anger and resentment in her voice after Alberta passed away. Worse, would she even mention her name? It was quite troubling to think that Alberta's death might not rouse any emotion in her daughter at all. But Jinx, ever the pragmatist, was excited at being unexpectedly handed information that could help them uncover why Lucy was killed, if not who did the deed.

"Maybe somebody killed Lucy for her collection," Jinx surmised. "Whatever that might have been."

Now that they had been given a reprieve, Alberta and Jinx continued to search the condo for clues, anything that could lead them to whatever it was that Lucy had been collecting. Unfortunately, while Jinx searched the bedroom with renewed focus, Alberta wandered the living room aimlessly filled with memories of her own fractured relationship with her daughter.

Absentmindedly she moved into the adjoining galley kitchen area, thinking of the time she and Lisa Marie argued over how to properly polish Grandma Marie's silverware. Alberta insisted the only way was with a combination of white vinegar and baking soda, while Lisa Marie proposed the absurd notion that ketchup would bring back its luster. Very quickly all thoughts of silverware were abandoned and replaced with a litany of every stupid idea the other had ever uttered. Alberta shuddered at how ugly she had sounded yelling at her daughter and how easily it was for Lisa Marie to mimic her tone. She threw out her hands to the side and shook them in an attempt to repel the memory from her mind and accidentally knocked over a pile of papers on the kitchen table.

"Dammit!"

"What's wrong?" Jinx yelled from the bedroom.

"Nothing . . . I'm *maldestro* . . . a klutz, I knocked over a bunch of papers."

Jinx entered the kitchen and joined Alberta in picking up the fallen debris. "No worries, let me help so I can feel useful, I didn't find anything in the bedroom," Jinx announced dejectedly.

"Maybe there's nothing here to find," Alberta said.

"Oh, how wrong you are, Gram!"

Jinx held up a small piece of paper that to Alberta looked like a business card with a key attached to it. "What's that, lovey?"

"This, Gram, is our first real clue!" Jinx exclaimed. "It's a key to a storage unit that I guarantee you houses Lucy's collection."

Alberta felt a wave of pride waft through her achy body for her accidental achievement. Maybe there was still some life left in the old girl yet.

# CHAPTER 8

*Belle parole non pascono il gatto.*

"I cannot believe you lied to me, Alberta!" Helen shouted from the driver's seat of the car. "Sisters aren't supposed to lie to each other."

"Oh, *Madon!*" Alberta shouted back. "You should talk! I had to find out you were leaving the convent from Father Sal."

"He's got a big mouth, that one!"

"And you, *Sister* Helen, have a tight one!"

Sitting next to Helen in the front seat of her aunt's beige Buick LaCrosse, Jinx just smiled and looked out the window. She was already used to the bickering that went on between her grandmother and her aunt and knew that it was part of their normal conversation. The sound was different than the fights her mother and Alberta had. Those were filled with one main ingredient: anger. Jinx had grown to enjoy Alberta and Helen's verbal sparring, because she knew that despite the volume of their voices they loved each other.

"You could've just asked me if I would mind driving the getaway car," Helen said. "You didn't have to lie to me and say that you needed a lift to the hairdresser. I should've known the two of you wouldn't go to the same beauty parlor. Adrianna might be good enough for you, Berta, but she would be lost trying to work on Jinx's beautiful hair."

"Thanks, Aunt Helen," Jinx beamed.

"I have beautiful hair too!" Alberta protested.

"You do not!" Helen shouted. "You have old lady hair that you try and make look pretty. You should cut it short and simple like I do and not worry about it."

Since the love between Alberta and Helen could get sidetracked amid their comments, Jinx thought it best to intervene before things got out of hand and their mission derailed.

"You both have very pretty hair that suits your styles and personalities," she stated. "And don't be mad at Gram, I told her not to tell you because I wasn't sure you'd approve of us sort of breaking and entering into Lucy's storage unit."

"Sort of?" Helen contradicted.

"Well, we do have the key," Jinx said weakly.

"That you stole after breaking and entering into Lucy's house!" Helen shouted. "Thou shall not steal, remember that one? Anybody?"

"Thou shall not renege on your word, Helen, remember that one?" Alberta asked. "You said you would be part of this little team, so now you're getting a chance to do just that. What the hell else do you have to do today anyway?"

"My shift at the shelter starts at four!"

"We'll be done in plenty of time, Aunt Helen, don't worry."

"Good, because tardiness puts a smile on Satan's face," she announced. "And remember, one beep means I see the fuzz approaching, and two beeps means I have to go and use the ladies' room."

Sighing heavily as she got out of the Buick, Alberta replied, "You're a regular Angie Dickinson, Helen."

A few minutes later Alberta was the one channeling Ms. Dickinson's iconic role as Sergeant Pepper Anderson on the 1970's TV series *Police Woman* as she and Jinx walked down the aisle of the U-Store-It Urself storage facility trying to act nonchalant, as if they had a legal reason to be on the premises. Alberta glanced ahead at Jinx, who was half a step in front of her and was impressed to see that her granddaughter possessed an even more purposeful stride. Jinx was definitely taking the lead, and Alberta was delighted to follow in her footsteps.

At the end of a long row of mint green metal units, Jinx looked down at the ticket she was holding and without pausing pointed to the right to indicate that was the direction their path should continue to take. This new stretch of units was electric blue and twice the size of the green ones, each one the size of a small, outdoor shed. When they got three-quarters of the way down the aisle, Jinx stopped and pointed to the left.

"Here we are," she announced. "Number 152."

"I wonder what we'll find in there," Alberta whispered.

"Only one way to find out," Jinx replied, holding the ticket in the air so the key dangled like an enticing carrot in front of them.

Gleefully, Alberta snatched the key from Jinx's hand and entered it into the lock. She felt like she was standing at the entrance to the tomb that housed the Holy Grail. But after she opened the door to the storage unit she felt like that entire piece of biblical folklore was a hoax.

"It's empty!" she cried.

"It can't be!" Jinx added.

Alberta entered the unit and pulled on a string hanging from a light fixture that housed a single, bare lightbulb. The unit was suddenly bathed in a harsh, fluorescent glow that made both women squint. When their eyesight adjusted they saw that Alberta was technically a liar.

"It isn't *completely* empty," Jinx said, trying to sound much more optimistic than she felt.

"Lovey, three empty cardboard boxes doesn't a collection make," Alberta replied. "I stand by my word, this place is empty."

"But within this emptiness, Gram, there still might lie a clue."

While Alberta pondered Jinx's cryptic comment, Jinx took out her cell phone and started taking pictures of the logo printed on the boxes.

"Wasserman & Speicher," Jinx said, pronouncing the second name *Spi-ker*. "Why do I know this name?"

"Oh my God! Really?" Alberta gasped.

"Yeah, it says so right here, look," Jinx instructed. "You know who they are?"

"Yes, but it's German and pronounced Spei-*sher*," Alberta corrected, "And you *should* recognize the name, it's the big real estate firm in town."

"Oh right, of course," Jinx replied. "But how do you know that?"

"It's the firm that I had to deal with when I got Aunt Carmela's house," Alberta explained.

"I thought you dealt with the crazy Italian lawyer."

"Giancarlo handled most everything, but there was

some paperwork I had to sign dealing with land rights since the house borders the lake, and all that was handled by Wasserman & Speicher."

"Okay, that makes sense," Jinx started. "But what doesn't make sense is why you look like you've seen a ghost."

Alberta took a deep breath, "Because Wasserman & Speicher is where Vinny told me Lucy used to work."

"That's a pretty big coincidence, isn't it?"

Joyce's question hovered over the table and mixed with the delicious aroma of the Entenmann's glazed cinnamon Bundt cake that served as the centerpiece. The women were gathered around Alberta's kitchen table playing canasta, eating dessert, and sipping flavored vodka out of small jelly jars. It was their weekly ritual, but this week, they were a bit distracted from their weekly ritual as the evening held an added attraction: discussing the latest details of the investigation into Lucy's murder.

"I mean the storage unit contains boxes that just happen to be from the real estate firm that handled the transfer of title on Alberta's house," Joyce concluded.

Not everyone shared her opinion. "It doesn't mean a thing," Helen said, inspecting her cards. "Lucy worked at the real estate firm, so it makes sense that she'd steal boxes to house her collection or just to store things. It's a well-known fact, everybody steals."

Ignoring Helen's cynicism, Jinx said, "It's definitely an interesting connection, Aunt Joyce, but I don't think it adds up to anything significant. I'm much more curious to find out what this collection is."

"And why the storage unit was empty," Joyce added, taking a sip of vodka. "Also too, fluffy marshmallow vodka is fluffilicious!"

"For Pete's sake, Joyce, will you stop saying that!" Helen shouted, melding five jacks. She slammed the cards so hard on the table that she woke Lola up from her nap. The drowsy cat purred at Helen before burying her head again into the oversized pillow that doubled as her bed.

"She's right, Helen," Alberta stated. "Lucy rents a huge storage unit and the only thing in there are three empty boxes? That's very strange, if you ask me. And, yes, this vodka really is delicious."

"I'm not talking about that!" Helen snapped. "I'm talking about the 'also too'! How many times do I have to tell you Joyce, it's redundant! *Also* means *too*, so what you're really saying is '*also, also*.'"

Shoving a bit of Bundt cake into her mouth, Joyce responded, "Maybe that's what I mean to say."

"Not so fast Aunt Helen, she could mean to say '*too, too,*'" Jinx added with a smile.

"I give up!" Helen declared. "And, also too, I won!"

She tossed down all her cards to reveal a score of 5,210. Helen may have lost the war on grammar, but she won the game of cards.

"Nobody's got the *malocchio* on you, Aunt Helen, that's for sure."

"What?"

"The evil eye thing that Lucy put on Gram from heaven or, you know, wherever she is."

"I know what the *malocchio* is," Helen corrected. "What I want to know is why your grandmother is teaching you such nonsense."

Alberta refilled the empty jelly glasses with fluffy

marshmallow vodka and took a long drink before replying. "It isn't nonsense, Helen. Lucy always put the horns on me when she was alive and that's exactly what she's doing now. It's the only reason I got dragged into this whole mess."

"I'm sorry, Aunt Helen, I should've known you don't believe in such things."

"What are you talking about?" Helen asked. "I devoted most of my life to the Catholic Church, of course I believe in the evil eye. I just don't believe Lucy's spirit put it on your grandmother's head."

"Well, I do," Alberta announced. "And I'm the one Lucy tormented practically her entire life, so I should know. End of discussion."

Despite Alberta's declaration, the discussion as to whether or not Lucy's powers could extend beyond the spirit world lasted for a half hour. When they came to a stalemate on the subject, they spent the next half hour debating if they should share their newfound information with Vinny and the police department. Alberta's instinct was to call her friend and fill him in on both the mysterious connection and the empty storage unit, but Jinx wanted to keep their intel private until they had more specific details to share.

"And just how are we supposed to get more details?" Alberta asked.

"Follow the facts, ladies," Joyce said. "Who else knows about this collection?"

"Just Enza and her boy toy, Donny, as far as we know," Jinx answered.

"Then go to the source," Joyce announced. "March right back over to Lucy's condo, but this time ring the bell instead of breaking in through a back window."

They all agreed that it was the smartest, most direct route to take, but they also agreed that Enza was not the cooperative type and was not going to be a willing participant in a straightforward Q&A session. They had to figure out a way to dupe her into telling them what she knew.

Standing at the kitchen sink, feeling the breeze from the lake coming in through the window, Alberta figured she would probably have as much luck engaging Enza in a substantive conversation than she would with her own daughter. Over the years she was sure Lucy had spoken about her in front of Enza and could guarantee that Lucy hadn't rambled on about her virtues. No, the dislike for Alberta would have been transferred from mother to daughter like some congenital disease.

She also realized that Enza wouldn't waste time speaking with Helen after their run-in at the wake. The woman looked like she had wanted to rip Helen's head off for her not-so-subtle comments. The only candidates for the mission were Jinx and Joyce.

"I agree, Gram," Jinx said. "But even if she doesn't hate us for being related to both you and Aunt Helen, what pretense could we use to try to have a sit-down with her?"

"How about dragging her butt into confession?" Helen suggested.

"I think Enza is beyond being swayed by an act of contrition," Alberta said.

"But she might be swayed by the power of the church!" Jinx announced.

Jinx explained that if she and Joyce were going to visit Enza they couldn't go as themselves, it would be too risky given the recent and distant pasts. What they needed to do was to go undercover. Sort of.

"You mean we should wear a disguise?" Joyce asked.

"No, just disguise our intentions," Jinx replied. "We should visit Enza as members of her mother's church, St. Winifred's of the Holy Well. Show up with a casserole or a fruit basket and tell her that we come to offer her the prayers of the congregation during this, her time of sorrow."

"So basically you want to use the Lord's name in vain?" Helen asked.

"I think He'd understand that it's for a good cause," Jinx replied.

"You know something, Jinxie?" Helen said. "I think you're right. Go for it."

"But be careful," Alberta added. "I trust Enza less than I trusted her mother."

"Also too, *belle parole non pascono il gatto*," Joyce added.

"Wow, Aunt Joyce, I didn't know you could speak Italian."

"She can't!" Helen barked. "That sounded like Yiddish."

"Shush, Helen!" Alberta scolded. "Joyce is right, fine words don't feed the cat. Sometimes you have to take action."

Helen pursed her lips and adjusted her eyeglasses looking every inch like the stereotypically stern nun who doubled as a Catholic schoolteacher. When she spoke, she sounded like one, too. "Also too, make sure when you take action and confront the cat, she doesn't scratch your eyes out."

As if sticking up for her species, Lola meowed loudly without lifting her head from the pillow.

\* \* \*

The second time Jinx entered Lucy's condo, she did so through the front door. Crawling with her grandmother through the back window, however, was an easier and more pleasant experience, as it turned out that Helen had been right and Enza was acting like a tomcat whose territory had been breached by two trespassing felines.

"I don't mean to be rude," Enza said, not meaning a word she uttered. "But I'm gluten and dairy free, so I can't eat macaroni and cheese."

"We're so sorry," Joyce said, accepting the tray back from Enza. "We also brought some fruit, which is free of any nasty gluten or dairy, so you should be fine."

"Is it organic?" Enza asked.

Before Joyce could answer and disappoint Enza for the second time, Jinx pulled something out of her bag. "How about a bottle of wine?"

Finally, the tiniest of smiles formed on Enza's otherwise expressionless face. "Now *that* I'll take."

Pushing their way into the living room, Jinx and Joyce sat down on the gold velvet couch before Enza could escort them to the door. She clearly wasn't happy having visitors, but other than throwing them out, she really had no choice except to act as a semi-gracious hostess. It was a role she failed at miserably.

Enza sat in a high-backed chair across from the couch that was made of the same velvety smooth material, but was the color of the burgundy wine she was clutching in her hands. Her grip around the neck of the bottle was so tight Jinx thought Enza was going to twist off the top with her bare hands and to hell with a corkscrew.

"So how did you know my mother?" Enza asked.

"We're members of her church, St. Winifred's," Joyce began.

"Of the Holy Well," Jinx finished.

"That place is still around?" Enza asked.

"Oh yes, it's thriving," Jinx said, even though she had never set foot inside the church so she didn't know if it was a beacon for the community or a blight. "People come from all over just to hear our chorus sing. Your mother had such a beautiful voice."

"My mother was tone deaf," Enza contradicted.

"But she sang from the heart," Joyce interjected. "And when you sing from the heart, God only hears the intention, not the sound."

Jinx and Joyce smiled at each other and it was obvious that they were enjoying this tête-à-tête far more than Enza was. In fact, she was hardly listening and kept glancing at the closed bedroom door. Jinx may have only been a private eye for a few days, but she knew what Enza was hiding in the bedroom, and that the *what* was actually a *who* named Donny.

Emboldened with this knowledge, Jinx felt it time to be more direct and not tap dance around the reason they were here. "I just can't imagine why anyone would want to hurt your mother, do you?"

Enza's eyes said *yes*, but her mouth said *no*. "I really have no idea . . . what did you say your name was again?"

"Gina Maldonado," Jinx said, thinking it best to use her real name since her nickname was so recognizable.

"I have no idea, Gina," Enza continued. "My mother

was a simpleton . . . I mean a simple person, who was nice to everyone, nice to a fault actually, and kind of lived in her own reality."

"She did love watching TV," Joyce ad-libbed. "She could spend hours watching reruns, old sitcoms, westerns, and she loved her soaps, didn't she?"

"Yes, she did love her stories," Enza answered, finally warming up to the conversation. "I feel like you two really knew my mother."

Jinx and Joyce both answered in the affirmative, quite enthusiastically, and at the same time. If Enza hadn't forced herself to have a coughing fit to cover up Donny's sneeze from inside the bedroom, she would've noticed that their response was manufactured and hardly sincere.

"I'm sorry, sometimes I get very choked up when I talk about my mother," Enza lied. She yanked a tissue out of a Kleenex box on the table next to her chair and dabbed at some imaginary tears. "So then, you must know about her collection."

Joyce almost dropped the tray of macaroni and cheese she was holding in her lap and Jinx dug her fingernails into an orange in the fruit basket.

"Oh, yes, of course," Jinx replied.

Joyce stepped on Jinx's foot in an attempt to remind her that they needed Enza to give them information about the collection and not the other way around.

"But, you know, only in the abstract," Jinx backtracked.

Suspicion crept into Enza's face and she sat back in the chair, crossed her legs, and for the first time relaxed in their presence. She was acting as if she were a woman with nothing to hide even though she was hiding her lover in the other room and clearly guarding a secret she had no interest in divulging.

"So, my mother never told you about her collection?"

"Not in so many words," Jinx replied, all bravado and confidence swept away by Enza's icy glare.

"How in the world is that possible?" Enza shrieked. "My mother couldn't keep a secret if her life depended on it!"

Joyce matched Enza's glare "Maybe it did."

After getting thrown out by Enza, Jinx and Joyce held a postmortem on the drive home and surmised that Lucy had a possibly valuable collection that her daughter knew about, but for some reason, now can't find. The only other link to the collection was that it might have been housed in a now empty storage facility and packed in boxes taken from Lucy's job. If there were any answers to be found, they could probably be found at Wasserman & Speicher.

"Well, there's only one way for us to get closer to the truth," Jinx announced.

"And what's that?" Joyce asked.

"It's time for my grandmother to go back to work."

# Chapter 9

*Chi ha nome, ha robe.*

The last time Alberta was employed, there was no e-mail, no Internet, no fax machine, nor was there a no-smoking policy. She also had a twenty-four-inch waist. It was a very long time ago. When Alberta opened the glass door and entered the rotunda of the Wasserman & Speicher building it was like stepping through a time tunnel.

For a brief period after graduating high school, Alberta had worked at the Kleinfeld Insurance Agency. She hated every second of it, so if she succeeded in getting a job here it would definitely be an improvement. The building itself was an upgrade.

Standing in the middle of the huge lobby on the speckled gray and white marble floor, Alberta noticed that the walls were painted off-white and trimmed in dark wood paneling. Directly in front of her was a floor-to-ceiling window that ran four stories high, the entire height of the building, allowing light to flood the lobby. Drenched in a downpour of sunlight, Alberta closed her eyes and could feel the warmth penetrating through the walls. It must get hot inside during the summer, she thought, but the view was well worth it. She thought it would be wonderful to be greeted by a picture-perfect blue sky and the swaying branches of the trees every morning upon arriving at work. All this could be hers, she thought, if only she could fake her way through the initial interview.

"I know I don't have an *enormous* amount of office experience," Alberta conceded. "But I worked at an insurance company before I got married and, well, I did raise two children and kept house. Plus, I've done tons of volunteering. Catholic Daughters of America, Sisters of Charity, PTA when my kids were little, back in the day . . . as they say. Oh, and I hosted our annual fire department fund-raiser, Blaze of Glory. At the end of the night we'd get a big bonfire going and then the firemen would show everyone the proper way to put it out. Making fire fun, that was our motto."

Denise Herb-Kaplan, the human resources administrator interviewing Alberta, was fascinated by her applicant. Regardless of age, gender, or race, the typical job seeker was never forthcoming about faults and thought it best to present a shell of a person devoid of personality. Alberta was refreshing, and if there was a position available, Denise would have given it to her. Unfortunately, there were no current openings.

"I'm so sorry, Alberta, honestly I am," Denise said, her tone more apologetic than it had ever been in her career. "But as we say in the HR world, there's just no room at the inn."

"Well if it's good enough for Jesus," Alberta replied. "Then it'll have to be good enough for me."

Alberta was more disappointed than she thought she'd be upon hearing the bad news. She was dejected, of course, because she wanted to make headway with the investigation, but she also thought it would be fun to be a member of the working force again after such a long hiatus.

Denise walked Alberta to the elevator and told her that she would definitely call her if a position opened up. And just as the elevator doors opened, one did.

"Alberta Ferrara?"

The man standing before Alberta was vaguely familiar, but in the kind of way that meant he could've said he was a former neighbor or a TV weatherman, and either way she would've believed him.

"I'm sorry, I don't believe I know you," Alberta replied.

"Sure you do," he replied. "I'm Marion Klausner."

And then she remembered. He wasn't a neighbor or a local TV celebrity, he was yet another old schoolmate. First Lucy, then Vinny, and now Marion? Ever since she moved to Tranquility it was as if she was reuniting with her past instead of moving toward her future. Was the universe trying to tell her that you can never escape your past? Or were all these chance meetings serendipity?

"Oh, *Madon!*" Alberta gushed. "Now isn't this a nice surprise."

"I believe the pleasure is all mine," Marion replied.

"Do you two know each other?" Denise asked.

"Ever since ninth grade," Marion replied.

"Really? That is . . . so incredible," Denise said a bit nervously in the presence of her boss. "Mr. Klausner is the president of Wasserman & Speicher."

"Well, what do you know?" Alberta mumbled.

Marion stepped out of the elevator and into better lighting and Alberta immediately saw the resemblance to the teenager she knew in high school. Marion's close-cropped hair was all silver now, but worn in exactly the same style as was memorialized in his senior class photo, parted on the right and swept over to the side, more fastidious than stylish. His blue eyes shined as bright as ever, his face was still smooth, though with the expected smattering of wrinkles no one can avoid, and his nose was still a tad too long for his face.

"I'm sorry I didn't recognize you at first, it's been so long," Alberta said apologetically. "But once you said your name, it all came rushing back to me."

Her comment made the blood rush to Marion's cheeks and his lips formed into a boyish smile. "*Chi ha nome, ha robe,*" he said softly.

"Is that Italian, Ma . . . uh, Mr. Klausner?" Denise asked.

"It certainly is," Alberta answered. "I can't believe you remember that."

Marion explained with an awkward mixture of sheepishness and pride that growing up he was incessantly teased for having a girl's name even though he always pointed out that John Wayne's real first name was Marion, which meant it was definitely a man's name. Despite that bit of trivia, each school year brought forth a new bully who taunted him for his moniker. Try as he might to rise above the put-downs, the constant ribbing pushed him into a depression deeper than the typical teenaged angst. But one of the things that always helped him rally against the ridicule was something Alberta said to him when they were sophomores, *Chi ha nome, ha robe*—"A good name is the best of all treasures."

"I don't know if I ever properly thanked you for those kind words," Marion said, still moved by the memory.

Alberta was filled with a different kind of awkwardness, one that she hadn't experienced in almost four decades, the feeling of being nervous in the presence of a good-looking member of the opposite sex. She remembered that it made you do and say inappropriate things. When she spoke, she knew she was right.

"You could make it up to me by giving me a job."

Marion smiled like a teenager, "Done. She can have Lucy's old job."

Denise burst into inappropriate laughter at hearing the comment. When she saw that Marion wasn't laughing along with her, she tried to stop laughing, but only wound up laughing harder. "I'm so sorry, excuse me," she said, still chuckling. "But, um, I thought that position had been phased out per, um, your request."

"It was," Marion confirmed. "But I've changed my mind. Welcome to Wasserman & Speicher, Alberta."


After giving Alberta a tour of the whole building, showing her important office landmarks such as the ladies' room, the kitchen, the supply room, and—most impressive—the outdoor lounge, which was off the third floor and on a clear day offered a view of Memory Lake, Denise brought Alberta to her desk. It was as if she had just been led to that elusive

Holy Grail, and this time she found it to be brimming with treasure.

"It's beautiful," Alberta sighed.

"I've never heard it called that before," Denise said. "But I'm glad you like it."

Alberta's new desk was quintessential eighties office chic, a heavy structure with thick legs and made of laminated knotty pine so it looked like smooth tan wood decorated with random black circles. There were several built-in shelves on the top and sides of the desk in a variety of sizes that Alberta couldn't imagine ever being busy enough to fill, and except for the office essentials—phone, computer, mouse, keyboard, pencil holder—the desk was bare. Behind her was a shelving unit and a bulletin board on which some papers and a calendar depicting a tropical beach hung by pushpins, but other than that it looked like all evidence that Lucy had ever occupied the area had been removed. Once again Alberta felt a pang of guilt for invading a dead woman's space. All for a good cause, she reminded herself.

"Lucy was Mr. DiSalvo's assistant, but since he's retired, Lucy has . . . sorry, *had* been acting as an office floater, helping out wherever she was needed," Denise explained. "Which will be good for you, because it'll break you in slowly and give you an overview of the company. We'll start you off on a temporary basis, which is just our company policy, but don't worry, I get the feeling that you'll be put on the permanent staff in no time at all."

Alberta didn't comprehend much of what Denise had just told her (though she did notice "floater"), but nodded her head and said, "That sounds wonderful."

Adjacent to Alberta's desk was an identical space;

the only difference was that there were many more papers and personal items covering the desk's surface, the shelves were crammed with files, and the bulletin board was one gigantic photo montage. It was the lived-in version of the space Alberta had inherited.

"Beverly sits over there," Denise advised, "She's Mr. Klausner's admin. And right over there is his office."

If Alberta didn't already know Marion was the head honcho, the size of his office would've given it away. His door was brown wood, laminated just like the desk, but a few shades darker, and flanked by two floor-to-ceiling glass panels so you could see right in. Inside the office, however, bunched up at the top of the window, were Venetian blinds that could be drawn to create complete privacy. The rest of the wall was the same wood as the door, and it seemed to continue for the length of the hallway. His office looked to be the same size as the first apartment Alberta and Sammy moved into after they got married. Her old friend with the funny name had done well for himself.

"That's some important-looking office," Alberta murmured.

"That's because Mr. Klausner is an important man."

Both Alberta and Denise turned around to see a woman standing behind them. Alberta's first impression was that she was one of those middle-aged women who was desperately trying to cling to her youth. Bleached blond hair, chunky jewelry, and a skirt and blouse combo in too-bright colors and too-small sizes. But she was impressed with the woman's footwear, because Alberta couldn't remember the last time she even attempted to wear shoes with a three-inch heel. Luckily there was something in the woman's eyes that led Alberta to believe that despite her age-inappropriate outfit, she possessed a genuinely good spirit, because the woman was going to be Alberta's closest office mate.

"Alberta Scaglione, I'd like you to meet Beverly LaStanza," Denise said, introducing the women to each other. "Alberta's going to be joining us as our new floater."

"You mean she's going to be the new Lucy."

Before Denise could chastise Beverly for making such an unprofessional comment, the woman took matters into her own hands.

"I'm so sorry," she said, tears welling up in her eyes. "It's just been . . . difficult since . . ." Her voice trailed off into nothingness, but she didn't need to finish her sentence for Alberta to know what she was going to say.

Later on as the two women sat at their desks, fresh cups of coffee in their hands, Alberta was hit with more feelings of guilt upon learning that her new acquaintance was having a much harder time processing Lucy's death than she was.

"I mean, one day she was sitting right where you are now and the next she's floating on top of Memory Lake," Beverly said, shaking her head in disbelief. "I just don't understand how something like this could happen."

"Neither can I," Alberta agreed. "It's like a bad dream. I keep thinking I'll wake up and Lucy will still be alive."

Beverly's head cocked to the side like a perplexed poodle. "Did you know Lucy too?"

Dammit, Alberta cursed herself, so much for being an undercover agent! Obviously, Marion knew of her connection to Lucy because they all went to high school together, but since he was the boss she didn't think he'd engage in small talk with the rest of the staff, and Alberta didn't think it wise to let everyone in on the truth, especially if her sole reason for employment was to collect information to uncover Lucy's murderer. She was taking a chance because some of Lucy's co-workers must have gone to her funeral, but thus far she didn't remember seeing anyone, including Beverly, and no one seemed to recognize Alberta.

Vinny had also pulled some strings and was able to keep Alberta's name out of the police report, identifying her only as a female resident of Tranquility, and subsequently, her name never made it into the papers as the person who had actually found Lucy's floating dead body. With one slip of the tongue, Alberta almost ruined all that careful maneuvering. She knew that if she wanted to play the role of a private eye, it was time to start acting like one.

"No, I didn't know her, but I read about the unfortunate news in the paper," Alberta lied. "I guess she reminds me of myself . . . we're both the same age, Italian, widows, live in the same area . . . it could just as easily have been me in that lake instead of her."

By the compassionate look on Beverly's face, it appeared that she bought Alberta's fib. "I know what you mean," Beverly said, her eyes once again moist with tears. She blew her nose and took a moment to compose herself, then added, "I only worked with her for a few years, but I really do miss my friend."

That comment haunted Alberta all the way home

and continued to gnaw at her conscience when she was filling Jinx and Helen in on the details of her day later that night. She focused on the facts and kept her feelings to herself, but even though she didn't speak it out loud, she was very disturbed that Beverly, who only knew Lucy for a short time, was much more upset about her death than Alberta was—and she had known Lucy for a lifetime. Maybe as she got older Lucy softened and started to treat people better. Alberta sighed despondently because she would never really know.

"How crazy is it, Gram, that your boss is somebody else you went to high school with," Jinx declared. "It's like everybody from Hoboken suddenly moved to Tranquility."

"It was a vacation spot for us back then," Helen confirmed. "We thought it was like the South of France or Palm Springs even, very fancy."

"From the looks of it, Marion is living a very fancy lifestyle," Alberta conveyed. "The building itself is beautiful, his office is huge, and he looks amazing for a man his age."

Helen pursed her lips and folded her hands around her coffee cup. "Do I need to remind you that you're there to find a killer and not a boyfriend?"

"*Ma, che sei pazzo?* I don't want a boyfriend!" Alberta exclaimed. "And if I did want a boyfriend, I can tell you that it certainly wouldn't be Marion. To me he'll always be a skinny little boy with pimples on his forehead no matter how polished he might look now."

"And boy, has Pimpleface gotten polished," Jinx said, admiring a photo of Marion that she uploaded onto her cell phone. "He's like the epitome of the distinguished gentleman even though he's got a lady's name."

"Lovey, Marion *is* a man's name," Alberta corrected. "Not the best man's name in the world like Joey or Frank, but a man's name all the same."

Still gazing at the photo on her phone, Jinx replied, "Well lady's name or not, your boss is kind of hot in a silver daddy sort of way."

"Let me see that," Helen ordered.

When she looked at Marion's photo she threw her hands up and rolled her eyes in disgust. "Don't waste your time with that one, he's already got a girlfriend."

"How the hell do you know that?" Alberta asked.

"Because I've seen him in action."

In between spoonfuls of ricotta cheese eaten right out of the container, Helen described the scene she had witnessed downstairs at Ippolito's Funeral Home the night of Lucy's wake. She was on her way to the ladies' room when she saw a man and a very distraught-looking woman huddled together in a corner. She could only see the woman from behind, but from the way her body was shaking and the sounds she was making it was obvious that she was crying. The man whispered something into the woman's ear, and just as he took her by the elbow, he turned around and he and Helen locked eyes. The man was definitely Marion. And Helen could tell by the gentle way he led the woman outside that the two were a couple.

"So get any thoughts of an office romance out of your head, Berta, and just concentrate on your work and finding out who offed Lucy," Helen instructed.

Which is exactly what Alberta did the next day. While Beverly was in Marion's office taking dictation, Alberta was reading through some of Lucy's old business e-mails to see if they could provide a link to her killer, but all they served to do was help Alberta familiarize herself with the company's real estate holdings. The phone rang.

"Wasserman & Speicher," Alberta announced, unexpectedly delighted by how corporate she sounded.

The voice on the other end of the line didn't sound nearly as corporate, but it certainly sounded Russian. "Lucy, it is me, Olive, we are still to meet for tonight?"

Alberta was about to tell Olive, whoever she was, that she had made a mistake and hadn't reached Lucy, when she remembered Helen's words. If she wanted to help Jinx solve this murder, she was going to have to start thinking more like a detective and not like a woman impersonating a detective.

"Oh, hi, Olive, how are you?" Alberta said.

"Me? I am a-okay," Olive replied, her tone of voice not so subtly suggesting that she hadn't called to make small talk. "And you? I will see you at seven?"

"Yes, absolutely, seven it is," Alberta confirmed. "See you then."

Just as Olive was about to hang up, Alberta remembered she had no idea where she was supposed to be at 7 p.m. For all she knew she might need to race to the airport to catch a flight to Moscow. "Wait! What's the address again?"

"You cannot be serious, Miss Lucy?" Olive screamed and then shouted something in Russian that Alberta was rather sure would translate to "What a friggin' idiot." "I do not understand how people in this country expect to do business when they cannot even remember simple details like an address. You have pen?"

Alberta jotted down the address where she was supposed to meet Lucy's mysterious comrade later that night and was again filled with a rush of adrenaline. Not only was Alberta finding undercover detective work to be exciting, but this second stint at employment was already much more satisfying than her first.

# Chapter 10

*Oro è che oro vale.*

Helen wasn't going to make getaway car driver her follow-up career to her decades spent in sisterhood, but she was proving to be a very reliable chauffeur. When Alberta and Jinx asked her to drive them to meet Olive a few towns over from Tranquility, she told them she and the Buick would be gassed up and ready to leave in fifteen minutes. Alberta wasn't the only one enjoying this excursion into the investigative arts.

But when they pulled into the parking lot of a grungy strip mall, they were introduced to the seedier side of undercover detective work. The Olive Branch Pawn Shop was located between The Rose Tattoo Parlor Shoppe and Johnny Giambona's Bail Bondsmen Service. It looked like Alberta really did hop an international flight, and the safe enclave of Tranquility felt as far away as the Kremlin.

"If you're not back in fifteen minutes, I'm calling Vinny for backup," Helen announced.

Once inside Olive's place of business things, thankfully, got a little less seedy. The musty odor and piles of mismatched items for sale made Alberta and Jinx feel as if they were at a quaint antique store some-where in Maine. Of course, one whose proprietress was a feisty Russian émigré.

"You must be Lucy," the woman from behind the counter sneered. "You're late!"

Olive Berekshnyav looked like she just stepped out of a KGB training video. Her steel-gray hair was pulled back into a bun that sat on top of her head, and her stout figure was covered in a dress of the same color that was both sleeveless and shapeless. She wore no makeup or jewelry, and her perfect posture would've made the most hardened military man weep with pride. Both hands were buried into the two pockets of her dress as she stared at them with contempt, but not suspicion. So, as Jinx had suspected, Lucy and Olive had never met, only spoken to each other on the phone. All Alberta had to do was impersonate a dead woman and they might finally find out what kind of collection Lucy had because the only reason Lucy would have to be in contact with a pawnbroker was to make a sale. Unfortunately, they still had no idea what Lucy was selling. Fortunately, that was about to change.

"So where is your collection?" Olive asked.

"What collection?" Alberta replied.

"Your *TV Guide* collection!" Olive shouted.

As Olive cursed them in Russian for their stupidity, Alberta and Jinx's eyes lit up with excitement as they grabbed each other's hands, both suppressing the urge to hug Olive for supplying the missing and very important piece to their puzzle. Lucy had a collec-tion of *TV Guide*s that she was obviously going to sell to Olive unbeknownst to anyone, including her daughter Enza.

"Yes, of course, my *TV Guide* collection," Alberta said backtracking. "I . . . uh, I didn't bring it."

Before Alberta and Jinx could offer up a reason as to why they didn't have boxes of *TV Guides* in tow, Olive did it for them. "It's because of her, isn't it?" Olive said with disdain as she pointed at Jinx. "The greedy daughter always gets in the way."

Despite the age difference, Jinx was up to the challenge, and when she spoke she sounded exactly like the forty-something Jersey-born gold digger that Enza Saulino was.

"We want mawe," Jinx demanded.

"What?" Olive replied.

"Mawe!"

"I do not understand what you are saying," Olive explained. "Your accent is thicker than the white winter snow of my beloved homeland."

"What Enza's trying to say," Alberta explained, "is that she, I mean we, want more."

"More?!"

Olive shouted so loud it wouldn't have been surprising if she was indeed heard back in the former Soviet republic she called home. "What did I tell you? In your own native tongue I spoke . . . *Oro è che oro vale* . . . Everything is worth its price, and the price for your collection is fifty thousand dollars. That was my offer and you accepted so you could add it to your retirement fund since your daughter keeps spending your money like it is her own!"

Jinx couldn't believe that someone would actually pay fifty thousand dollars for a bunch of magazines. But she couldn't dwell on that, she had a role to play. "I don't care what my mother agreed to, we want mawe," she repeated. "I mean, you know, more."

Olive stared at them with such contempt that the temperature in the pawn shop fell so rapidly it felt as if they were standing in the middle of the Russian tundra two seconds before the onslaught of a blizzard. "You listen to me, comrades, Olive Berekshnyav is a businesswoman who keeps her word, she is not some money-hungry daughter or a weak-willed woman," Olive seethed as she leaned over the glass-topped counter that Alberta and Jinx were grateful still separated them from the furious pawnbroker. "You agreed to the fifty thousand dollars and now you insult me by asking for more? Get out! Get out of Olive Berekshnyav's store and never come back!"

Driving back home the chill of Olive's words was about to get chillier.

"You know what this means, right?" Jinx started. "Lucy may very well have been killed for her *TV Guide* collection."

"How I used to love reading the *TV Guide*," Alberta mused. "Not the new version, the old ones that were small and the same size as the *Reader's Digest.*"

"That was a little before my time, Gram, but I do remember them," Jinx said. "I just can't believe someone would have killed her for it."

"I think you're both missing the point," Helen said, her eyes focused on the road.

"What point is that?" Alberta asked.

"Whoever knew about Lucy's collection probably knew that she was about to sell it, which is why they stole it from her storage unit and killed her," Helen stated. "But since they haven't tried to sell the collection themselves, they must still have it."

"You're absolutely right about that, Aunt Helen."

"I know," Helen agreed. "We can cross off Enza and Donny from the list of potential thieves because neither of them would've wasted any time selling the collection, so the next likely suspects would have to be someone she worked with."

"Right again," Jinx said. "You're really good at this."

Helen sighed, "Working for the Catholic Church for so long, you get used to being surrounded by sinners."

Once again, Alberta wanted to have a discussion with her sister about why she truly left the convent, but the backseat of the Buick was not the ideal place to engage in a heart-to-heart. Alberta would have to concentrate on solving one mystery at a time.

"So, what should we do with this information?" Alberta asked.

"I'll meet you at the office tomorrow," Helen announced. "It's time I took my sister to lunch to celebrate her new job."

At precisely noon the next day, Helen was standing in front of Alberta's desk ready to take her to lunch when she was informed that there would be an addition to their party.

"Marion's at an off-site meeting today, so Beverly is free to join us," Alberta announced.

"Listen to you, 'off-site,'" Helen teased. "It's like you've been a working girl all your life."

"It's just like riding a bicycle," Alberta replied.

"You don't know how to ride a bike," Helen said.

"Shut up."

Alberta introduced Beverly to her sister and soon

after the preliminary hellos and reassurances that she wouldn't be intruding on their sisterly lunch, the three women were sitting at a red vinyl banquette at China Chef. The restaurant was actually an all-you-can-eat buffet so the plates in front of the women contained a smorgasbord of Chinese specialties: egg rolls, pork fried rice, dumplings, lo mein, shrimp with lobster sauce, General Tso's chicken, and beef and broccoli. Every food category imaginable was represented.

While the women ate they shared snippets of their lives. Alberta and Helen learned that Beverly had never married and had been born and raised in Tranquility.

"I'm what used to be referred to as a townie," she said. "That was when Memory Lake was more of a vacation spot for the folks from your part of Jersey and not the full-fledged community it is today."

"You must've seen a lot of changes over the past decades," Alberta observed.

Nodding her head in agreement, Beverly replied, "Oh yes, lots of changes." Then she added with a wistful hint to her voice, "Though I still seem to stay the same."

"In a sea of change everybody needs an anchor," Helen said, crunching on an egg roll. "Is that what you were for Lucy?"

Alberta almost dropped her fork into her moo goo gai pan. She was used to Helen's brusque nature, but was surprised that her sister would be so callous, especially when she had told her how upset Beverly was over Lucy's death. She quickly learned that the direct route is sometimes the best to take when looking for answers.

"Oh Helen, I hope so," Beverly replied, seemingly

grateful to talk about her dead friend. "I didn't know her that long, she used to work on another floor until a few years ago, but we were close and, well, neither of us have . . . *had* I guess is the right way to say it, any family or good friends around here, so we did rely on each other."

"And what about Marion?" Helen asked. "Do you play the same role for him?"

This time Beverly didn't reply with such genuine candor. For a moment she froze and stared down at her food until she found the strength to speak again. But when she did, she continued to gaze at her plate and not look Helen in the eyes as she had only seconds before.

"I'm not sure what you mean," Beverly mumbled.

"I mean you've been Marion's secretary for a very long time, isn't that right?"

"Yes," she replied, still more interested in her food than making eye contact. "Almost twenty years."

"Such an important man as Marion, he must rely on you to keep his ship running smoothly," Helen elaborated. "You must be his anchor too."

"I'd like to think so." Finally, Beverly looked up from her plate, her face a curious combination of so many conflicting emotions, but she had only one sole purpose: to leave the table as quickly as possible. "Excuse me, I need to use the ladies' room."

When Alberta was certain Beverly was out of earshot, she hissed at her sister. "What the hell was that about?"

"You can be so naive, Alberta," Helen replied. "Can't you see for yourself?"

"See what?"

"Beverly is having an affair with the boss."

Chalking it up to Helen's many years of being cloistered in a convent and not an active participant in the real world, Alberta told her sister that she needed to curtail her active imagination. Helen, however, stood her ground and explained that she didn't come to the conclusion that Beverly and Marion were having an affair based on an intuitive hunch, but rather cold hard facts.

"Beverly is the woman I saw Marion consoling at the wake."

"What?" Alberta cried. "You said you didn't get a look at the woman's face."

"I didn't," Helen confirmed. "But the backside of that woman is quite unique. I'd recognize it anywhere, and her hair isn't what Mama would call subtle. She most definitely was the woman who Marion was all over, whispering in her ear, draping his arm around her shoulder, touching her elbow. I may have taken a vow of chastity, but I'm not stupid, Berta, I know the difference between a friendly touch between a man and a woman and a touch that's the product of something much more intimate."

Simultaneously impressed and shocked, Alberta realized that Helen could once again be right. Why couldn't Beverly and Marion be having an affair? They were both roughly the same age, Marion was handsome and Beverly, despite her attire, wasn't a bad-looking woman. Plus, in the short time she had been working at Wasserman & Speicher, she had noticed that Beverly wasn't a very good assistant. She thought it was because she was still in shock over Lucy's death, but maybe it was because she just stunk at her job, and the only reason Marion kept her on the payroll was because she was better lying on a bed than sitting behind a desk.

When Beverly returned to the table, she announced that she must have eaten something bad and wasn't feeling well. The women quickly paid for the check and were almost out the door when they got another surprise that made Beverly turn even whiter.

"Marion! I thought you were at that meeting all day," Beverly declared.

The faintest flicker of alarm appeared on Marion's face, but his fluster quickly dissolved into calm. "Hello, Beverly. Everybody has to eat lunch, isn't that right, Alberta?"

"You're asking an Italian about the importance of food?" she joked.

"And this must be your sister Helen," he added. "I haven't seen you in years."

Alberta held her breath waiting for Helen to answer, hoping that she would keep her typical blunt demeanor in check and understand the importance of concealing certain bits of information. Luckily, her sister didn't disappoint.

"No, I don't believe so either," Helen lied. "Not since you and Berta graduated high school."

"Time surely does fly, doesn't it?" Marion asked rhetorically. "Now, if you ladies would excuse me, there are some boring businessmen over there that I need to get back to."

Beverly reached out and grabbed Marion's arm and the look of fear returned to his face once again. "Mr. Klausner, I think I ate something that doesn't agree with me," Beverly said, releasing her hold on him to clutch her stomach. "I should go home."

"Of course," he replied. "I'll see you tomorrow."

But when tomorrow rolled around, Beverly didn't. The next day, Friday, another absence. Not courageous enough to bring up the subject with Marion, Alberta asked Denise if she had heard from Beverly and was told that she hadn't, but then added with a conspiratorial whisper that this wasn't abnormal behavior on Beverly's part.

"She, um, does this quite a bit," Denise admitted before scurrying back to her office.

In between answering Marion's phone calls, ordering lunch for a department meeting, and alphabetizing files, Alberta called Beverly's cell phone and home numbers, but never once got hold of her or received a return call. For most of the day and the entire drive home, Alberta imagined Beverly was lying in a pool of blood on her living room floor and half-expected to find the woman floating in the lake exactly where she had found Lucy.

"You're taking this crime-solving thing a bit too far," Helen barked.

"This time you're wrong, Aunt Helen," Jinx said. "Gram's senses are being awakened after lying dormant for so long. I think you're on to something."

"I hope Beverly is all right," Alberta said. "She really is such a lovely woman."

"Only one way to find out, Gram," Jinx announced. "Time for another break-in."

Standing outside Beverly's front door, they realized that it wasn't going to be nearly as easy to break in as it was to get into Lucy's condo. Beverly lived on the first floor, and her building, along with an adjoining garage, was surrounded by a very tall privacy fence equipped with a security alarm system, so there would be no shimmying through a back window. Also too, as Joyce would say, she lived right off a shared public space where some people were sitting on benches and others were walking their dogs so anyone could see them trying to jimmy the lock or breaking her front window to crawl through. They would have to try and enter the old-fashioned way.

Alberta knocked on the front door and called out for Beverly in a voice a few notches above normal, but not quite a yell that would startle the neighbors. She did this a few more times.

"Can I help you?"

Alberta and Jinx turned to the right to see the face of an elderly woman peering out at them. The rest of the woman's body remained inside her condo.

"Hello," Alberta said cheerily. "My name's Alberta and this is my granddaughter, Jinx. We're looking for my friend Beverly, do you know where she is?"

"Jinx? I thought I had a funny name—Ruthanne— but Jinx? Now doesn't that just take the cake?"

Stepping out onto the terrace that connected both condos, they saw that Ruthanne's body was as elderly as her face. In her slippered feet, she stood just under five feet tall, and her blue and yellow floral house-dress hung loose over her bony frame. Her updo looked like it was a few days overdue for a trip to the beauty parlor, but her face, although wrinkled, radiated warmth and kindness that reminded Alberta of long-passed relatives and reminded Jinx of her grandmother.

"Don't you worry about Beverly, honey," Ruthanne

said with a twinkle in her eye. "I'm sure she's just gotten lucky."

"Does she like Atlantic City too?" Jinx asked.

Ruthanne laughed so hard at Jinx's comment that she had a coughing fit that made her extend her arm to grab hold of her doorframe so she wouldn't fall over. The loose skin underneath her arm continued to jiggle even after her coughing subsided.

"Oh no, honey, not that kind of lucky," Ruthanne continued. "The kind of lucky that makes her leave looking like that sad sack Bette Davis and come back home looking like Lana Turner. You know, like her *you know what* don't stink."

"You mean she's with her boyfriend?" Alberta inquired.

"I can't be one hundred percent sure, being that I only came back a few days ago from my sister's. She lives in one of those fifty-five and older communities in Barnegat," Ruthanne said. "Costs a fortune, but they provide three meals a day. Since Dolly, that's my sister, can't cook to save her life, it's worth every penny."

Alberta couldn't think of anything worse than not being able to cook her own meals but didn't want to get on Ruthanne's bad side, so she said, "That sounds amazing."

"It was! And even if it wasn't, I still would've went," Ruthanne explained. "I had to get away from all the noise."

"What noise?" Jinx asked.

"The construction! For the past few months they've been working on the outdoor space, ripping it up and planting a whole new garden," Ruthanne said. "Isn't it beautiful?"

Alberta and Jinx looked around at the landscape

and had to admit that it was pristine, but it still didn't answer their main question. "It is," Alberta started. "But do you have any idea where Beverly is?"

"Has to be with her boyfriend," Ruthanne replied. "Nothing else matters to her in this world except her fella."

Later that night as Helen was once again beating them at canasta and they all agreed that cucumber-flavored vodka was no match for fluffy marshmallow, three-fourths of the group assumed Ruthanne must have been referring to Marion.

"I know he's the obvious choice," Alberta said, scooping Lola up in her arms, "But I just don't know if I believe it."

"That's because you're a Greedy Gretchen," Helen declared. "And you want Marion all to yourself." In defense of her owner Lola meowed loudly. "*Sta 'zitto!* You should know a hussy when you see one, Miss Gina Lollobrigida." At the sound of her full name, Lola meowed even louder and squirmed in Alberta's arms.

"Oh come on, Helen, I do not."

"Then do like Joyce says and follow the facts," Helen argued. "And all the facts lead to Marion being Beverly's secret lover."

Helen accented her comment by throwing down some cards to reveal that she had over 5,200 points and was the canasta winner for the sixth week in a row.

"Again!" Alberta cried. "If I didn't know you better, Helen, I'd swear you were cheating."

"No cheating necessary, not when you know how to play the game."

"Well, one game Beverly is losing at is the game of finance," Joyce announced.

"What are you talking about, Aunt Joyce?"

"I was waiting for a lull in the evening to tell you what I found out," Joyce explained. "Beverly's credit score is a dismal 410, and that condo you couldn't get into is in foreclosure."

"That's so sad," Alberta cried.

"That's so impressive," Jinx cried next. "How'd you find that out?"

Joyce explained that even though she hadn't been a part of the financial world as a wheeler and dealer for the past several years, she still had many friends who were active members of the industry. "You'd be surprised how easy it is to obtain private financial information about someone."

"And how easy it is for a good person to turn bad," Alberta said, a shiver racing down her spine. They all knew what she was referring to, but allowed Alberta to finish her thought. "If Beverly was hurting for money, she could have killed Lucy, stolen her *TV Guide* collection, and decided to leave town to find someplace less risky to sell it."

"But Gram, how could she do that?" Jinx asked. "Beverly and Lucy were friends."

Alberta smiled weakly at her granddaughter's innocence. "It's like Olive said, lovey, everyone has their price."

# CHAPTER 11

*Ogni cuffia è buone por le natte.*

The early bird may catch the worm, but the early temp catches the boss worming through his assistant's desk. At least that's what Alberta discovered when she went into work earlier than usual Monday morning.

The previous night Alberta had been plagued by upsetting dreams associated with Lucy's murder that kept her from getting a restful sleep. The dreams couldn't be categorized as nightmares, but the scenes and images conjured by her sleeping mind were definitely disturbing. After lying awake for several hours, Alberta decided to get up at 5 a.m. and take advantage of the situation by getting an early start to the day. She never thought she'd catch Marion trying to take advantage of Beverly's absence.

She turned the corner of the hallway and in the distance saw the unusual sight of Marion sitting at Beverly's desk gazing intently at the computer screen. Not only had she never seen Marion sitting at Beverly's desk before, but every time she went into his office or walked by and peered in through the windows, he always seemed to be doing something other than working on his own computer. He would either be on the phone with his back to his PC, sitting on the couch talking to a colleague, or standing with his hands in his pants pockets staring out the window. She hadn't been in his employ for very long, of course, but she never once saw him working on a computer. Until now.

Just as Alberta was about to clear her throat or drop her employee entrance card on the tiled floor to make some noise that would announce her presence, Marion looked up and caught her watching him.

"What are you doing in so early?"

Although startled, Alberta quickly regained her composure once she realized the truth was on her side. "I couldn't sleep," she replied honestly. "So, I thought why not come in early and continue to acclimate myself to my new surroundings? So much has changed since the last time I was a working girl." Not the least of which was her fearlessness when talking to her boss. "Like, isn't your assistant supposed to start your computer in the morning and not the other way around?"

"My assistant is also not supposed to suddenly quit on me," Marion said. "But that's exactly what she did."

Since Alberta already knew it was very likely that Beverly had skipped town, she almost forgot to feign shock over hearing the news. She was further distracted watching Marion try to conceal the fact that he was closing out all the files he had opened on her computer. Why was he hiding what he had been looking at? After all, wasn't he the boss and didn't he essentially have the right to rifle through anyone's computer who was on his payroll? She would contemplate those questions later. For the moment she needed to act surprised.

"She quit?" Alberta cried. "Why on earth would she do such a thing?"

"I wish I knew," he said, eyebrows and shoulders rising. "I do know that Beverly was a flighty woman who had a tendency to be impulsive and make decisions based on emotion rather than logic, but this is drastic even for her."

Nodding her head to illustrate that she understood Beverly had always been a flight risk, Alberta mentally cataloged the fact that Marion spoke of Beverly in the past tense. She wasn't sure if that was an important clue or a simple slip of the tongue, but she did think it odd that he would speak of her in that way, especially if he had only just found out she had quit. Was he one of those men who, if he felt betrayed, turned his back on you immediately and forever? Was Beverly already dead to him even after such a long relationship, whether that relationship had been passionate, platonic, or something in between?

"But quitting your job is such a major decision; she must have been thinking about it for a while at least," Alberta gushed. "You had no idea she wanted to leave?"

"None," Marion confirmed as he leaned back in Beverly's chair, now quite relaxed, his foot bouncing up and down as if tapping the air. "Denise received an e-mail from her this morning with nary an explanation, just stating that effective immediately she was resigning from her position as my secretary . . . or executive assistant as she preferred to call herself."

"That seems so sudden," Alberta observed. "Did she say where she was going or if she had another job?"

"Nothing, except that she was quitting," Marion replied. "And she didn't even have the decency or courage to send the e-mail to me. I take personal offense that she would circumvent protocol and reach out to HR instead of me."

Alberta didn't remember much about office protocol from her first stint as a working stiff, but she did believe that sending a resignation notice directly to human resources was the proper way to handle leaving a job. Wisely, she kept that thought to herself. Her thoughts about Beverly were handled differently.

"I have to say that I am stunned by all of this, Marion," Alberta began. "I didn't know her all that well—and, not for nothing, we never really know anyone completely—but, from what I did know of Beverly, this doesn't sound like her at all."

"Like I said, she could be . . . impetuous," Marion replied, choosing his adjective carefully. "But not for nothing, as you say, I must admit that she was a very good secretary and now, of course, I can't find anything, which is why I was looking on her computer."

That makes sense, Alberta thought. After working for Marion for so many years it would be reasonable that Beverly would have worked autonomously and handled many of the mundane, yet necessary, daily tasks on her own without consulting Marion. With her suddenly gone, he would be at a loss as to how to get the simplest thing done. Alberta then wondered why she was trying so hard to convince herself that she hadn't caught Marion in the act of doing something wrong. Perhaps it was because she so desperately wanted that thought to be right.

"If you need any help, Marion, please just ask," Alberta offered.

"Really? Because I know the perfect way you can help me."

"Tell me what I can do," Alberta said.

"Be my new secretary."

It took Alberta only three seconds to reply. Although when she did, she wasn't entirely sure if she was replying as an undercover detective trying to get closer to the truth or as an understanding woman trying to get closer to a man.

"Nothing would make me happier."

An hour later, sitting in Denise's office, her happiness was put to the test.

"Looks like somebody is moving up the corporate ladder at breakneck speed," Denise said, her words much more enthusiastic than her tone.

Alberta explained that it was happenstance, she was in the right place at the right time and didn't expect to remain in the position for very long. "I completely understand that I'm still in the probationary period and, honestly, I'm not sure I'm going to be able to fill Beverly's shoes, speaking of which, I found a bunch of her shoes in her bottom drawer," she confessed. "Anyway, I'll do the best I can, of course, but if I don't feel I can hack it or if Marion . . . is that okay if I still call him Marion? Mr. Klausner sounds so formal. If Marion isn't satisfied with me, I will not take it personally and I will move aside so someone else can take over."

Denise's slightly condescending smirk in response to Alberta's honesty could be interpreted as vaguely inappropriate for someone working in HR. There was, however, no ambiguity when it came to her explicitly inappropriate comment. "I have a feeling you'll be able to satisfy *Marion's* every need."

Alberta wasn't sure if she should be flattered or insulted. She decided to take the third option and acted confused. "I'm not really sure what you mean by that, Denise."

Denise knew that Alberta knew exactly what her comment meant, so she decided to be as blunt as possible to make sure she got her point across. "If you ever repeat what I'm about to tell you, I will deny it to my grave," Denise said leaning forward and dropping her voice to a whisper. "Marion likes all the secretaries here at Wasserman & Speicher. And he likes them in that Sally Field way . . . he really, *really* likes them. Not only that, but he likes the secretaries to like him back." Sitting back in her chair, Denise smirked, "*Capisce?*"

"*Capisce,*" Alberta repeated, then added, "I think."

Sighing harshly, Denise said, "I really don't think I can speak any plainer than that."

Alberta could feel the tension in the room and knew that if she asked more questions she would risk Denise either getting suspicious as to her motives or getting aggravated with her interrogation, but she was desperate to find out if Marion and Beverly really were having an affair or if Marion was just an old-fashioned skirt chaser who never really made contact with his target.

"So you think Beverly quit because she found out Marion was cheating on her?" Alberta asked as innocently as possible. Alberta thought she saw a flash of anger swipe across Denise's face, but the woman suddenly tossed her head and waved her arms animatedly, and any trace of hostility was gone.

"Between you, me, and the lousy wallpaper in this office, that's my guess," Denise confided. "Now I have no proof and, personally, I admire the business Mr. Klausner has created. Just to be clear not one person has ever brought charges of harassment against him and most employees stay until retirement age, which was just around the corner for Beverly, *but*—and this is a very big *but* with a capital *B*—when it comes to women, I don't trust him. And neither should you."

At that moment, Denise's cell phone rang and the sounds of a trumpet filled the room playing a tune that was vaguely familiar to Alberta, but she couldn't recall its title. Denise glanced at her phone, but instead of answering the call, she muted the sound. By the look of her tightly pursed lips, Alberta could tell she didn't want to speak to whoever was on the other end. By the way her hands were folded on top of her desk, it was clear that their conversation had also come to an end.

"You're a grown woman, Alberta, and I know you can handle yourself, but at some point Mr. Klausner will make his intentions known, so please . . . consider yourself warned."

It took only two days for Denise's prophecy to manifest itself. Alberta was sitting at her desk munching on slices of fresh mozzarella and tomato trying desperately to decipher Beverly's color-coded calendar system—so far the only thing she could determine was that green meant an in-house meeting and yellow meant a conference call, but she had yet to figure out what blue stood for—when she saw Marion walk past her desk and circle the interior of the office for the third time. Just when she had decided he was wearing one of those devices that count how many steps you take in a day, he stopped in front of her desk, tiny beads of sweat forming on his forehead, and she realized he was actually circling his prey.

"Let's have coffee tomorrow," he said. Although she knew he meant for his words to sound like an order, he was so nervous that they sounded more like a question.

Could this anxious man standing before her really be the notorious lady-killer? Could he really have continued an affair with Beverly while pursuing other women in the same office? That would require a certain savoir faire, like the businessman version of Tom Jones or at least Engelbert Humperdinck, and Marion was acting much more like Jim Nabors, and not the smooth-voiced crooner, but the goofy sitcom soldier. There was only one way for Alberta to know what Marion's intentions were and that was to agree to the date.

"I'd like that, Marion," she replied earnestly. "Thank you."

Her acceptance seemed to boost his confidence and he literally bounced up and down on his heels a few times. "Wonderful," he beamed. "We've been spending so much time as boss and employee, we haven't had a chance to be just Marion and Alberta like in the old days."

That was a bit of a stretch, Alberta thought, since back in the old days they hardly had any interaction. Yes, they knew each other, but they weren't friends in high school and never hung out in the same crowd. Come to think of it, Alberta couldn't remember what crowd Marion did hang out with, if any. How egotistical, she thought, to feel pity for a man who had clearly become a success. Interesting how the impressions made early in life are hard to shatter despite evidence to the contrary.

"That would be nice," Alberta lied, "It'll be fun to reminisce about the, um, good old days."

And, of course, pump Marion for information and see if he knew anything about Lucy's *TV Guide* collection or Beverly's disappearance. Those were the real reasons she had agreed to have coffee with Marion at a little café away from the prying eyes of the rest of the Wasserman & Speicher employees, at least that's what she tried to convince herself. She had a harder time convincing her family.

"Ooh, Grandma's caught herself a silver fox!" Jinx exclaimed, as she strained the water out of a pot of ravioli.

"Don't be ridiculous, Jinx," Alberta protested. "Marion just wants to talk about old times."

"And create some new memories," Joyce interjected.

"Just don't lose sight of the mission," Jinx said. "He might be able to supply some answers to our questions."

"Like why is my sister falling for a man she hardly knows," Helen snapped.

"I've known Marion since I was a teenager," Alberta corrected. "He's harmless. A bit *ungatz*, but harmless."

"*Ogni cuffia è buone por le natte*," Helen said.

"She's right about that," Joyce added.

"I seriously need to brush up on my Italian if I'm going to hang with you gals," Jinx said. "She's right about what?"

"Men are men, Jinxie," Helen said, "Young, old, married, single, gay, straight, they're all the same."

"What Helen's trying to say is that men all want the

same thing, a little action, a quick roll in the hay or on the office couch," Joyce clarified.

Alberta threw her hands up in the air so quickly she almost knocked over the plate of ravioli Jinx was setting down in front of her. "*Ah, Madon,* Joyce, not you too!"

"You forget, Alberta, I've worked with CEOs, I know what they're like," Joyce informed. "Now forgive me, but I have to ask, do you have protection?"

"What do I need protection for?" she cried. "I'm having coffee with him, not breakfast in bed."

"Don't you remember what Sister Bernice always said?" Helen asked. "One thing leads to the other."

"*Santa Madre di Dio!* You three are insane!" Alberta shouted. "The only reason I agreed to go out with Marion is to uncover more clues, not to have sex with him. For Crise sake, you make me sound like cousin Gertie!"

"Let's not get carried away, Berta," Helen said. "I never called you a street whore. All I meant to imply is that it seems like you might be falling for the man you're supposed to be investigating. I don't want to see you cross the same line Beverly did."

"Speaking of crossing a line," Alberta said, her face puckered up like she just sucked on a rancid lemon. "What did you do to this ravioli, lovey?"

Ignoring Alberta's pained expression, Jinx grinned broadly. "It's gluten-free pasta stuffed with dairy-free cheese."

Alberta, Helen, and Joyce all looked at Jinx as if she had committed a mortal sin. "Why on God's green earth would you do something like that?" Alberta asked, her eyes wide with disbelief.

"I'm trying to be more health conscious, Gram,"

Jinx explained. "You said so yourself that you needed to cut back, so I'm taking some of your old recipes and updating them."

Helen spit out a half-eaten ravioli onto her plate. "That's blasphemy!"

"Also too," Joyce said, forcing herself to swallow one of Jinx's creations. "They're disgusting."

"Oh, come on!" Jinx protested. "They're not that bad. Gluten-free pasta just, you know, takes some getting used to."

Alberta shoved the plate away from her. "Sorry, lovey, but I'd rather be force-fed food from the Olive Garden for the rest of my life."

Helen took a swig of mango kiwi vodka to cleanse her palate and smirked. "You better hope your rendezvous with Marion leaves a better taste in your mouth than Jinxie's concoction."

"Trust me," Alberta said. "I'm not letting that man anywhere near my mouth."


Her family's laughter was still ringing in her ears the next day as she sat across from Marion at a bistro table at Mama Bella's Café. The small restaurant was only a short block from the office, but its Mediterranean decor and ambience, complete with soft lighting, statues of cherubs in various stages of undress, and piped-in music that ranged from traditional Italian folk songs to Dean Martin's greatest hits, made it feel like it was a continent away.

Their conversation was just as distant, and they spent the bulk of their time discussing the whereabouts of former classmates, the idiosyncrasies of certain teachers, and of course Marion's unusual name. Alberta once again apologized on behalf of her class for teasing him about it, but he assured her that he had long since reconciled himself to the fact that some people would always mock him for his moniker. "Life isn't for the weak," he said, and Alberta heartily agreed.

It was, however, for the patient. Marion was on his third cup of coffee, and the closest he got to flirting with Alberta was to confess that he had a crush on her freshman year. Flattered, Alberta admitted that it was sweet to know someone liked her back then, because she thought she was the most hideous creature ever allowed to roam the planet. Marion assured her that was far from the truth and the only reason he never asked her out on a date was because he considered her to be out of his league.

"Better late than never," Alberta blurted and immediately regretted her words. So much for playing it cool and trying to get Marion to trip up on his words and reveal some secrets. "Not that this is a date . . . it's just coffee, but you know what I mean."

Laughing good-naturedly, Marion said that he did understand and was happy Alberta agreed to step out of the office with him. "A man can only talk escrow, closings, and real estate development for so long before he wants to take a bulldozer to every high-rise he's helped build," he admitted. "It's nice to just sip coffee and chat with an old friend."

This time, when Marion called Alberta an old friend she didn't wince, she didn't silently contradict him, but rather thought the reference was sweet and perhaps accurate. Maybe she had remembered the past too harshly, too dismissively, and maybe if she looked deeper she'd recall that she and Marion had shared some fun times together. She'd have to make do with her memories, because it didn't appear that Marion was interested in making any new ones.

"I have to get back to the office tonight," Marion announced, standing up from his chair. "Do you need me to walk you back to your car?"

It was a good thing that Alberta was an expert when it came to hiding her disappointment. "Oh no, I'm going to sit here and finish my cappuccino," she replied. "I'm awfully surprised they make such a good one."

"Thank you, Alberta, this was nice," Marion said. "I'll see you in the office tomorrow morning."

And that was that. No kiss good-bye, not on the lips or even her cheek. He didn't shake her hand or brush her shoulder with the tips of his fingers as he walked away. There was absolutely no physical contact whatsoever. And despite her previous protestations to her family, she had hoped there would be *something*. So, despite all her grand talk she had to be honest and admit that she was upset because Marion had behaved like such a gentleman.

Sitting in front of her now cold cappuccino all thoughts of Lucy and Beverly were gone from her mind and the only person Alberta felt sorry for was herself.

# CHAPTER 12

*I frutti proibiti sono I più dolci.*

The next morning it was business as usual for both Alberta and Marion. It was as if yesterday's field trip had never happened.

Alberta looked into Marion's office and saw that he was marking up a contract with a red pen, head down and eyes focused on the legally binding words he was reading instead of trying to steal glances at his new secretary, whose lipstick, incidentally, was a slightly glossier pink than it had been the day before. Even when he reached for the coffee cup that Alberta had placed on his desk a few minutes earlier, he didn't lift up his head and allow his eyes to stray in her direction. He remained fixated on his job at hand. For the moment, work, and not some woman, seemed to be Marion's mistress.

The more she thought about it, the harder it was for Alberta to believe that Marion was the lecherous boss Denise made him out to be. He and Alberta had shared friendly conversation over a few cups of coffee and nothing more. He never made a pass at her or even allowed suggestive innuendo to enter into their dialogue. He was in his office redlining a contract, being nothing but proper and professional, while Alberta was at her desk rummaging through a huge file trying to find something called a quitclaim bill of sale and harboring nothing but improper and unprofessional thoughts about her boss. Alberta turned page after page of the file in search of the elusive document, but her eyes glazed over and she couldn't concentrate. She was not only ashamed of herself, but also very confused.

Could Denise be well intentioned, but not so well informed? Maybe she was trying to warn the newest member of her staff of the potential romantic pitfalls of the job but doing nothing more than spreading unsubstantiated rumor. And could Jinx and her family simply be judgmental? Maybe they just assumed Marion and Beverly had an affair because that was the easiest, most convenient solution as to why a man would befriend a woman.

Even though Alberta was on red alert, she hadn't noticed Marion showing any signs of emotional distress since Beverly's departure. He didn't seem at all frazzled that the secretary with whom he had allegedly been having sex was no longer an intercom's buzz away. Ever since he found out Beverly quit, he hadn't been trying to call her incessantly, he wasn't asking people if they had heard from her, nor had he made up some lame excuse to leave the office to meet with her and beg her to come back to work. He wasn't acting at all the way a scorned lover should act.

Was Alberta—with a little help from her colleague and family—making a mountain out of a molehill, or a philanderer out of an employer, as this case may be? Or was she so desperate for affection from the opposite sex after spending years in an emotionally unsatisfying marriage that she had imagined the first single man she met who fell into the appropriate age bracket had instantly fallen in love with her? Dear Lord, Alberta thought, what would Jessica Fletcher say? Only a few weeks on the job as an undercover sleuth and already she was letting her emotions cloud her reasoning. She had agreed to join forces with Jinx to do a job, and it was time she started to act like the superspy her granddaughter believed she could be. Right after she mastered the skills required to be a super secretary.

"Alberta," Marion said, his voice rising out of the intercom speaker. "Could you please pull the Hampton Estate file from the Safe Room?"

Alberta pressed the red button on the machine so Marion would be able to hear her response, "Absolutely! Will do! Right away!"

Brimming with can-do determination, she swiveled around in her chair, but before she rose, she swiveled back, and pressed the red button a second time. "Marion?"

"Yes."

"Any chance you could tell me where the Safe Room is?"

Marion led Alberta down a flight of stairs and then a long hallway, which was in an area that Alberta had never been. Clearly, they were headed somewhere that was not a designated stop on Denise's introductory tour for new hires. To the right was a large double door made of steel that was padlocked but definitely not soundproof because she heard a loud, whirring noise coming from behind the door.

"That's the computer room," Marion explained in

answer to Alberta's quizzical stare. "Only Ruchir in IT has the key, and even I don't have clearance to get in without his say-so."

"Ruchir?" Alberta questioned. "I don't think I've met him yet."

"He works off-site," Marion replied. "Saves quite a bit of money to outsource certain departments."

At the end of the hallway was an identical double door that served as a dead end. It was also their destination. "And this, Alberta, is the Safe Room."

Unlike the computer room, which was kept locked the old-fashioned way, access to this room was monitored in a much more twenty-first-century fashion, through an electronic passcode.

"I guess Denise didn't take you down here originally because you were starting out as a temp," Marion said. "And, really, only a few of us still use this area."

"It looks like whatever's behind these doors is highly personal and confidential," Alberta commented. "I feel like I'm about to be given the keys to the kingdom."

"I hate to dispel such a lofty idea," Marion said, his lips spreading to form a wide smile, "But it's nothing more than a relic of the past."

Marion went on to explain that most of their files and documents were archived off-site and stored online, but there were many files that were too old and too important to completely discard, so they were kept here under electronic lock and key. Originally the files were kept in a safe, complete with a seven-number combination, which is why today it was still called the Safe Room.

"I don't readily admit this to most people," Marion

said lowering his voice, "But this room is more nostalgic than necessary."

He paused for a moment and stared directly into Alberta's eyes. "Truth be told, I sometimes find it hard to let certain things go."

Was this his attempt at flirting? Alberta couldn't be sure, because this time there were no beads of sweat on his forehead, just a twinkle in his eye. But boy, was Jinx right, Marion really had grown into a very distinguished man.

Wait! What was she doing? Alberta silently chastised herself because she wasn't supposed to be thinking of Marion as a man, she was supposed to be thinking of him as a suspect. Or, at least, a link to the real suspect. She needed to hold tight to logic and not romantic notions.

"I know what you mean, Marion," Alberta said. "But that's why God invented the paper shredder."

After a moment, Marion's body convulsed into laughter, and he actually bent over and slapped his hand on his thigh. He reached out to touch Alberta's forearm, and despite the invisible armor she tried to cover herself in, she felt an electric shock that almost made her flinch.

"You are such a breath of fresh air," he said. "Would you like to know another secret?"

Trying not to hyperventilate, Alberta answered, "What girl doesn't want to hear a man's secrets?"

"The passcode to this room is my nickname," Marion disclosed. He then added with a chuckle, "Can you guess what it is?"

Her mind racing, Alberta thought back to what the kids used to call Marion when they were in high school, but she hardly doubted that he would use

Girly Boy or Sissy Name as his secret password in a professional setting. Since she didn't know his likes, dislikes, hobbies, or what his favorite *anything* was, she didn't have a clue as to what his password could be. However, when he told her the four-letter-word that would open the door when punched into the keypad, she felt like an idiot because it was so obvious.

"Duke," he replied.

"Of course!" Alberta cried.

If the nickname was good enough for John Wayne, the original Marion, it was good enough for his namesake.

An hour later, while Marion was at a lunch meeting, Alberta finally found the quitclaim she had been looking for all morning. It was a crumbled, three-page document from 1964 that looked to be a carbon copy of the original since some of the typed information appeared to be smudged. She smoothed out the pages, walked over to the copier to make a copy, and returned it to the file on her desk. She stapled the new copy, but when she went to paper clip it to the front of the file before bringing it into Marion's office, she noticed that the pages were still unstapled—obviously the stapler was shooting blanks.

Alberta didn't feel like walking to the other side of the office to the supply room, so she opened the top drawer of Beverly's desk, where she knew her former office mate kept her personal stash of supplies. She found a small container of paper clips, a ruler, a rather risqué Betty Boop pencil sharpener, multiple bottles of Wite-Out, and another stapler that upon further inspection was also out of staples.

When she tried to open the bottom drawer, she was surprised to find it locked. She could have sworn she had seen Beverly open both drawers when she was sitting at her original desk, but maybe her mind was playing tricks on her. Upon second thought she distinctly remembered seeing Beverly grab a piece of special "From the desk of Marion Klausner" letterhead from the bottom drawer, then kick it shut with her foot before spinning around to put the letterhead into the electric typewriter that was behind her.

Alberta spun around in her chair and looked at the typewriter with the same curiosity she did when she first saw Beverly pounding its keys because she couldn't believe such an old piece of machinery still had a place in a modern office. She laughed to herself because she felt like she was staring at a kindred spirit. Who would have thought that at her age she would have been welcomed back into the workforce?

Unable to resist, Alberta flipped the typewriter's power button on and watched in amusement as the antique came to life. Various lights flickered until they shined dimly around the edges of the plastic covering, the cylindrical platen inched upward a few times accompanied by a clicking sound while the ribbon cartridge slid slowly to the left and then did a quicker slide to the right and then back to the left where it remained in position. When the typewriter was completely resuscitated, it produced a low hum that seemed to cry out to Alberta and say, "Please use me! I still have some life left in me yet!" She was about to find out the old clunky machine also had a purpose.

Alberta grabbed a piece of regular stationery from her desk and placed it behind the platen. She then held her finger down on the Return key and watched as the piece of paper was sucked into the body of the

typewriter to emerge securely fastened to the roller.
It was now ready, willing, and able to be struck by the
still-eager keys.

For a few seconds Alberta's fingers lay motionless
on top of the thick plastic keys while she wondered
what she should type. It was as if she felt compelled to
choose words that would be profound and meaning-
ful. After a moment of contemplation, she thought of
the perfect phrase. Slowly and deliberately she typed:
Alberta & Jinx—Lady Detectives.

She hit the Return key a few times so the letters
rose above the metal piece that held the ribbon in
place and she could have an unobstructed view. Then
the key suddenly jammed and she heard a clanking
noise every time she hit the button.

"Oh, for Crise sake please tell me I didn't break
this thing," she muttered to herself.

She lifted up the plastic top that covered the ribbon
and immediately saw the problem. A small key, similar to one that would unlock a mailbox, had been
taped to the underside of the cover, gotten loose, and
had fallen between the platen and the ribbon cartridge. What an odd place to store a key, Alberta
thought, unless it was put there to keep it hidden
from prying eyes!

Feeling adrenaline once again pump through her
veins, Alberta used the key to open up the locked
desk drawer and was overwhelmed with pride when
she heard the tumbler click and the drawer slide
open. She did it! She solved the mystery of the unlocked drawer. It was a small victory, but she would
take it.

She quickly surveyed the contents of the drawer
and found that it only contained a box of the special

letterhead and a notebook. Why would Beverly keep such mundane contents under lock and key? She opened up the notebook and immediately understood why.

Looking around to make sure she wasn't being watched, she stuck the notebook into her shoulder bag and tossed the key back into the drawer. Now that she had stolen—well, *relocated*—the once secure valuable, there was no need to keep the key hidden. She couldn't wait to share her news with Jinx and the others.

"I have proof that Beverly's love for Marion may have been unrequited," Alberta announced at a table filled with Entenmann's mini blueberry muffins and blueberry vodka. "*I frutti proibiti sono I più dolci.*"

"I thought we already agreed that she and Marion were having an affair?" Joyce inquired. "Now you think she considered him to be forbidden fruit?"

"Yes!" Alberta squealed.

"Are you talking about Beverly or yourself?" Helen asked.

"Shut up, Helen!" Alberta snapped. "Beverly loved her boss from afar. Any comment about the two of them doing anything more . . . *intimate* is just hearsay."

"Well I say they were having an affair," Helen said. "I know what I saw at the funeral parlor and I know how these things go, Berta."

"Aunt Helen," Jinx started. "No offense, but you spent most of your life in a convent and not mixing in with the public, so maybe Gram's right about this."

Popping a muffin into her mouth, Helen rolled her eyes and shook her head. She leaned forward, pointed a bony finger at Jinx, and asked, "What do you think I did when I was a nun? Kneel on a pew and pray the day away? For ten years, I taught English at St. Dominick's to girls on hormonal overload, and then I counseled battered women for the next twenty. In between I got a degree in social work and ran a homeless shelter. Along the way, I learned a thing or two about how to read people."

"Wow, Aunt Helen!" Jinx cried. "I had no idea."

"That's 'cause you never asked!" Helen shouted back. "Don't assume you know anything about a person until you learn the facts."

"And what facts do you know about Marion?" Alberta asked. "That he put his arm around Beverly at a wake?"

Waving her hand dismissively at Alberta, Helen replied, "It's not what he did, it's how he did it."

"Ladies, can we focus, please," Joyce interjected. "Alberta, what proof do you have that Beverly's love for Marion was unrequited?"

From underneath her chair, she pulled the notebook and plopped it onto the table in between the bottle of vodka and a box of muffins. Since the cover of the notebook was a picture of several kittens battling over balls of pastel-colored yarn, it didn't quite have the dramatic effect Alberta was hoping it would.

"Marion didn't love Beverly back because she was a crazy cat lady?" Helen asked. "That doesn't bode well for you, Berta."

"No, smarty-pants!" Alberta yelled. "Because it's filled with all of Beverly's passwords, and they're all variations on Marion's nickname, Duke."

"Ooh, Gram, it's like the smoking notebook!"

Helen picked up the notebook, opened it up, and

randomly started reading in a voice devoid of emotion. "Beverly and Duke, Bev and Duke, Bev loves Duke, Bev Loves Duke forever . . . and that's spelled with the number four, I heart Duke . . ."

"We get the point," Joyce said. "You could be right, Alberta."

"Thank you."

"Then again," Joyce added. "You could be wrong."

"How can I be wrong?" Alberta shouted. "The proof is right there."

"We don't have any more proof than we did before," Joyce stated.

"Oh, come on! Beverly was like a teenager, she was in love with Marion or at least had a severe crush on him," Alberta said. "These are not the writings of a woman in a happy relationship with a man."

"I think you might be right about that."

Helen's comment stunned the group into silence. It wasn't often that she agreed with her sister, and they were all anxious to find out why this time was different.

"Have you noticed that all the passwords start with Bev and none of them say Duke loves Bev or Duke and Bev forever, spelled correctly or not?" Helen observed. "Now this doesn't actually tell us if they were or weren't having an affair, but I'm pretty sure it tells us that their relationship was one-sided. Marion might have been sleeping with Beverly, but he definitely didn't love her."

Jinx popped two muffins into her mouth at once. "Boy, do I have a lot to learn about men."

"I think we all do," Alberta said, a bit dejected. "I read over that notebook a couple times already and never picked that up."

"Berta, that's because I learned more about men while in a convent than you ever did while in a marriage."

Downing her glass of vodka, Alberta whined, "And here I thought Marion was a gentleman."

"Don't judge the guy too harshly just yet, hon," Joyce said, refilling Alberta's vodka glass. "Who knows what really lurks inside anyone's house."

"Oh my God! That's it, Aunt Joyce!" Jinx cried. "Are you free tomorrow morning?"

"I'm retired, sweetie, I'm free every morning!"

"I'll pick you up at eight," Jinx said. "It's time we found out what's lurking inside Beverly's house."

# CHAPTER 13

*Aiutati che Dio ti aiuta.*

Even though it was risky, Jinx had decided that the only way to break into Beverly's condo in broad daylight was to act as if it was a completely natural thing to do and not something illegal. So, while Joyce stood in front of her holding a bag of groceries as camouflage, Jinx used a bobby pin to fiddle with the lock to the front door.

"How are you doing, hon?" Joyce asked, her eyes surveying the open courtyard and her lips barely moving.

"They make it look so easy on TV," Jinx grunted.

"Uh-oh," Joyce groaned.

"Just give me a second," Jinx said, "I think this might be working."

"Time's up," Joyce said. "Hello there, ma'am."

"Jinx, is that you?"

Frightened, Jinx whipped around until she saw the elderly woman staring back at her. "Ruthanne! I am so glad to see you."

Without waiting for the older woman to reply, Jinx took a deep breath and concocted a story that was fully detailed, very convincing, and a complete fabrication.

"Me and my grandmother, who you probably remember from our last visit," Jinx started.

"Italian, snazzy haircut, could stand to lose a few pounds," Ruthanne stated.

Ignoring the urge to snap at Ruthanne for her less-than-flattering comment about Alberta, Jinx continued. "My grandmother couldn't be here today because she accidentally broke her foot."

"Oh, that's a shame," Ruthanne remarked. "Can't lose any weight sitting on your rump with a broken foot."

In less than five seconds Jinx's expression changed from friendly to fierce. Just as she opened her mouth to yell at Ruthanne for speaking rudely about her grandmother, Joyce coughed loud enough to remind Jinx she needed to steer the conversation away from getting revenge for Alberta and back to a way of getting into Beverly's condo.

Taking a deep breath, Jinx continued her fake explanation of why she and Joyce were there in the first place. "Even though my grandmother was laid up, she was still trying to get in touch with Beverly, but she couldn't reach her. We started to get worried that something bad had happened to her like maybe Beverly had fallen and broken her hip and was lying on the floor half-dead or in a coma unable to get to the phone. Then we remembered that we had an old key to Beverly's condo, so since my grandmother is stuck on the couch, my Aunt Joyce and I thought it would be nice to bring over some groceries for Beverly, you know, in case she hadn't eaten in a few days, but when we got her and realized that our key wasn't just old, it was the wrong one, and it doesn't work."

Ruthanne was so desperately trying to keep track of what Jinx was saying that she didn't even notice she was holding up a straightened-out bobby pin and not a key. She was also touched by the fact that they would care so much about Beverly that they'd go to such trouble to find out if she was okay.

"But I'm afraid it's all for naught," Joyce said. "Because we don't have the right key."

Pulling out a ring of keys from her housedress, Ruthanne declared, "Well then, this is your lucky day! I'm the building manager and I've been dying for an excuse to go inside Beverly's place and see what's going on."

As giddy as a child on the last day of school before summer vacation, Ruthanne let them into Beverly's condo. She flicked on the lights and Jinx and Joyce both squinted their eyes instinctively out of fear that they would actually see the woman's dead body on the living room floor. But all they saw was an empty room.

"Just as I expected," Ruthanne said, snidely. "The woman has no taste."

Jinx and Joyce tried not to get pulled into a conversation about Beverly's sense of style or lack thereof, but they did feel as if they had stepped into a living room that hadn't been redecorated since Shabby Chic was a design breakthrough.

As Ruthanne continued to rant about the ugliness of the all-beige furnishings and accessories, Joyce put the groceries down on the kitchen table and then followed Jinx into the bedroom. Ruthanne was just entering the room when she heard Joyce scream.

"Oh my God, is she dead?" Ruthanne shouted, clutching the doorjamb.

"No, I saw a snake!" Joyce shouted, her dark skin almost the color of Jinx's olive complexion.

"A snake!" Jinx screamed, jumping on the bed.

"Not on my watch!" Ruthanne cried.

The second Ruthanne was out of the room, Joyce grabbed Jinx's shaking hand and told her that she had lied, there was no snake, she just screamed as a diversion to get Ruthanne out of the condo.

"Why did you need a diversion?" Jinx asked, jumping down off the bed.

Joyce got on her hands and knees and pulled out a cell phone that was wedged between two shoeboxes underneath Beverly's bed. "To retrieve this."

"Aunt Joyce, you're amazing! This has to be Beverly's, it's got a cute little kitten on the phone case," Jinx cried. "But oh no! If this is her phone, then there's no way Beverly left town voluntarily."

"You're right," Joyce agreed. "Who leaves town without their phone?"

And who has a hatchet handy?

"Where is it?!"

Upon seeing Ruthanne run into the room wielding a hatchet, Jinx and Joyce screamed and backed into a corner of the bedroom.

"I think I saw it slither into the bathroom!" Joyce shouted.

Dutifully, Ruthanne ran out of the room in search of her prey, leaving Jinx and Joyce alone holding each other tightly and crammed in between the wall and Beverly's dresser. After a few seconds they tiptoed out of the room and passed the bathroom just in time to see Ruthanne step into the shower with the hatchet perched over her shoulder.

"What kind of woman owns a hatchet?" Jinx asked, as they ran out of the condo.

"Well, truth be told, I kept a butcher knife in my desk when I was working on Wall Street," Joyce said. "A girl's gotta protect herself."

"There's only one way we can help protect Beverly," Jinx declared.

"How's that, sweetie?"

"Find out what's on this cell phone."

Three hours later, after not being able to reach Jinx or Joyce on their cell phones, Alberta panicked and called Vinny. She quickly regretted her decision.

"What are you talking about, Alfie?" Vinny growled. "Are you ladies doing something you're not supposed to be doing?"

What did she expect when she called a cop to tell him that her granddaughter and sister-in-law might be missing and that it somehow might be related to Lucy's murder? Did she think he was going to respond calmly and disinterestedly? Or was he going to react the way he did, concerned and suspicious that Alberta and company were sticking their big Italian noses where they didn't belong? Now Alberta needed to backpedal to throw Vinny off the scent.

Unfortunately, her attempt at dismissive laughter sounded strangely reminiscent of what Ida Lupino would've sounded like had she been cast as an ingenue in a film noir movie in the 1950s. It just didn't work. It also made Helen pause her game of solitaire to give her sister a look that confirmed just how unconvincing she sounded and made Lola stroll in from the living room to investigate.

"We're not doing anything that we shouldn't be doing, Vinny, trust me," Alberta said, hoping her white lie would work. "I'm just concerned because Jinx and Joyce went out this morning, I haven't heard from either one all day, and they're late for canasta."

"Canasta?" Vinny mocked. "I didn't think anybody still played that. Do you follow it up with a game of mah-jongg?"

"Don't get smart with me, Vincenzo," Alberta replied. "Canasta is a game of skill—you should try it sometime."

"Maybe one of these days you'll have to invite me over," he quipped. "Now, don't think I haven't forgotten why you called. Why in the world would you think Jinx or Joyce would be in danger?"

"Have you forgotten that Lucy was murdered and her murderer is still running around out there somewhere?"

"Of course, I haven't forgotten," Vinny said, not bothering to disguise his resentment. "What do you think me and my guys have been doing every day since you found her body in the lake?"

Duly chastised, Alberta apologized and softened her tone. She knew that Vinny was holding his own investigation separate from hers, but she also knew that Tranquility hadn't seen a murder in decades so his investigative skills were probably rusty. Although she knew that she should, she didn't want to reveal that they were looking into the murder on their own, because she knew he was going to tell her to keep their noses out of police work, and he wouldn't be entirely wrong. They had no business doing what they were doing other than that they felt compelled to bring a criminal to justice. And in Alberta's case, to regain a feeling of self-worth that had been eluding her for years.

Vinny's reaction would also be a blow to her ego. She knew that Vinny, like most of the other men in her life, would tell her that she wasn't qualified to be an investigator. For starters, she was a woman, plus she was too old, too dumb, too fat, and too everything else to solve this mystery. She wanted to prove Vinny, and by extension every other man in her life, wrong.

"Of course, I know that you're working around the clock to find Lucy's killer," Alberta said, trying to find the right combination of fear and humility in her voice. "But the fact is that the killer is still out there, and that's why I'm worried."

Alberta waited for Vinny to yell at her and tell her that she was worrying about nothing and that Lucy's murder was an anomaly in an otherwise peaceful enclave, but the yelling never came.

"You have a right to be worried," he said quietly. "Just between you and me, Alfie, we haven't made much progress. DNA results haven't yielded anything significant, no witnesses, all our interviews haven't given us any new leads. Frankly, I'm surprised that the rest of the community hasn't been making more of a fuss about things. I think we have a few more days before all hell breaks loose and people start demanding answers that I just don't have."

*Maybe I should share my information with Vinny,* Alberta thought. Looking at her sister, it was as if Helen could read Alberta's mind and she knew that she was on the verge of telling Vinny what they had discovered. She wasn't about to let that happen.

And she wasn't going to be subtle about it. The fork hit Alberta in her shoulder so hard it made her drop the phone. "For Crise sake, Helen! What the hell are you doing?"

As Lola scurried out of the kitchen anxious to get away from the sisterly squabbling that would undoubtedly follow, Helen scrambled to the floor to pick up the phone before Alberta could get to it and covered the mouthpiece with her hand. "You were about to tell boyfriend number one what we found out," she whispered harshly. "And that would've screwed up Jinx's plan to solve this crime without the police's help."

Ignoring most of what Helen said, Alberta replied, "Boyfriend number one? Who the hell is boyfriend number two?"

"Marion, of course," Helen disclosed. "And for all I know there's a boyfriend number three that you haven't told us about yet."

"*Ah, Madon*, you're *pozzo*!"

"And you're an idiot if you think Vinny is going to let you continue your private investigation after you show him all your cards."

Reluctantly, she knew that Helen was right. Vinny was an old, trusted friend, but he was also the chief of police. She grabbed the phone out of Helen's hand and was desperately trying to think of something to say to cover up the commotion when she was literally saved by the bell. Seconds after the front doorbell rang, Jinx and Joyce ran into the kitchen.

"Sorry we're late, Gram!"

Greatly relieved to see her granddaughter and sister-in-law alive, she quickly got rid of the fuzz.

"They just showed up!" Alberta cried exuberantly. "Looks like one case has been solved."

She put the phone back into its cradle and before she spun around she started yelling at the latecomers. "Do you know how worried I've been? Haven't you checked your cell phones? I thought the two of you were the killer's latest victims!"

Jinx hugged and kissed Alberta, knowing that such physical affection always got her out of a jam with her grandmother. This time was no exception.

"I was helping Aunt Joyce set up her cameras around the lake and it took longer than we expected," Jinx explained.

"Oh right, your photography," Helen said dismissively. "Still doing that?"

"Yes, I'm still doing that, Hel," Joyce replied. "You know how much I love my art."

"I also know how much you love your money," Helen added.

"I've said it before and I'll say it again," Joyce announced. "I will not apologize for being rich."

After retiring early from a long and financially successful career, Joyce devoted much of her spare time to her favorite hobby—painting. Her forte was painting landscapes and she would often get up at dawn to capture the lake at sunrise and paint undisturbed while most of the town was still fast asleep.

But she also wanted to capture how the lake looked during the night. It was Helen who gave her the inspiration when she said, "Why don't you take a picture of it? It lasts longer." That snide remark gave Joyce the idea to buy a camera that she could program to rotate and take pictures at ten-second intervals at various times throughout the night. She then could paint landscapes based on the photos without losing any sleep. Now, her paintings were bestsellers at local fairs and showcased in small art galleries throughout the area. So, Helen had inadvertently helped Joyce make more money, even though Helen was quick to point out that Joyce had more money than God. And since she was once a former Bride of Christ, she should know her ex-father-in-law's finances.

"If we could move on from discussing my net worth, you might be interested to know that Jinx and I found another clue," Joyce began. "We found Beverly's cell phone underneath her bed."

"You what?" Alberta cried.

"And in what universe is setting up cameras around a lake more important than sharing that tidbit?" Helen inquired.

Joyce ignored Helen and instead asked Jinx if she had found any incriminating evidence on Beverly's phone, but Jinx revealed that she couldn't get into the phone because it was password protected. Normally that would be a problem, but since they had a notebook with all of Beverly's passwords it wouldn't be an issue.

Alberta placed the kitty-covered notebook on the table, and Lola came bounding back into the kitchen as if Alberta had opened up a bag of her favorite treats. Jumping up on the table, she plopped down next to the notebook and started licking the image of the cat's face.

"Looks like Lola's got a boyfriend too," Helen quipped.

"What?" Jinx and Joyce asked.

"Never mind," Alberta replied. She then picked up

Lola and placed her on the floor. "And you know the table is off limits, missie. We have work to do."

Alberta started looking through the list of passwords, but couldn't immediately find the one she was looking for. "She has lots of passwords, but they aren't labeled clearly," she explained. "A few of them have initials next to them though."

"Look for a 'CP,'" Helen suggested.

"What's that stand for?" Alberta asked.

"Cell phone," the three other women said simultaneously.

"*Managia!*" Alberta cursed. "Of course. What would I do without you three?

Armed with a goal, Alberta reexamined the contents of the notebook and at the bottom of the first page found what she was looking for. "BevnDuke," she said. "Try it."

Jinx typed in the letters and the cell phone unlocked. She let out a shriek that would have made Victor Frankenstein proud. "It's alive!"

The others immediately went into a mantra of "What's it say? What's it say?" as they formed a semicircle behind Jinx, peering over her shoulder to read the texts she was scrolling through.

"Oh, I feel bad," Alberta said. "These things are private, Beverly never meant for anyone to read them . . . except her and, of course, whoever they were being sent to."

"Pish posh!" Helen shouted. "*Aiutati che Dio ti aiuta!*"

"I agree!" Jinx screamed.

"You know what she said?" Joyce asked.

"I've been brushing up on my Italian so I don't feel *stupido* around you ladies," Jinx explained. "Aunt

Helen said something about God helping people or something like that, right?"

"Heaven helps those who help themselves," Helen confirmed.

"Fine! So help us out, Jinx, whose texts are those?" Alberta asked

"These are between Beverly and Marion," Jinx answered. "There's a ton of them and they are definitely NSFW."

"What's that mean?" Joyce asked.

"Um, not suitable for the workplace," she said.

Helen grabbed the phone from Jinx so she could read the texts more clearly. "According to these," Helen started. "They were doing a lot more than just working."

"What's that word mean, Hel?" Alberta asked, pointing at a text that Marion had sent to Beverly.

"Gram, you don't want to know," Jinx said, grabbing the cell phone back.

"Remember that thing Sammy always wanted you to do to him that you always refused to do?" Helen asked. "Well, Beverly did it every Thursday at noon."

"*Caro Signore!*" Alberta gasped. "I guess I'll have to make sure that I have lunch plans on Thursday in case Marion wants to continue the tradition."

"Here's a text from Lucy!" Jinx interjected, changing the subject.

The mention of the dead woman's name brought them all back to reality, to the real reason they had committed petty theft: They wanted to find out who murdered Alberta's old, if not dear, friend. The exchange of texts between Beverly and Lucy revealed that they were much closer than Alberta and Lucy had ever been and shared lunch dates, movies, and the occasional weekend shopping excursion together. And that Beverly also knew about the *TV Guide* collection.

"Look at this," Jinx said, pointing to the phone. "Beverly asks Lucy if she was going to keep her appointment with Olive, and Lucy says yes."

"That means she was definitely planning on selling her collection," Joyce said. "But never got the chance to do it."

"Whoever killed her saw to it that she didn't keep her appointment," Alberta surmised.

"Also too, from what the cell phone is telling us, that person looks to be Beverly," Joyce declared.

The horror of Joyce's statement sunk into Alberta's mind slowly like poisonous quicksand. "Oh dear God," she muttered. "Do you really think Beverly could've killed her friend just for a collection of old magazines?"

No one really knew how to answer such a bizarre question. To avoid having to respond, Jinx next scrolled through the list of phone calls and found some information that could potentially contradict everything they had just learned. Marion's name only appeared on two calls, both of which were made by Beverly, and besides Lucy there was only one other name that popped up with startling frequency.

"I think Beverly might've been two-timing Marion," Jinx announced.

Stunned, Alberta asked, "Why do you say that?"

"Because she exchanged over fifty phone calls with some guy named Sal DeSoto in one four-day period," she said. "And there's a ton more between her and Sal in her deleted phone calls list, which she, you know, never deleted."

"You think Beverly was having an affair with Sal, while she was having an affair with Marion?" Joyce asked.

"Beverly was definitely *not* having an affair with Sal," Helen said, definitively.

"Why do you think you know everything?" Alberta yelled.

"I don't know everything!" Helen yelled back. "But I do know this."

"How?" Alberta shouted. "How do you know this?"

"Don't you recognize the name, Berta?" Helen asked. "Sal DeSoto is Father Sal!"

"Oh my God, Helen!" Alberta cried. "You do know everything!"

"You really know this Sal, Aunt Helen?"

"Know him? I worked with Father Sal for over thirty years," Helen confirmed. "He's many things, and celibate is one of them. Why do you think he's such a cranky SOB?"

"But if she wasn't having an affair with Father Sal," Joyce started, "why was she so tight with a priest?"

"Because she had something to confess!" Alberta declared triumphantly.

"That must be it! Beverly did something bad, she felt guilty about it, and she needed to confess her sins!" Jinx exclaimed. "And who better to go to for confession than a priest?"

"Pure conjecture," Helen barked.

"There's only one way for us to find out the truth," Jinx said.

"What's that, lovey?" Alberta asked.

"Looks like Sister Helen is going to have to come out of retirement."

# CHAPTER 14

*A cane scottato l'acqua fredda pare calda.*

A few hours later, Sister Helen returned home after an emotionally draining day at work.

"I need a drink," Helen announced, "And make it a strong one."

"How about some mango-flavored vodka?" Joyce suggested.

"I need something stronger," Helen said. "Make it apple."

"How is apple stronger than mango?" Alberta asked.

"Don't question me, Berta!" Helen shrieked. "I just had a visit with the ghost of my religious past, and it wasn't a pleasant experience."

Jinx poured Helen a healthy glass of apple-flavored vodka and placed it on the table in front of her. "I'm sorry you had to come face-to-face with the life you left behind, Aunt Helen, but it was the only way to find out the truth. Tell us what happened and don't leave out any details."

Helen took a swig of her vodka and let the apple-infused warmth linger in her mouth before swallowing.

Once she felt the burn start to spread out to the rest of her body, she was ready to tell her story.

When she sat across from Father Sal in his office, Helen was reminded of everything she disliked about the Catholic Church. While she had devoted her life to near-poverty and charitable service, this priest was sitting, quite literally, in the lap of luxury. As a realist, Helen understood that helping the unfortunate while living like Mother Teresa in the bowels of Calcutta was hardly practical or, in her estimation, necessary to teach God's word. However, she also didn't think it should be preached from an ergonomic, Italian leather, fully reclinable chair with three-speed massage control. From the soft buzzing sound that had filled the spacious office, Helen surmised that Sal had the setting on low.

A terribly graphic Italian phrase had popped into her head: *A cane scottato l'acqua fredda pare calda.* Roughly translated into English, it meant "A burnt child dreads the fire." It also meant that the burnt-out former nun dreaded revisiting the rectory, and a shiver went down Helen's spine as she felt the first sparks lick at her feet. She didn't want to be in this impeccably decorated office, sitting opposite this impeccably decorated priest, but she didn't want to disappoint her niece. And although she would never admit it out loud, she didn't want to disappoint her sister or sister-in-law either. As a modern-day spinster and, most undeniably, an Italian woman, family was vitally important to Helen. So instead of running from the impending inferno, she fanned its flames.

"If I remember correctly, this is your favorite," she said, placing a bottle of Chardonnay on top of the mahogany desk. "I didn't have room for glasses in my pocketbook, but I believe you keep some in the lower left-hand drawer of your desk for special occasions."

"You remember correctly," Father Sal replied, opening the drawer. He placed two small, gold-rimmed tumblers onto his desk, and then produced a bottle opener. After he uncorked the bottle of wine, he declared, "I guess this can be considered a special occasion."

As Helen sipped her wine, she watched Sal pour his second glass. Everything she despised about the man came into focus. She knew that as a former nun, or simply someone who considered herself Christian, she shouldn't despise anyone for their appearance, but she thought Sal was an illustration of the Catholic Church's hypocrisy.

She noticed that his fingernails were not only manicured but supported a sheer topcoat of polish. The two gold rings on his left hand, one sporting a diamond, the other a ruby, were more expensive than all the items in Helen's jewelry box, and his thick black vintage eyeglasses looked like something her own father would've worn, but she could tell Sal's were made by a current designer and, therefore, over-priced.

Somehow the wrinkles on his face had been smoothed over, and Helen wasn't sure if he was wearing makeup or if he visited the same Botox doctor Enza frequented. And just like Enza's, his eyebrows were perfectly arched thanks to an expert plucking. His hair was the same bottle-black color, without the hint of gray that surely should have appeared on top of his sixty-seven-year-old head. Nothing about Father Sal's appearance was honest, but she was hoping that the conversation would be different, which is why she poured him a third glass of Chardonnay the moment after he had finished his second.

"So are you enjoying civilian life, Helen," Father Sal asked. "Or do you clamor for the days of discipline and rigidity that is our norm?"

Helen smiled and adjusted her eyeglasses. She wanted to tell the pompous priest that he knew very little about leading a rigid or disciplined life, but opted to maneuver the conversation into Sal's preferred territory: gossip.

"It's a bit of an adjustment, I will admit, but I'm keeping busy and doing things I didn't have a chance to do as a nun," Helen said. "Like reconnecting with old friends."

Father Sal raised his glass and placed his right hand over his heart. "*Ai vecchi amici*," he praised. "To old friends . . . like you and me."

Helen swallowed hard and replied, "Yes, just like you and me." She took a quick sip of wine to wash away the bile that was rising in her throat and added, "And Beverly LaStanza."

The mention of Beverly's name caused Sal to have a choking fit and almost topple over backward in his chair. Finally upright, he clutched his desk to maintain his balance and chugged the last of his wine to maintain his composure. "You know Beverly?"

"Bev and I go way back," Helen lied. "Such a sin about her and Marion though, isn't it?"

Luckily, Sal was as emotionally weak as Helen remembered, and all he needed was a gentle push to help him cross the line and break priest-penitent privilege. It didn't hurt that he had never learned to hold his liquor and was already inebriated, but Helen refused to feel bad about being an enabler if it got her the desired results. And as the words quickly poured out of Father Sal's mouth, she knew this reluctant return to her religious past had been well worth the visit.

"She was like a German clock, that one," Father Sal began. "Every Wednesday and Saturday she would be first in line for confession at twelve-thirty on the dot and every confession was the same. *Bless me Father for I have sinned . . . with my boss.* I tried to tell her that premarital sex with an unmarried man couldn't be considered that big of a sin for a woman of her age, but Beverly, as I'm sure you know, Helen, is an innocent soul, almost childlike."

Helen had no idea if Beverly acted her age or her shoe size, but she agreed with Sal in order to keep his monologue flowing. "She could be a regular Shirley Temple."

"Ah, but sadly, she turned into a Shirley Temple Black," Sal replied, downing his fourth tumbler of wine.

Helen had no idea what Sal meant by his comment, but again she chose to play along. "Black as charcoal, that one," she said.

"I tried to warn her, Helen, I truly did," Sal professed. "But she wouldn't listen to me. Oh no, no, no, she was beyond my grasp and that of our church because she was in love with Marion and was convinced that he loved her and was going to propose to her simply—and here's the kicker—because he had promised that he would. Can you believe she could be so gullible? She could sometimes think like a child, as if what she was told was the truth. But as the years went by and Marion didn't produce an engagement ring to slip on her finger, she realized that her fantasy of upgrading from the boss's secretary to his wife was slipping away, and it was time to take matters into her own hands."

Father Sal paused so Helen pushed. "Did she propose to him?"

"No, she decided to get revenge."

"What kind of revenge are we talking about, Sal?" Helen asked. "Venial or mortal?"

"Oh Helen, how I wish I knew. How I truly wish that I knew," Sal replied. "But that's the last thing she said to me when she made her confession on Wednesday, that she was going to get her revenge, and I haven't seen her since. It's been a whole week and I'm dying from the suspense. Talk about a cliffhanger. Who cares about who shot J.R.? I want to know what Beverly did to get revenge on her lover!"

Finally, Helen and the priest had something in common.

After she conveyed all this information to the rest of the gang, the women were more convinced than ever that Beverly possessed the temperament and the motive to be Lucy's killer, but also that Marion was a wolf in perfectly tailored sheep's clothing.

"Be careful, Alberta," Joyce said, pouring out four glasses of the apple-flavored vodka. "I spent my career working for and with men like Marion and they cannot be trusted. They're friendly on the outside but rotten to the core."

Alberta knew that she could be naive where men were concerned, having spent her entire life with only one man, but she was nonetheless confused.

"Beverly was the one whose heart was filled with revenge and Marion's the villain?"

"It's not that cut and dried, Gram, and two rights don't make a wrong," Jinx said, placing a plate of lasagna in front of her grandmother. "But the only reason Beverly wanted revenge is because Marion lied to her for so many years and took advantage of her."

"If I had a nickel for every time I watched a new secretary get taken for a ride by some executive," Joyce shared. "Heck, I'd be richer than I already am."

"I understand what you're saying and I know that those types of things happened and, unfortunately, still happen in the workplace all the time, but I know Marion, and he's different," Alberta said. "I just have a hard time believing that the quiet man who took me out for a friendly cup of coffee, who has also proven to be a respectful businessman, is this evil *bellimbusto*."

"Stop living in the past, Berta. Evil can be subjective, but a gigolo . . . not so much," Helen said. "And the facts are proving more and more that that's what your boss is." She ate a piece of Jinx's lasagna and wasn't as confident. "I wish I could be as certain about this food. Jinx, honey, what is this?"

"Vegetable lasagna with gluten-free pasta," she informed.

"Again with the gluten-free!" Helen yelled.

"I promise you Aunt Helen, you'll get used to the taste."

"But why?" Helen yelled even louder. "Why would you want to get used to such a bad taste? Gluten-free anything makes no sense unless you're allergic to it or have that celiac disease. Any other reason for eating the stuff means you don't have normal taste buds."

"It's called healthy living, Hel," Joyce interjected, swallowing a huge mouthful. "I like it."

Shaking a fork at Joyce, Helen replied, "That's because you're only Italian by marriage and you don't know any better!"

"I will say, lovey, that it's an improvement over your last attempt," Alberta conceded. "But mainly because I don't think you can ever have enough vegetables. Remember Great-Grandpa's vegetable garden he had out on the fire escape in Hoboken, Helen?"

Helen pushed the plate away from her and cried, "Don't try to lure me away from the topic at hand with happy memories, Berta, it won't work!"

Continuing to eat, Alberta said to Jinx, "Well, I tried, lovey."

"Thanks, Gram," Jinx replied. "I know it's not for everyone, but too many carbs and rich foods aren't good for you. It's unhealthy."

"Listen to me, Jinxie, as a woman who has lived a lot longer than you have," Helen lectured. "What's unhealthy is to deny yourself simple pleasures, and one of the simplest, most satisfying pleasures that God gave all his creatures here on earth is the joy of eating good food. And I'm sorry to be the one to have to tell you this, but gluten-free anything just ain't good food!"

"Maybe it's time you stopped living in the past, Helen," Alberta said, munching on some broccoli. "Foods, like bosses, change."

Jinx's eyes popped open, glowing like two light-bulbs. "Would you like to prove that, Gram?"

Suddenly the kitchen was filled with silence and the sound was panic-inducing. The women had come to learn that whenever Jinx made a proclamation at the kitchen table it usually entailed them engaging in some undercover work. They reacted like Italian Pavlovian dogs, both excited and scared to receive their latest assignment.

"Prove what?" Alberta asked nervously.

"Your boss's innocence," she replied.

"As long as it doesn't entail me compromising my own innocence, I'm willing," Alberta said.

Jinx explained that Marion was linked to both Lucy and Beverly because they worked at Wasserman & Speicher, so that's where they had to go to dig into Marion's past.

"Ladies," Jinx announced. "It's time for another break-in."

# CHAPTER 15

*Non guardare a caval donato in bocca.*

Alberta had only been Marion's secretary for two weeks, and already she knew his schedule well enough to know that he spent Saturday mornings playing golf at the Tranquility Country Club with a rotating roster of business colleagues. This Saturday he was scheduled to play eighteen holes with Elliot from accounting, who was notorious for hitting at least two balls into the sand trap, so even if they unexpectedly came back to the office after playing for some work emergency, the coast would be clear for several hours. That meant that Alberta and company would have more than enough time to do their snooping and make an exit without being seen.

Alberta had previously been advised by Denise that her employee ID card would give her access to the building on weekends for any office-related emergency that might arise, even though Denise told her that in her nine years of working at Wasserman & Speicher, such a weekend emergency had yet to arise. So, the worst-case scenario would be that if Alberta was later questioned as to why she was at work on a

Saturday morning she could simply say that she left her pocketbook at her desk and needed to retrieve it in order to engage in some weekend retail therapy after a hard week's work.

At 7 a.m. on a Saturday morning the building was eerily quiet so any small noise the women made would be heard by anyone else who might be around. To avoid any suspicion, they decided to act natural, as if they truly were on the premises at such an odd hour to retrieve Alberta's forgotten belongings.

They stepped off the elevator, and once they turned the corner, Alberta couldn't hide the feeling of pride that crept into her voice, "Here's my desk."

"Ooh, it's fancy, Gram!"

"Also too, it's expensive," Joyce added. "They don't make desks like this anymore."

"If we're done fawning over the office decor, can we get to work?" Helen sniped.

Prior to arriving, Alberta instructed them on the floor plan so they knew exactly where Marion's office was located. Jinx quickly surveyed the area to make sure they weren't being watched and then announced to the ladies that their work could begin.

With Helen standing guard in the hallway, Alberta, Jinx, and Joyce entered Marion's office. Jinx immediately took out the small fingerprint kit she borrowed from work that Wyck boasted he used in order to figure out who was stealing his lunches from the fridge and began lifting Marion's fingerprints from his phone, keyboard, and various spots on his desk. When she was finished, it was Alberta's turn to take over. Her job was to type in Marion's password and get into his computer since he had given her his password one morning last week when he was running late and couldn't log in remotely through his phone because he forgot to charge it overnight. Confidently, Marion typed in "Duke1907," the year of John Wayne's birth, but her confidence waned dramatically when a prompt appeared on the computer screen stating that the password was incorrect.

"Are you sure it's right, Alberta?" Joyce asked.

"It was the last time I used it," she replied. "But he must have changed it."

"Oh no!" Jinx cried. "We can't hack into his computer if we don't know the password."

"Do you think he kept a notebook like Beverly did with all his passwords listed?" Joyce questioned. "Maybe not one with a cute kitty cat on the cover, but possibly one with a picture of John Wayne? Or a traditional western motif?"

"I don't think so," Alberta said. "I never noticed one."

"Try Alberta Klausner," Helen said smugly, still standing outside the office.

"Helen!" Alberta cried. "That is ridiculous!"

"It might be ridiculous, Gram," Jinx said. "But it worked."

If Alberta's scream didn't result in someone rushing into the office to inspect what the commotion was about, nothing would. They were obviously alone and could rifle through Marion's e-mails undisturbed.

Joyce immediately recognized some of the names of Marion's business colleagues from her days working on Wall Street. She opened a few and confirmed that they were filled with the usual business jargon and what she liked to call empty language, which constituted business speak. Just to be on the safe side she printed a few of the longer ones to read later. They went through several screen lengths of e-mails before they came to a name that made them all gasp.

"That's Father Sal!"

"What?" Helen shouted from her post.

"Marion e-mailed Father Sal," Alberta confirmed. She quickly read one of the e-mails and it gave them all the information they needed. "He was seeking his counsel because he knew that leading Beverly on with no intention of marrying her was wrong."

"I told you he was a cad," Helen sniped.

"Technically, a cad with a conscience, Aunt Helen," Jinx said. "Since he was e-mailing, you know, an ecclesiastic."

"This means you have to go meet up with Father Sal again, Helen," Joyce declared. "He knows more about Beverly and Marion's relationship than he's letting on, which means he might know more about the *TV Guide* collection and maybe even Lucy's murder."

Tired of shouting from the hallway, Helen entered with her own declaration. "Absolutely not."

"You have to, Helen," Alberta said. "You're the only one who can get Father Sal to talk."

"Do you know how it makes me feel to have a sit-down with him?" Helen confessed. "It reminds me of everything I dislike about my religion and why I left the convent."

"Aunt Helen, will it make you feel better if I go with you this time?" Jinx asked.

Softening a bit, Helen—like Alberta and Joyce—realized there was little that Jinx could ask of her that she could refuse. "Well . . . that might make a tiny bit of a difference."

Jinx hugged Helen tightly and squealed, "Hashtag ThankYouAuntHelen!"

"I have no idea what that means," Helen replied. "But you're welcome."

On their way out of the building, Jinx announced that Father Sal would be presiding over a service at St. Winifred's at 9 a.m. "I'll meet you at the side entrance of the church at 8:45 and we'll ambush him right before he's about to go on for his big number."

"Where are you going?" Helen asked.

"I have a quick errand to run," she replied. "I know of a way to make sure Father Sal answers all of our questions."

After she ran off, Alberta commented, "I'm not sure if that girl is adding twenty years to our lives or if she's going to put us into early graves."

Standing outside of St. Winifred's, Helen looked around for Jinx, but only saw a few older women climb the stairs of the church and a lone novitiate walking down the grassy path leading to the rectory. At 8:47, Helen dialed Jinx's number on her cell phone and although she could hear her niece's ringtone fill the quiet morning air, Jinx was nowhere to be found. Because she was in disguise.

"Aunt Helen, over here."

Helen whipped around and saw that the novitiate was Jinx dressed up as a nun.

"What in the world are you doing?" Helen whispered harshly.

"Don't you love it?" Jinx cried proudly. "I figured Father Sal would be more likely to spill the beans if he knew that I was, you know, playing for the same team."

"You might win over Father Sal, but I'm not sure if

you're going to make Our Father all that happy," Helen said. "Where'd you get that thing?"

Jinx explained that she borrowed the costume from her roommate, Nola, who taught English and creative writing at St. Winifred's Academy and also ran the school's theater program. Last year, they had put on a critically acclaimed production of *The Sound of Music*, and Nola had some of the costumes in storage in their apartment.

"Your roommate is Nola Kirkpatrick?" Helen asked.

"You know her?"

"She asked me to act as a consultant on that production," Helen replied. "It was terrible!"

"But it got great reviews from *The Herald*," Jinx stated. "I looked them up."

"I don't care if it got five stars in the *New York Times*," Helen retorted. "Their Liesl looked like she was sixteen going on thirty-five, and the girl who played Brigitta whined so much about everything I wanted to offer her up to a Nazi so she could really have something to complain about."

Ignoring her aunt's critique, Jinx was shocked with how small her world was becoming. "I can't believe you know Nola!"

"And I can't believe you're dressed like that!" Helen hissed. "Now let's get inside before we both get struck by lightning."

Helen led the way through the side entrance of the church and saw Father Sal fussing with his stole to make sure both hemlines lined up properly. "Sal, we need to speak with you," Helen said, her voice just loud enough to alert him that she was prepared to cause a scene if he didn't comply. When he turned around, he was surprised to see she had company.

"Helen, I'm about to go on," he pouted. "Pardon me, Sister. I didn't see you there."

"That's all right, Father," Jinx said. "I'm Sister . . . um, Maria."

"Hello, Sister Maria," he replied. "Perhaps we can meet later and talk."

"We're going to talk now, Sal," Helen interrupted. "Or else the six ladies in there waiting for mass to start are going to hear how you broke church confidentiality and told me all about Beverly's confession."

"Are you th-th-threatening me, Helen?" Sal stammered.

"No, I'm blackmailing you," she replied. "As a priest, you should know the difference."

Before Sal could protest any further, Helen lied and said that Sister Maria was Beverly's niece, who was concerned about her aunt's whereabouts. Helen added that she also wanted to know why Marion, in addition to Beverly, was seeking his counsel. While Father Sal stuttered to try and come up with a retort, Helen told him that she knew all about his e-mail exchanges with the CEO, so it would be foolish of him to deny the relationship. Cornered, Father Sal had no other option but to acquiesce to Helen's demands. He was about six months from officially retiring and living the rest of his life on a Vatican pension with two other former priests at a spacious ranch house in Palm Springs, and he didn't want anything to interfere with his plans. For over forty years he had avoided scandal, and he wasn't about to let an ex-nun and a curious novitiate ruin his record.

"Like most men, Marion was a coward," Sal announced. "He didn't want to marry Beverly, but he didn't have the guts to tell her the truth."

"So, he just strung her along?" Helen said.

"You could position it that way if you were so inclined," Sal admitted reluctantly.

"And like most men," Helen began. "You sat back quietly and let him do it."

Father Sal pulled back the heavy red velvet curtain that separated them from the small stairwell leading to the altar and looked out nervously. Helen didn't have to peek to know that the altar boys were waiting impatiently, shifting their weight from one leg to the other as they held bottles of incense and a gold chalice. She knew that some of the women were sitting quietly in the pews, but most were whispering to each other about the latest town gossip, oblivious that such activity was frowned upon by the church's landlord: God. She hated disrupting mass, but knew that Father Sal wasn't going to answer her questions unless he was pushed further.

"So, you enabled Marion, isn't that right?" Helen insisted.

"Now you s-s-see here, Helen . . ." Sal stuttered.

"Don't deny it Sal," she countered. "Marion confessed to you that he lied to Beverly about his intentions and you did nothing to put an end to it."

"Yes, all right, what could I do?" Sal argued. "Marion was a weak man, and he fed Beverly lies for years, until he couldn't any longer," Sal replied.

"Did Beverly . . . I mean, my aunt, give him an ultimatum?" Jinx asked.

"I think so. At least, that's what she said she was going to do," Sal replied. "The last time we talked."

"So, you don't know if she really went through with it before she disappeared?" Helen asked.

Sal was growing very uncomfortable standing in

the entrance to the church disclosing confidential information when he was supposed to be saying mass. It was bad enough that he was secretly counseling two people who were involved with each other, but now one of them had gone missing.

"Look, I tried my best to get Marion to tell Beverly the truth, and I tried even harder to get Beverly to open her eyes to the real kind of man Marion was," Sal admitted. "But you know as well as I do, Helen, that sometimes you can put a glass of water right under a thirsty horse's nose and he'll still refuse to take a drink."

Sadly, Helen understood. Through her many years of service she had met men and women who were incapable of seeing the truth about their partner no matter how horribly they were treated. Acting like a martyr was part of the human condition.

"Did my aunt give any indication that she was scared of Marion?" Jinx asked.

Sal's face turned a shade of gray that Helen thought looked quite attractive in contrast to his deep purple robe, but it was an indication that he was shocked by this statement. "Scared of Marion?" Sal repeated. "No, he was weak, not dangerous."

Before Helen could ask a follow-up question, they were interrupted by the older of the two altar boys. "Father Sal," the boy said. "We kind of can't get started without you."

"I'm sorry, Jason," he said. "Tell Virginia to play 'Make Me a Channel of Your Peace,' the long version, the ladies always love to sing along to that one."

"Sure thing, Father."

The boy stared at Helen and Jinx suspiciously before retiring back into the church, presumably to follow Father Sal's instructions. The priest, however, wasn't finished giving orders. "I'm done with this, Helen," he announced. "Done with this whole thing. Follow me."

Moving so quickly that his robes rippled behind him, Father Sal bounded out of the building with Helen and Jinx close behind him. He dashed across the alley and into the rectory where he lived without looking back, confident that his interrogators would follow him, which they did, until they reached his bedroom.

It was only because of instinct that Helen paused at the door before entering, since she couldn't remember the last time she walked into a man's bedroom. The room was small and sparsely decorated—a gold cross over the twin bed, a chest of drawers, scuffed and wooden, a nightstand holding a few books and a lamp, and a small writing desk and chair. Helen was surprised by the threadbare nature of the room, especially in comparison to his office, and couldn't believe that Sal hadn't spruced it up a bit, knowing his penchant for excess. She was actually impressed by how frugally he lived.

She was so thrown by Sal's living conditions that she didn't think it odd that he was standing on the chair rummaging through the top shelf of his closet until Jinx whispered in her ear.

"You don't think he's looking for a gun, do you, Aunt Helen?"

"No, priests usually carry those in their robes," she deadpanned.

Sal jumped down off the chair and whirled around to reveal his find. "This is yours."

Helen looked at the small package Sal was holding and wondered what he was talking about. Was this a setup? Some kind of peace offering? An unwanted gift from an obsessive parishioner? "What is it?" she asked.

"It came in the mail a few days ago," Sal said. "From Beverly."

"Oh my God!" Jinx shouted before realizing such an exclamation wasn't appropriate for a woman of her position. "I mean, Gee willikers!"

"You've spoken to Beverly?" Helen asked.

Father Sal's coloring took on a gray pallor again and he shook his head. "No, from her attorney," he replied. "He was instructed to send it to me in case she . . . um . . . disappeared."

*"Non guardare a caval donato in bocca,"* Helen replied.

"I don't think the box is big enough to hold a horse or just its mouth," Jinx whispered. "And neither would make for such a nice gift anyways."

Ignoring Jinx's feeble attempt at translating her Italian, Helen continued on with her inquiry. "What's in the box, Sal?"

"I don't know and I don't want to know," Sal said, offering the package to Helen. "You asked me for a favor and now I'm asking one of you. Take this package off my hands and do with it what you will. I don't want any part of it or them."

Hesitating only slightly, Helen grabbed the package from Sal and felt as if she had just taken candy from a baby. She knew that Sal wanted to get rid of the box for purely selfish reasons, so he could no longer be connected to Beverly, but she also knew that she was accepting it for the same selfish reasons, so she could get closer to the truth.

"On one condition, Sal," Jinx said. "I mean *Father* Sal."

Breathing deeply and trying to control his temper, Sal replied, "And what would that be, Sister Maria?"

"This . . . *transaction* stays among the three of us," she replied. "No more breaking priest-civilian confidentiality. No more clandestine counseling. We don't want to hear that you've gone blabbing to the police that you gave us evidence."

Once again Sal's pallor turned ashen. "You think whatever is in there could be used as evidence?"

"I guess you'll never find out," Jinx answered smugly.

When they returned to Alberta's kitchen, Jinx was still wearing her nun's outfit and Helen was still wearing a proud smile. "She's a lot tougher than we were at her age, Berta," Helen beamed.

Alberta looked at her granddaughter wistfully. She was incredibly proud that Jinx had grown into such a confident, self-assured woman, and she hoped one day she'd get to congratulate Lisa Marie for being such a good parent. Until then she had a job to do, which was finding out who killed Lucy. She was about to get one step closer.

"Oh, *Madonna mia*!" Alberta exclaimed. "Look at this!"

The three women didn't need to be ordered, they were already circling around Alberta and looking inside the box, stunned to see three *TV Guide*s staring back at them.

"This means Beverly must have stolen the collection," Jinx said.

"But why would she send three *TV Guide*s to a priest?" Joyce asked.

Suddenly cold and unsteady, Alberta sat down, the enormity of the situation finally hitting her. "Don't you see? This was her way of confessing that she killed Lucy."

# CHAPTER 16

*Il blu è il colore più solitario*

As Alberta's comment hovered above them just as Lucy's body had hovered on top of Memory Lake, the four women shoved the unpleasant thoughts from their minds as they tried to make sense of the three *TV Guide*s. But at first glance none of them could deduce what the three celebrities gracing the covers had in common or how their images could be connected to Lucy's murder.

"These *TV Guide*s have got to form some sort of clue," Joyce suggested. "Separately they don't mean anything, but together they may help us solve this crime."

"The John Wayne reference is obvious," Alberta offered. "Marion's named after him, so it makes sense that it would be included." She was about to pick up the *TV Guide* with the photo of the Duke on the cover when Jinx grabbed her hand to stop her.

"Don't touch it, Gram," Jinx said. "I know it's wrapped in plastic, but you could still muss up any fingerprints that might be on it."

Each *TV Guide* was in a protective plastic covering

like a Ziploc bag, which was standard practice among collectors to prevent magazines, comic books, or any kind of ephemera from getting damaged. Alone, it didn't mean much, but it did give further proof that these were part of Lucy's larger collection, because if they were just random *TV Guide*s someone had found, they would be less likely to be covered.

"Sorry, lovey," Alberta said. "I keep forgetting I have to think like a detective."

"We're all learning how to do that, Gram," Jinx replied. She then pointed to the *TV Guide* in the center of the box, "Who's that woman? She's very familiar, but I can't remember why."

Helen laughed heartily, "Which is why you stink at being a nun."

"What are you talking about, Aunt Helen?"

"That's Peggy Wood," Helen answered. "She played Mother Superior in *The Sound of Music,* so she's basically your boss."

"I loved her in that movie!" Jinx exclaimed. "But she looks so young in that photo."

"Before she was urging Maria to climb ev'ry mountain, she was the star of her own TV show," Helen explained. "It was called *Mama,* kind of a sitcom that took place at the turn of the century."

As Alberta, Joyce, and Helen reminisced about the long-forgotten show and the early days of TV in general, which they agreed were much better than the types of shows that passed as entertainment today, Jinx was busy searching for information on her smartphone. Alberta thought Jinx looked odd still clad in her nun's outfit feverishly searching on her phone— an ironic mix of old versus new, but nonetheless unsuccessful in finding more details.

"I can't find anything useful about Beverly's mother online," Jinx reported. "Just that her name was Anna, she died in 1991, was predeceased by her husband, and survived by her only daughter, nothing else."

Alberta walked to the other side of the kitchen and stood before the many bottles of flavored vodka that decorated the counter. She wasn't sure what the occasion called for and couldn't decide between peppermint or strawberry. Neither sounded right and she knew there had to be another choice. That was it!

"I don't think it's about Beverly's mother," Alberta suggested. "But Marion's."

"Now look who's starting to think like a detective!" Jinx exclaimed. "Do you remember her name, Gram?"

"Oh, *Madon*, no, not really," Alberta replied. "Wait yes! Yes, I do!"

"What was it?" Jinx asked.

"Something German!"

"Well, that narrows it down," Helen answered in her trademark snarky tone.

Unfortunately, technology failed them again and Jinx wasn't able to find an obituary about Marion's mother. Taking off her wimple, Jinx untied her hair from its bun and let it fall loose over her shoulders. She looked even stranger now as her long black wavy hair fell over her tunic. Worse, she felt less like a detective than she did a nun.

"I got nothing. Gram, can you remember anything at all about her?"

Alberta closed her eyes and pressed two fingers to her forehead as if the pressure would release a memory. It worked.

"She used to make those pfeffernüsse cookies and

Marion would bring them to school on International Foods Day," Alberta shouted triumphantly.

"I stand corrected, that really does narrow things down," Helen said. "It doesn't help us at all, but it does bring an air of specificity to the investigation."

"Also too, it brings with it an air of hunger," Joyce added. "I could really go for some pfeffernüsse right now. Does Entenmann's make any?"

"I don't think so," Alberta replied. "But how hard can they be to make?"

"Are you forgetting that you stink at baking?" Helen reminded her.

Grabbing a cookie tray from the cabinet next to the stove, Alberta said, "No, but if I can learn how to be an amateur detective, I can learn how to be an amateur baker."

The kitchen instantly turned into a bustling factory of culinary delight, if not necessarily expertise. Alberta arranged the flour, sugar, and spices on the counter as Joyce retrieved a carton of eggs and butter from the refrigerator. Helen, still skeptical, foraged through the cabinets above the kitchen counter until she found the extra virgin olive oil and a small bottle of multicolored sprinkles. She knew pfeffernüsse didn't call for multicolored sprinkles, but they might make the cookies look better than they would most certainly taste. All thoughts of baking, however, were interrupted by Jinx's outburst.

"Oh, *Madonna mia*," Jinx cried.

"Honey, if you're going to shout in Italian, you really have to work on your accent," Helen reprimanded. "Maybe watch that Meryl Streep in the movie about the bridges."

"I found Marion's mother!" she cried again.

"On your phone?" Alberta asked.

"Where else?" Jinx commented. "I mean, seriously, what did you people do before the Internet? How did you learn anything?"

"From the library, the Funk & Wagnalls—" Joyce replied.

"Funk and what?" Jinx questioned, not sure if she heard her aunt correctly.

"Never mind," Joyce said. "What did you find out?"

"Guess who used to bake an award-winning pfeffernüsse?" Jinx shouted. "Helga Wasserman Klausner, that's who!"

"Helga!" Alberta exclaimed, pounding her fist on the kitchen counter and causing the flour to rise up like a cloud. "I told you her name was German."

"And her maiden name is Wasserman," Joyce pointed out. "As in Wasserman & Speicher."

All thoughts of making or eating pfeffernüsse were put on hold as this new revelation filled the women with a curiosity that displaced any hunger pains. There were coincidences in life that linked random occurrences and then there were facts that when connected could hardly be considered random. If Marion's mother's maiden name was one-half of the name of the company at which her son worked, it could only mean that Marion was more than just running the company, it meant that he owned the whole damn thing.

While walking back to her desk with a fresh cup of French vanilla coffee on Monday morning, Alberta set out to see if she could really turn coincidence into fact, and the best way to legitimize rumor and innuendo was to interview someone who lived for gossip.

"Hi Denise, how have you been?"

"Busy as usual, Alberta," she replied, closing one file and then opening up another. "How about you?"

Seizing the opportunity, Alberta accepted Denise's casual pleasantry and turned it into an invitation to enter her office. She swung the door behind her a bit harder than necessary so that it almost closed as she sat in the chair on the other side of the HR executive's desk. From Denise's forced smile, Alberta knew that she didn't want any company, but she also knew that Denise could never pass up the chance to chat about fellow employees. Especially if those employees were higher up the company ladder than she was.

"I heard an interesting rumor the other day," Alberta started. "About Marion."

Immediately, Denise's attention was captured. She made a pronounced effort to try and keep her eyes focused on her file, but she kept twirling the strands of her short black bob, which was something Alberta had noticed she did every time she talked about the personal matters of the professionals she worked with. It was her *tell*, and Alberta wasn't about to let her mark off the hook.

"He's much more than just the CEO, isn't he?" Alberta asked.

Twirling her hair rapidly, Denise couldn't resist engaging in the conversation and gave up all pretense of being interested in her work. "I told you Alberta, no, I warned you, that Marion has what some might like to call, enhanced interpersonal skills," Denise said. "Personally, I cannot confirm or deny, but that's what the scuttlebutt's been since I started."

Slyly, Alberta turned around to make sure that no one, especially Marion, was standing in the doorway before she continued. "No, I'm talking about his familial relations, specifically his mother, Helga Wasserman."

Denise's jaw literally dropped, and she was silent for several seconds. During the silence her face turned beet red. "Why do you care about Marion's mother?"

Alberta should've been silenced by Denise's harsh tone, and it was clear that she was about to cross a line. But what other choice did she have? Slink out of Denise's office like a coward or lift her foot up and step right over that line. Proudly, Alberta continued, "It seems that Marion's mother is the founder of Wasserman & Speicher."

Denise glared at Alberta for a moment and Alberta felt as if she was going to be thrown out of the office with an official reprimand going into her personnel file. But the look evaporated and Denise simply shook her head, saying that she had never heard of such a thing nor did she think that the real estate firm was a family business. "I was told that the parent company was based somewhere in Germany," she disclosed. "But I couldn't even tell you the name of the town."

For some reason Alberta didn't believe Denise, but could hardly find fault with an HR executive who didn't disclose company secrets. She did, however find Denise's dismissive attitude unnecessary. "If you don't have any more rumors to spread," Denise said, "We both should really get back to work."

A few hours later, as Alberta and Joyce sat side by side on the Adirondacks facing the lake sipping fresh-brewed iced tea, the former Wall Street executive proved that she still had more business acumen than Denise would ever be able to acquire.

"I called a few of my old colleagues, and I can confirm that Helga Wasserman Klausner is indeed the founder of Wasserman & Speicher," Joyce announced. "Which makes Marion a lot more than just a flunky."

"But why would he keep something like that secret?" Alberta asked. "Especially from his own human resources department."

As Joyce closed her eyes to let the sun warm her face, she explained one of the primary rules of corporate America to Alberta: Businessmen typically kept information close to the vest and didn't like to reveal secrets that rivals could use against them. It was called survival of the fittest in the concrete jungle. While it was unusual to keep the fact that his real estate firm was a family-run business, it was a smart strategic move that allowed him to be viewed as merely another employee, objective and a high-level cog in a wheel instead of an emotionally invested son who had inherited the family empire from his mother without having had to work hard for the title. Staying autonomous gave him power.

"It's almost as if he approaches business the same way he approaches his personal relationships," Alberta considered. "He's as detached from his company as he was from Beverly."

Joyce reached out to hold Alberta's hand. "Looks like my favorite sister-in-law is growing up."

Alberta gave Joyce's hand a squeeze and laughed. "Come now, Joyce, we all know Helen's your favorite."

Their raucous laughter seemed to stir up the breeze, and both women reveled in the cool wind, their friendship, and the faint smell of honeysuckle that suddenly wafted over them. They inhaled deeply and smiled. Even though they were still haunted by the fact that someone their age who lived nearby had been murdered, they knew they had so many reasons to rejoice. They were healthy—God bless—near family, and while they might be in the sunset of their lives, they got to see the sun set every night over their favorite lake.

"That's it!" Alberta exclaimed. "Memory Lake!"

"I know, honey," Joyce replied, patting Alberta's hand. "I love it, too.

"No, the third *TV Guide*, it has to do with Memory Lake," Alberta said. "Where Lucy was murdered."

Alberta went on to explain that the first two *TV Guide*s more than likely related to Marion, his nickname and his mother, and the third *TV Guide*, depicting an image of Lloyd Bridges as the star of the late 1950s TV series *Sea Hunt,* had to do with Memory Lake.

"That's a brilliant deduction, Alberta," Joyce proclaimed, "but how do they all work together?"

Grimacing, Alberta stared out at the lake as if the body of water would feed her the answer. It didn't. "I don't know, but we're getting closer, Joyce, I can feel it," she said. "The one thing that bothers me is Beverly. I'm not convinced that she just disappeared."

Joyce confessed that she shared the same uneasiness. "You think she might be dead too, don't you?"

"God forgive me, but I do," Alberta said quietly. "I was thinking that maybe we should contact her accountant, the one who sent Father Sal the package. What do you think?"

"I have a better idea," Joyce said, standing up

abruptly. "I think I know someone who might know more about Beverly's disappearance than she's letting on."

Once again Beverly's condo was locked, and once again Ruthanne came to the rescue. This time, however, she was much better dressed than the last time Joyce saw her and without a hatchet.

"I'm so sorry, Ruthanne, but it looks like you're on your way someplace fancy," Joyce said, schmoozing with the building manager.

Blushing, Ruthanne ran her hands down her skirt and actually pivoted from side to side to show off her jacket-and-skirt combo that was a very intense shade of pink. "Do you like it?" she asked. "I just picked it up at that new boutique in town."

"You're a liar."

Joyce was arguably more stunned by Alberta's outburst than Ruthanne was.

"Alberta . . ." Joyce said, the word wringing out between clenched teeth in three very long syllables. "Ruthanne here is our friend."

Waving her hand dismissively in the air, Alberta continued. "You didn't just buy that outfit and you know it. Now, tell me where you got it, and don't lie to me."

Flustered, Ruthanne stammered nervously. When it was clear she couldn't come up with a cover story, she confessed. "Oh, all right already, don't get your bowels in an uproar! It's Beverly's, but it serves her right! She hasn't returned any of my calls and she hasn't returned here so I . . . well I . . . *borrowed* some of her clothes. But even if she does return, she won't miss this one, she has five of the same outfit all in different colors."

"Were there any in navy?" Alberta asked gravely.

"No," Ruthanne replied. "And trust me, I looked. It would look lovely in navy and really set off my hair."

Without saying another word, Alberta turned and left. Joyce muttered their good-byes to Ruthanne and assured her that they wouldn't tell anyone that she had gone on a shopping spree in Beverly's closet. Her secret would remain with them. Inside the privacy of her car, Joyce turned to Alberta and wanted to know what her secret was. She could tell from Alberta's frightened expression that she was not at all upset that Ruthanne was wearing Beverly's clothes and that something else much more frightening was going on.

"Alberta, what's wrong?

"*Blu è il colore più sola*," Alberta whispered, more to herself than to Joyce.

Joyce quickly translated the Italian saying in her head. "Blue is the loneliest color? What are you talking about?"

Looking straight ahead, Alberta explained why she was so upset. "The reason there isn't an outfit in navy is because Lucy was wearing it when they found her in the lake. Whoever killed Lucy, killed her in Beverly's condo and then deliberately changed her clothes before dumping her in the lake."

Slowly, Joyce began to look as scared as her sister-in-law. "You mean someone dressed her in one of Beverly's outfits? *After* killing her? But why would someone do that?"

Shaking her head, Alberta finally looked at Joyce, her eyes filled with fear. "I don't know why *someone* would do that, but I think I know why Marion would."

# CHAPTER 17

*Mammone.*

Joyce wished that she could tell Alberta not to jump to any conclusions, but the facts they were uncovering were starting to tell a different story.

Since Marion was having an affair with Beverly, it was a likely assumption that he would have a key to her condo or would at least be an invited guest and could come and go without suspicion at any time of day or night. If Lucy were indeed killed in Beverly's condo, which was another likely assumption because she was found dead wearing Beverly's clothes, Marion would have had no problem gaining entry to the premises to carry out the deed. It was also obvious that Beverly knew about Lucy's *TV Guide* collection and its monetary worth, so it was yet another likely assumption that she would have shared this news with the person she loved the most, aka Marion.

Perhaps Beverly and Marion planned to steal the collection to sell it and keep the money. It was a logical conclusion, but while Beverly definitely needed the extra cash since she was financially challenged, why would Marion, who ran and owned his very lucrative family business, need a measly fifty thousand dollars? And would he really kill someone for that amount of money? And if so, could greed lead him to kill Beverly too so he wouldn't have to split their windfall?

Then again, if Beverly was the murderer, why would she dress Lucy in an outfit that could so easily be linked to her own wardrobe? She could have planned to say that Lucy borrowed the outfit, not realizing the fatal mistake that Lucy hated the color navy and wouldn't be caught dead—figuratively or literally—in a navy blue ensemble. But here were other nagging questions too. If Beverly were such a close girlfriend of Lucy's to know of her secret collection, wouldn't she also know about her secret hatred of navy blue? And if Marion were the murderer, why would he change Lucy's clothes? He was always impeccably dressed, but wasn't that taking the idea of being a fashion victim a bit too far?

After laying out the facts, they were left with the belief that both Marion and Beverly had motive and opportunity to kill Lucy, but they were still no closer to pointing an unwavering finger at either one of them as the definitive prime suspect. As the co-founders of the unofficial Ferrara Family Detective Agency, Alberta and Jinx understood that it was time to ramp their sleuthing up a notch.


*The Upper Sussex Herald* employed eleven people, and all of them liked Jinx, which was good because she was always wandering into places where she had no business wandering. Like the broom-closet-sized, windowless office that housed the one computer loaded with software linking it to all of New Jersey's correctional facilities and government agencies. It was also the only office whose door was marked "Private." A warning that Jinx ignored.

While running Marion's fingerprints through the computer, Calhoun entered unexpectedly and startled Jinx, causing her to whip around and almost drop the coffee cup she was holding. At six feet three and exactly one hundred and sixty-two pounds, Sylvester Calhoun was often described as a tall drink of water. His lanky frame easily towered over Jinx's, especially since she was wearing flats and not her usual three-inch heels, so she knew that he only had to tilt his head slightly and he'd have a clear view of the computer screen. And if that happened, nothing was going to stop the investigative reporter from investigating why Jinx was running one of Tranquility's most prominent businessmen's fingerprints through the criminal justice system. She wasn't going to quell Calhoun's instincts as an investigative reporter, but she could quench his appetite as a man.

Seductively, she put the pointed end of his green paisley tie into her mouth and moistened it with her saliva, all the while deliberately avoiding eye contact with her wide-eyed colleague. She dabbed the wet tip of the tie onto his chest and pretended to wipe away imaginary drops of her hazelnut coffee.

"I wouldn't want to be the reason your shirt is covered in stains," Jinx purred.

"No worries," Calhoun nervously replied. "My kid usually spits up on me at least once a day."

Knowing that Calhoun had recently become a new father, she figured he had also become an old husband and was craving some affection from the opposite sex.

"Baby spittle on a man's dress shirt is super attractive," Jinx said. "Coffee blotches, not so much."

Calhoun flinched at Jinx's repeated dabs and finally took over cleaning duties, pressing his tie into the wet spots on his shirt. "You think so?" he asked. "About the baby spittle, I mean."

"Absolutely!" Jinx enthused. "It shows that you're a hands-on dad and not one of those absentee fathers who still believes a wife is best when barefoot and pregnant. It's a total turn-on, you know, to most women."

As she spoke, Jinx stepped counterclockwise so Calhoun had to follow suit, and soon he was standing in front of the computer and facing the door. He had no idea that behind him the computer was desperately trying to find a match for Marion Klausner's fingerprints.

"Well, I hope women will be watching the six o'clock news," he stated. "I'm going to be interviewed this afternoon about the tax fraud scandal I uncovered involving the mayor's former brother-in-law."

"Johnny Kaplan?"

"That's the one," Calhoun confirmed. "The piece is set to air tonight."

Jinx hid her immense disappointment that Calhoun was going to hit the local airwaves and frowned at the announcement. "In that case, you're probably going to want to clean up," she declared. "TV magnifies everything, so a tiny stain that might look sexy up close could come off as kind of gross on the small screen."

Calhoun looked instantly worried. He might be a veteran reporter and a harried father, but he was still a man, which meant that he was helpless.

"What should I do?" he said, a hint of desperation etching into his voice. "I don't have another shirt at the office."

"Go into the fridge in the break room, there's a bottle of seltzer behind the unclaimed Chinese take-out," Jinx instructed.

Calhoun's worried expression deepened. "That's Mary Margaret's seltzer, and she's very territorial about her soft drinks."

"Tell her it's an emergency," Jinx ordered. "Now go."

Alone again in the tiny office, Jinx chuckled to herself, thinking that men could be so predictable. She looked at the computer screen and gave a high five to the empty air when she received confirmation. Marion Franz Klausner's fingerprints were already in the government's database, which meant that Marion was a criminal. Or at least had been arrested at some point in his life for a crime that he may or may not have committed. It was good enough for Jinx.

Heart racing, she typed the information on the computer screen into her cell phone and quickly turned off the computer in case she was interrupted again. She snuck out of the room, making sure that no one saw her scurrying back to her desk. By the time she got there, Marion's rap sheet was on her phone's screen.

Weeks before he graduated from Rutgers University he was involved in a date rape scandal that, based upon the very small number of hits generated, was largely brushed under the rug. Of course, the alleged crime took place well before the dawn of the Internet, so it could have been widely covered by the press at the time, but now in the technological age, it was a mere footnote.

Scanning the one article she could find, Jinx discovered that an unnamed female student accused Marion of date-raping her, but after two separate and independent investigations spearheaded by the college and the state, the allegations couldn't be supported and the charges were dropped. Marion was only mentioned by name once in the article and never quoted, but his mother, Helga, was quite the blabbermouth.

"I know all too well what it is like to be condemned and considered guilty before proven innocent by the public," Helga was quoted as saying. "I have been suspected of terrible things simply because I am German and now my only son has been suspected of a terrible thing only because he is handsome, smart, and wealthy. Look at his handsome face, it is the face of an angel, a handsome angel who will go on to do great and remarkable things. And this girl, this evil girl who said my son did this deplorable thing, you watch her and you will see that she rots in hell."

Wow, Jinx thought, sounds like Marion's mother was the original helicopter parent. But after reading the quote again, Jinx realized that her mother probably would've said the same thing if she had been accused of committing such a heinous crime. And she knew without question that Alberta, Helen, and even Joyce would speak out as strongly against any person who dared incriminate her, and they would be vocal proponents of her innocence and her good name.

While she couldn't fault the mother for protecting the child, she had the nagging suspicion that the child had not learned his lesson. She felt it was time to go directly to the source and probe deeper into Marion's weak spot. After all, she might not be a mother, but she had already proven to be a very smart sister.

"I know you're used to meeting with Father Sal, but he's so overwhelmed these days counseling the bishop and balancing the church's precarious budget, not to mention returning the endless stream of phone calls from the Vatican."

"Yes, he's a very busy and influential man," Marion confirmed. "In fact, the last time we met, he said he wasn't sure if he could continue our sessions due to his schedule, but I'm grateful that in his absence he had the forethought to connect the two of us."

Jinx brushed the black cloth of the nun's headpiece with the back of her hand as if it were a strand of her own long hair and silently cursed herself since it was an inappropriate gesture for the woman she was portraying. But since Marion was staring into his coffee cup pensively, he was unaware that Jinx was behaving badly or that she wasn't who she claimed to be.

"Sister Maria," Marion said. "I must confess . . ."

"Please do," Jinx interrupted.

"You're younger than I thought you'd be," Marion stated.

Jinx nodded her head and smiled politely even though she was disappointed that he hadn't confessed to something more salacious, like murder, or at least a date rape that he committed decades ago.

"When I received the call to meet you here," he continued. "I just assumed that you would be a contemporary of Father Sal's, not someone so young."

Jinx smiled again, this time thrilled to know that he didn't recognize her voice as the person who called him to set up the interview. She had channeled her grandmother's thick New Jersey Italian accent and posed as Father Sal's secretary to lure Marion out of his office and across town to a diner that was once a local hotspot, but was now frequented primarily by tired truck drivers and kids craving disco fries late at night. Neither of them ran the risk of being recognized.

"I stopped drinking the sacrificial wine at the early morning masses," Jinx laughed until she noticed Marion's raised eyebrows. "Sorry, a bit of nun humor. I keep forgetting that it doesn't go over so well with non-parochials." Her comedy routine having failed, Jinx thought it best to hit hard and convince Marion that they shared an important connection.

"Father Sal thought my background in psychology might help me better counsel you," she lied.

"You studied psychology?"

"Yes," she lied again. "At Rutgers University."

"What a coincidence. That's my alma mater."

Marion smiled broadly, and although Jinx stared intently, she couldn't detect a crack in his veneer. If he was remembering his near-criminal past, he gave no indication and looked like a man momentarily lost in his college glory days. She needed to drag him into the present.

"So, your relationship with Beverly seems to be the latest in a long line of failures and is the most recent demonstration of a lifelong problem," she stated bluntly. "Which is your inability to commit to one woman."

Opening his mouth, Jinx thought for sure that Marion would protest, but he simply let out a deep breath. He didn't argue with Jinx's accusation; in fact, he appeared to rejoice in it.

"Thank you, Sister, for being so honest and, pardon me for appearing so forward, but for being a woman," he replied. "Father Sal is a very good listener, but even though he's a priest he's still a man, and try as he might, I don't think he ever thought what I was doing was really . . . wrong."

"I'm not here to judge what's right and wrong," Jinx maintained.

"I know that, but it's refreshing to hear my issue portrayed so plainly," Marion said. "Ever since I started dating in college, I would lead a girl on, make her think that we had a future, and then break things off just as she was expecting me to get down on one knee. Sometimes I even went so far as to insinuate that I would ask her to marry me and twice . . . I'm so ashamed to admit this . . . but twice I even bought a ring. Each time I swore that I would never do it again, that I would never break another woman's heart, but I did it again and this time I fear I've gone too far."

Jinx almost choked on her coffee and had to swallow hard not to spit in Marion's face. "What do you mean *too far?*"

For a moment Marion looked away at nothing in particular, but also at something very significant. Jinx assumed he was looking at Beverly's tear-stained face. She was wrong.

"I should have broken things off years ago, but I really hoped that it would work out this time," Marion said, his voice filled with emotion. "I know that it would have made her so very happy and that's all I ever wanted to do, you must understand that, everything I've ever done was to make her happy."

"Beverly?"

Shaking his head vehemently, Marion replied, "No, of course not. I'm talking about my mother."

At the same time, Alberta was conducting her own investigation at the Tranquility Library and her conclusions would point her in the same direction.

After spending about an hour on the computer in the library's Business Resource Room searching the Internet for articles on Wasserman & Speicher, Alberta still hadn't uncovered anything new about the real estate firm that she hadn't already learned on the job or in one of the many press releases that were constantly being e-mailed to all employees from the firm's communications department. Until she took a cue from the original Sister Maria from *The Sound of Music* and decided to start at the very beginning.

Before Marion there was Helga and before Helga there was the Wasserman family. If they owned the company Marion now ran, it would be important to find out about how the company started. Or more specifically, how the family started. Alberta typed *Wasserman* into the computer, and multiple random links popped up, including one that showed *wasser* was the German word for water. Who the hell was Waterman, Alberta thought?

Defeated, she then retyped in Wasserman & Speicher and noticed that not only did links pop up with the word *water*, but also with the word *memory*.

She did some further digging and was astonished to discover that *speicher* was the German word for memory. The German words for water and memory making up one company's name, could it just be a co-incidence? Alberta couldn't cover her mouth fast enough to stifle her gasp when she realized that Wasserman & Speicher could be loosely translated to mean Memory Lake, the same place where Lucy's dead body had been found.

Without realizing it, Alberta started to mutter to herself. Although her specific words weren't overheard by the few patrons milling about the library, her inco-herent whispering did attract the attention of the li-brarian who was restocking the magazine racks directly behind her.

"Excuse me, may I help you?"

The fingers that unexpectedly tapped her shoul-der felt like bolts of lightning. Alberta turned around in her chair so fast that she knocked the magazines out of Sloan's hands. "Oh, I'm so sorry!" she gasped.

"Not to worry," he replied, bending down to pick them up. "Happens to me all the time when I frighten a pretty woman."

Startled even further by the librarian's flirtatious comment, Alberta blushed when she apologized once again. "It was my fault," she admitted. "I was so lost in my reading that I didn't hear you come up behind me."

"No need to apologize," he said. "It's nice to see someone using the library for research, helps to keep me employed. I'm Sloan McLelland, by the way."

"Alberta Scaglione," she replied, reaching out to shake his hand.

The first thing she noticed was that Sloan's hand

was softer but much stronger than her husband Sammy's ever was. And the second thing was that she recognized his name. "I know that name," she said.

It was Sloan's turn to blush. "You must have read my articles in *The Herald*."

"Yes! They were wonderful and so informative," Alberta gushed. "Who knew Tranquility had such a rich history?"

As a third-generation Tranquilitarian, which is what the long-standing residents called themselves, Sloan knew all about his hometown's past, so Wyck thought he was the perfect person to write a multi-part series of articles highlighting the triumphs, events, and occasional scandal of the town's first hundred years. Wyck also thought having the articles written by a local would give them a hokey home-grown feel. He, along with most of the town, was quite surprised to find that they were not only very well written but impeccably researched, funny, and rather touching. The series served as a wonderful reminder to the fast-paced modern world of Tranquility's strong and sturdy roots.

"I guess I am sort of a big fish in a little pond now," he admitted. "I've been given the lofty, though largely ceremonial, title of town historian."

"Then you're just the man who can help me!"

Sitting in a folding chair in his cramped office, Alberta explained that she was trying to find out a bit of information on the new company she had just started to work for. All she had to do was mention the name of the firm and Sloan started spouting random bits of information about Wasserman & Speicher that she had never heard of. She tried to write notes, but found that she couldn't keep up with Sloan's excited monologue. She also found it a bit hard to focus on his words and not his appearance.

He was clearly not Italian, and so he, like Marion, was different than most of the men she had known all her life. He was at least six feet, probably a few inches taller, and even though he was definitely in his sixties, his tight-fitting dress shirt showed off his muscular chest and arms and that he had the body of a much younger man. Most of his hair was still dark brown, although there was quite a bit of gray on the temples, and his features were long and pointy instead of round and blunt like the rest of the men in her family. Taken individually, Sloan's nose, ears, and chin looked birdlike, but together they somehow appeared strong. When she caught a glimpse of his profile she silently remarked that he looked just like a matinee idol from the golden age of the movies. She had just launched into a daydream that featured Sloan as a bare-chested swashbuckler and her as his scantily clad mistress when she heard him start talking about Memory Lake.

"What a second," she interrupted. "What did you say?"

"Memory Lake isn't a real lake, it's manmade."

The lake Alberta stared at every morning, every night, and the occasional afternoon was a fake. How could that be?

"It was created by the original owners of Wasserman & Speicher when they came over from Germany," Sloan explained. "They turned what was previously flat, barren land into a beautiful crystal blue lake several miles wide. I found out so many details about the company, but most of it was cut out of my articles during the editing process. Wyck, he's the editor, he didn't think it was . . . forgive the expression . . . *sexy* enough to be included. I know I found some old blueprints during my research, but I can't remember where I put them. I'll see if I can find them, though, they're really fascinating."

Try as she might, Alberta couldn't wrap her mind around the idea that a lake could be built where beforehand there was no water. Sloan wasn't an engineer, so he couldn't shed any light onto how Memory Lake was built, but he was able to offer more insight as to why.

"Helga, the matriarch, wanted to be reminded of where she grew up . . . in Konstanz . . . on the shores of Lake Constance," Sloan added.

"But I thought his family lived in Hoboken, New Jersey," Alberta said, careful not to mention that it was her hometown as well.

"They did," Sloan confirmed. "But the story goes that the family was going to build the company there until they took a vacation here and Helga fell in love with the area. There was more than enough land to buy and build the lake she wanted, and rumor has it that Helga was an incredibly strong-willed and wealthy woman, some might even say overbearing, so from everything I uncovered it looks like whatever Helga wanted, Helga got. Just look at what happened to your boss."

"Marion?"

Sloan nodded his head several times. "Helga wanted her only son to live the American Dream, and considering what a big deal he's become, I'd say she succeeded."

Alberta didn't quite understand what this information meant or even if it would make any difference in their investigation, but she was certain that it felt good to make a new friend. And the way that Sloan smiled when Alberta thanked him for his help, it was obvious that he felt the same way.

While walking to her car, however, Alberta's thoughts strayed to the man she reluctantly considered her old friend. But was that who Marion really was? She hardly remembered him from her youth and she hardly knew him now. And everything she thought she knew about him had just changed after learning about the origins of Wasserman & Speicher and Helga's role in its creation. All this new information gave Alberta more insight into the type of man Marion really was.

Across town Jinx sat in the driver's seat of her Chevy Cruze and had a similar thought. The man Marion appeared to be on the outside was quite different from the person who lurked within. Regardless of how accomplished, successful, and rich Marion might be, at his core he was the quintessential mama's boy. As the Italians would say, he was a complete *mammone*.

It made both women question what else he might be hiding.

# CHAPTER 18

*Calme acque sono profonde.*

A wise Italian once said that when the world becomes too difficult to deal with, the best way to escape is with food. That person never tasted one of Jinx's recipes.

"*Gesù, Maria, e Giuseppe!*" Alberta exclaimed. "Who taught you how to cook down there in Florida? A prison chef?"

"Gram! It isn't that bad and you know it."

Pushing her plate away from her, Helen shook her head. "This has about as much flavor as a Eucharist without any of the hope."

"Lovey, I thought you said this was risotto?" Alberta asked.

"It is," Jinx swore. "Except I made it with couscous."

Downing a glass of citrus-flavored vodka, Helen said, "That's like making a hamburger with tofu. It might look like a hamburger, but it tastes like crap. Just like this."

Taking a bite of her own concoction, Jinx chewed slowly and thought she knew how to solve the problem of her culinary failure. "It just needs a few more spices."

"You could use every spice imaginable and it wouldn't help," Alberta said. "Face it, lovey, you're a terrible cook."

Jinx laughed and hugged Alberta, "You say the sweetest things to me, Gram."

Hugging Jinx back even harder, Alberta replied, "If you can't speak honestly with your family, you might as well get rid of your voice."

"In the meantime, get rid of this fake-soto thing," Helen said, "Because the smell is starting to give me a headache."

Jinx grabbed their plates, removed them from the kitchen table, and started to bend over to place a plate on the floor in front of Lola, who was patiently waiting for her next meal.

"Don't you dare serve that *schifezza* to my Lola!" Alberta proclaimed, rescuing her pride and joy from a meal she'd definitely regret. "You think I'm going to feed my baby something I wouldn't eat?"

Jinx rolled her eyes dramatically, "A thousand pardons, Queen Lola. I bet Aunt Joyce will like it—she loves to try new things."

Helen refilled her glass with more citrus vodka and remarked, "She might try to be on time for once."

Just then the back door burst open and brought with it the wind and rain from the evening storm as well as a drenched Joyce. "Oh my God! It's like the two of you are psychically linked or something!" Jinx shouted.

"Helen, prepare to eat your words," Joyce announced.

"Fine with me," she said. "They can't possibly be worse than what Jinx just tried to serve us."

While Helen remained seated waiting to find out

why she had to eat her words, Alberta let Lola jump out of her arms and ran to get a clean towel so Joyce could dry her face and hands. Jinx took her aunt's wet raincoat and hat and hung them on the hall tree next to the front door. Joyce sat across from Helen at the table and took her wet galoshes off and placed them on the bench underneath her still-dripping coat.

"It's really coming down out there," Joyce said, rubbing the fresh towel over her face. "And with the wind off the lake there's a bit of a chill in the air."

"I'll make some tea to warm you up," Alberta said.

"That would be perfect."

"How about some risotto, Aunt Joyce?"

Helen caught Joyce's eye as she shook her head slowly from side to side.

"Thank you, Jinx, but I'm too excited to show you what I found," Joyce said. "And prove to Miss Helen once and for all that pursuing my art is a worthwhile endeavor."

The women watched quietly as Joyce took a plastic tube out of her bag and unscrewed the top. She then turned the tube upside down and pulled out a large rolled-up poster that was over two feet long. Tossing the tube back into her bag, she proceeded to unfurl the poster, but it was so big and took up almost the entire circumference of the table, that Helen had to pick up her glass and the vodka bottle or else risk them being spilled.

To make the poster lie flat, Alberta and Jinx held down two of the corners with their fingers while Helen placed the vodka bottle on the third. Ever inquisitive, Lola hopped onto the table, plopped down on the fourth corner, and purred triumphantly.

"Okay, Lola, this time you can stay on the table," Alberta said. "But don't make it a habit."

They were all gathered on one side of the table behind Joyce and saw that they were looking at a dark and very grainy supersized photo of Memory Lake.

"You call this art?" Helen asked.

"No, I call this a clue," Joyce replied.

She explained that while she was developing the film from her overnight, automated photo shoot a few weeks ago that captured shots of Memory Lake in the middle of the night, she noticed something strange. Most of the photos were exactly the same landscape just with different lighting thanks to the shifting position of the moon and then, of course, the appearance of the early morning sun. But in a few of the photos from the northernmost part of the lake, there was an odd blur, like a shadow, first in the lake, then on the banks of the shore, and then once again in the lake itself.

"So, I blew up the photos to see if I could make out what the shadow was and voilà!" Joyce pointed to the enlarged photo on the table, her finger underneath the indisputable figure of a person standing on the banks of the lake. "Do you see it?"

"Yes!" Jinx squealed. "What's a man doing there in the middle of the night?"

"Are you sure it isn't a bear?" Helen asked, skeptical as ever.

"Have you ever seen a bear carry an attaché case?" Joyce asked.

"Helen does have a point, Joyce, the photo's so dark it looks like he's completely black," Alberta said.

Joyce described that after she blew up the rest of the photos they provided a timeline and showed that the man appeared on the surface of the lake, standing next to it carrying the briefcase, then a few minutes later reappeared still holding the case, only to enter the lake again and disappear.

"Almost like he's deep-sea diving?" Jinx asked.

"Exactly!" Joyce hollered. "Which explains why he looks like he's completely dressed in black. He's wearing a wet suit."

"But why would you go deep-sea diving with a brief-case?" Alberta asked.

"To make some kind of business transaction," Joyce stated.

"I've heard of paying off people under the table," Helen said, "But under the water? That's ridiculous."

"Not if your business transaction is illegal," Joyce replied.

The teakettle started to whistle, so Alberta left her place at the table to turn off the flame on the stove and pour four cups of tea. Now that the show-and-tell portion of the evening was over, Joyce rolled up the enlarged photo, much to Lola's displeasure, and returned it to its case. Jinx grabbed some lemon wedges and milk from the fridge and placed them all on the table along with the sugar container from the counter. Helen cut up the loaf of Entenmann's lemon pound cake in two-inch slices, and using napkins as plates, the women helped themselves to dessert while Joyce continued to explain her theory.

"Remember the e-mails I printed out from Marion's computer when we snuck into his office?" she asked. "One of the men Marion was e-mailing, a guy named Johnny Kaplan, who is somehow related to the mayor, is now in jail for tax fraud."

"That's the guy Calhoun exposed!" Jinx exclaimed.

"Who?" the three other women asked.

"He's the investigative reporter at the paper who gets all the juicy stories. Boy, is he going to be shocked when I scoop him on this."

"We don't have a scoop yet, but we're getting close," Joyce advised.

She continued to explain that three of the other men that Marion was e-mailing, none of whom lived in the area, had been indicted on drug-smuggling charges. It doesn't appear that the mayor's distant relative was involved in any sort of illegal drug activity, but since the details of the crimes were being kept quiet and the investigation was ongoing, allegations might arise at some point. The only reason Joyce found out as much as she did was because she was still in touch with many of her former business contacts.

"It's always smart to maintain professional relationships even after you retire," Joyce declared. "And to top it off, a VP who used to work for me bought one of my paintings for two hundred bucks."

"That's amazing!" Alberta shouted.

"Congrats, Aunt Joyce!"

"That's all you got?" Helen barked.

"I told you, Hel, it isn't about the money," Joyce stated. "But it is about you eating your words and admitting that my painting is worth the time and energy I put into it. Look how much we found out thanks to my artistic process."

Helen sipped her tea slowly and placed the cup on the table. Before she spoke, however, she removed her eyeglasses to clean them with the apron of the tablecloth. When she put her glasses back on she finally spoke. "I'll admit that your *hobby* has proven to be a valuable diversion for you, but it's also distracted us from the real issue here."

"Which is?" Alberta asked.

"Do I have to spell out 'drug smuggling' for you people?" Helen shouted. "If Marion was e-mailing these men who've been convicted of selling drugs, don't you think it's possible that he's involved as well?"

Alberta looked at Jinx, who looked at Joyce, who looked back at Alberta. "I hadn't thought of that," Alberta admitted.

"I know you haven't!" Helen yelled. "Because you're all too busy congratulating Joyce on selling some ugly paint-by-numbers of your precious lake that you haven't been listening to what's important."

"Aunt Helen's right. Marion could be the man in the photo, so maybe he was doing a drug deal."

"I don't have any business experience in the field, but from what I've read, dealing drugs isn't an easy occupation," Joyce said. "Why make it harder by swimming in a lake?"

"What if the lake really isn't a lake?" Alberta announced.

While the women were jabbering about Alberta's riddle, she was on the phone calling the library, expecting to be greeted by a voice recording. She was delighted to hear Sloan's voice on the other end of the line.

"Sloan, it's me, Alberta."

"Alberta, how nice to hear from you."

"I didn't think anyone would still be there at this time of night."

"We stay open late on Tuesdays, so I guess you can

say this is my lucky day. Or, more precisely, my lucky night."

"Well I'm hoping you can make it *my* lucky night. Sloan, did you ever find those blueprints you told me about?"

Sloan was grinning so boyishly he was thankful Alberta couldn't see his face. "I have them right here, as a matter of fact. I was going to call you in the morning to see if you'd like to come in to take a look at them."

"How about right now?"

"Now? Oh, well . . . the, um, the library's about to close in five minutes."

"Then come over to my place, 22 Memory Lake Road."

Alberta placed the phone back on its cradle on the wall and turned around to see all three women staring at her, smiling like three Cheshire cats after finding the inhabitants of their favorite mouse hole holding an extended family reunion.

"Was that Sloan McLelland, Gram?"

"You know him?" Alberta asked as nonchalantly as possible.

"Kind of . . . I met him once or twice at the *Herald*," Jinx answered.

"He's the town historian," Joyce said.

"The very *cute* town historian," Jinx added.

"Oh, *Madon!*" Alberta cried. "You're too much, Jinx."

Suddenly flustered, Alberta felt her cheeks grow hot. She started rearranging the canisters on the kitchen counter and then proceeded to tidy up the kitchen table, which didn't need tidying, just to busy herself.

"Well, I'll be," Helen drawled like a Southern Italian belle and poured some citrus vodka into her teacup. "Had I known we'd be acceptin' gentleman callers tonight, I would've made an appointment to get my hair washed and set."

A half hour later, Sloan was sitting at the kitchen table drying his wet face with a towel and being stared at by all four women. He was, of course, surprised to see that Alberta wasn't alone, but since Tranquility was a small town, he found himself surrounded by familiar faces. He remembered meeting Jinx at the *Herald* and knew Joyce from serving on various town committees together, but didn't realize she was a relation.

"I'm the black sheep of the family," Joyce joked.

"You are not, Joyce!" Alberta remarked. "You're just what we call Black Italian."

"Which is kind of like Black Irish," Joyce added, turning her head so her long gold earrings shimmied. "But with bling instead of a brogue."

"And who's this lovely creature?" Sloan asked as Lola weaved in and out of his legs before scooping her up in his arms and rubbing her underneath the chin. Lola let out an indecent purr that left no room for doubt that she enjoyed being in Sloan's presence as much as the others.

"That's Lola," Alberta replied.

"Like Gina Lollobrigida?" Sloan asked.

"Yes!" Alberta cried. "But Lola for short because Jinx's real name is Gina too, and I didn't want either one of them to be confused."

"I know she was the poor man's Sophia Loren," Sloan said. "But I always loved Lollobrigida. She was a fine actress, and you, Lola, are a fine feline."

Clearing her throat loudly, Helen asked, "Is anyone going to introduce me to Berta's new friend?"

"Sorry, Hel," Alberta said, still laughing. "Sloan, this is my sister Helen, who—and this is kind of funny—actually used to be Sister Helen. She's a former nun."

"Very nice to meet you," Sloan said. "So, you must know Father Sal."

"Unfortunately," Helen replied dryly.

Alberta took an unhappy Lola from Sloan's arms and sat down next to Sloan so she could steer the subject away from ecclesiastical bashing and toward the reason she had invited the librarian over to her home in the middle of a rainstorm. "Did you bring the blueprints?"

Once again, the ladies cleared the kitchen table to make room for an oversized document to be spread out and examined. At first glance the blueprints were hard to read since they weren't the originals, but copies that were faded, crinkled, and smudged after so many years of being in storage. Sloan, however, relished having an interested audience, so he embarked on a mini-lecture that brought the slightly damaged Xeroxed copy to life.

The women listened as he spoke, trying to connect his words to the details he was pointing at on the blueprint and not just watch his long, slender fingers move gracefully over the document, when they finally heard him say something so intriguing that it broke the spell his appearance had over them.

"A tunnel?" Jinx asked.

"Yes, for some reason a tunnel was built from the sub-basement of the Wasserman & Speicher building that leads directly into Memory Lake," Sloan explained. "Probably something to do with the structural soundness of the lake itself or perhaps an escape route."

"An escape route?" Joyce asked.

"Well, the original building was built in the late forties, and Helga and her family barely got out of Germany during World War II," Sloan explained. "So maybe she thought there'd be another war and she'd need a secret way to escape the Nazis. No one really knows. But according to these blueprints, the tunnel comes out right here."

The women shrieked when they saw that the tunnel's exit was the northernmost part of the lake, exactly the same location where they saw the diver in Joyce's photo. Sloan didn't realize why they were so excited, but he was still thrilled that he had found an audience as enthusiastic about Tranquility's past as he was. Their passion did make him curious, though.

"A few years ago that opening was closed up permanently after a family of deer got trapped inside. No one even knew it existed, but the town plugged it up," Sloan continued. "May I ask why you're so interested in the lake?"

After a short pause, Helen answered for the group, "We're just hungry for knowledge." She shot a devilish glance at her sister and continued, her voice dripping with sarcasm. "Some of us are hungrier than others."

The moment Alberta ushered Sloan out the door,

Jinx and Joyce giggled like schoolgirls and couldn't help ribbing Alberta about her new man friend.

"I used to say this about my Anthony—*Calme acque sono profonde,*" Joyce said. "But I think it applies to Sloan as well."

"You're right about that," Helen agreed. "Still waters usually run deep."

"Of course, my Ant was quietly running around with other women and cheating on me," Joyce remembered. "But Sloan appears to be the monogamous type, Alberta, so you shouldn't worry."

Shaking her head good-naturedly, Alberta said, "If you would get your minds out of the gutter, ladies, you'd see that this means the *TV Guide*s really are one big clue showing us where the collection is."

"I'm sorry, Gram, my head is still picturing you and Sloan kissing in a tree as well as in the gutter, so I'm not following you."

Smiling as she waved a finger at her granddaughter, Alberta explained her hypothesis, "Add them all up. *Sea Hunt* plus *John Wayne* plus *Mama.* If John Wayne went on a sea hunt to remember his mother, where would it lead him?"

All three answered at the same time, "To Memory Lake!"

"I think Lucy's *TV Guide* collection is at the bottom of Memory Lake," Alberta shared, proud of her deduction.

Joyce hated to be the one sticking the pin into Alberta's happy bubble, but she needed to state the obvious. "Looks like we've come to the point where we have to hand this investigation over to Vinny and the police. Unless one of you secretly knows how to deep-sea-dive."

Unable to contain her enthusiasm, Jinx shouted, "I do!"

"Really?" Alberta asked.

"Well not, you know, technically," she admitted. "But thanks to covering the Tranquility Waterfest, I know someone who can teach us. What do you say, Gram? Are you ready to tackle yet another new experience?"

Alberta hesitated only slightly. She had wanted to be a part of her granddaughter's life and make up for all of those lost years, so she wasn't about to miss an opportunity to grow even closer to Jinx just because it meant spending some time underwater.

Throwing her hands up in the air, Alberta shouted, "Why the hell not?"

# CHAPTER 19

*Danari fanno danari.*

At the end of their third scuba-diving lesson, Alberta had already learned that the word "scuba" was an acronym that stood for "self-contained underwater breathing apparatus," how to balance her breath against the surrounding water pressure, the most effective ways to use her fins to travel in any direction underwater, and most exciting, that she looked two sizes slimmer in her wet suit. She told Jinx that it was like wearing a full-body Spanx, but much more comfortable.

"I feel like Esther Williams," Alberta declared as she sat on the side of the pool. "And before you ask me who that is, google her name."

"I know who Esther Williams is, Gram," Jinx replied, hanging onto the pool's edge, her body still in the water. "Mom and I used to watch old movies all the time."

Alberta forced herself to smile to hide her sadness. She was glad that Jinx had fond memories of her mother; she just wished that Jinx's mother had fond memories of hers. She considered her estrangement with Lisa Marie to be the biggest failure of her life, and as time wore on she grew less and less confident that the fence separating them would be mended. Ah well, she thought, at least she was sharing time with her granddaughter. And using muscles that she never thought she had.

"Should I be worried that my thighs are burning like they're on fire?" Alberta asked.

"It means they're thanking you for bringing them back to life," Freddy said.

"That's very sweet of them, Freddy," Alberta replied. "But a nice thank-you card would've sufficed."

Freddy Frangelico was their scuba-diving instructor, and Alberta thought he looked like a young Clark Gable. He had the wavy black hair, the dimples, the devilish grin, and, most endearing, the large floppy ears. By the way he catered to Jinx's every need, she could tell, frankly, that he gave a damn.

"You're doing great, Mrs. Scaglione," Freddy announced. "And if it weren't for Jinx here, you'd be my number one student."

Shooting a conspiratorial glance at Jinx, Alberta replied, "I'll gladly take a backseat to my granddaughter any day, especially if you're behind the wheel."

Underneath the water, Jinx tugged on her grandmother's foot, and the two women laughed at Alberta's obvious attempt at matchmaking.

"I have a break for a few hours, Jinx," Freddy announced. "Any chance I can take you to lunch?"

Feeling her heart start to beat a bit faster in her chest, Jinx squeezed Alberta's foot harder and replied, "Sure, Freddy, I'd like that."

Squatting next to Alberta, he extended a hand to

Jinx and helped pull her out of the pool. He then proved he was as polite as he was strong. "Mrs. Scaglione, would you like to join us?"

Alberta didn't need to see Jinx shake her head behind Freddy's back while mouthing the word "No" to understand that she should decline the offer. There were some situations that were simply inappropriate for grandmother-granddaughter bonding, and lunch dates were one of them. Plus, she had a time clock to punch.

"Thank you, but I need to get back to work," Alberta stated. "I only took a half day off."

Ever the gentleman, Freddy replied, "Next time then."

"It's a date," Alberta said, winking at Jinx.

Just as she turned to go, Freddy said, "Oh, and tell Denise that we're doing a brush-up class for certified divers next Saturday. She's due for some retraining."

Did everyone in Tranquility know everyone else? She loved the sense of community—it really was like one big, extended Italian family—but she had to admit that it was disconcerting to know that a person's private business had no chance of remaining private. It seemed that everyone she met was connected to someone she already knew. The sacrifice of living in a small town, she guessed.

"Will do, Freddy," she replied. "You two enjoy your lunch."

Back at her desk, she tried to focus on listening to Marion's dictation tapes and typing his correspondence but was distracted. It wasn't hard to translate the recording, as his diction was as impeccable as his attire, but it was becoming harder to play the role of his secretary now that she was becoming more successful playing the role of detective. The more she found out about Marion, the less she thought she understood, and worse, the less she respected the man.

When they first reconnected, she thought he was the sweet, older version of the shy, misunderstood teenager from her past. Despite the fact that she was only in his presence as a ruse, she couldn't deny that he had unlocked long-dormant feelings and was happily surprised to feel that she might be able to have another shot at romance. It wasn't entirely Sammy's fault, but by no stretch of the imagination could her marriage be described as romantic, not even in the early newlywed days. Alberta and Sammy didn't have a sweeping love affair. They had a marriage, which was imperfect, hard, familiar, and unenvied. Sammy always made Alberta feel like a wife, but Marion had made Alberta feel like a woman. Even though she knew the fantasy of the perfect relationship was an illusion, it was nice to know that she still possessed the vulnerability and curiosity necessary to allow another man the chance to fill the emotional void she felt after Sammy's death.

However, after learning more about Marion from her conversations with Denise and from snooping into Beverly's life, Alberta realized Marion could never be that man. He was far less honorable than she had made him out to be, he seemed to hold an unhealthy fascination with his mother, and now there was the real potential that he was truly dangerous. Whether or not he was involved in Lucy's murder, he had ties to drug dealers. She couldn't comprehend how anyone could be involved with those people who hurt so many lives. As she listened to his erudite speaking voice on the tape and watched him in his office methodically mark up a contract, Alberta realized it was all a cover-up.

A further distraction was the series of text messages she had been receiving from Joyce. The first asked if she was back at work. The second wanted to know when she was leaving work. The third inquired if Marion was still on the premises. Finally, at ten minutes to five, Joyce sent a fourth saying that she was on her way up to meet Alberta, and that Alberta should play along with whatever Joyce said and did.

Intrigued, Alberta wasn't sure what game Joyce was playing, but until she arrived she needed to continue playing the game of dutiful secretary. She knocked on Marion's door but waited to enter until he looked up from the contract he was marking up.

"Here you go, Marion, all your letters await your signature."

Alberta placed the correspondence in the inbox on Marion's desk and was about to turn to leave when Marion's question stopped her.

"Is everything all right, Alberta?"

She tried desperately to keep her face an impenetrable mask so her true feelings would remain hidden. She was scared that she was getting in over her head, frightened that she was putting herself and her family in danger, and questioning her judgment not to tell Vinny and the police everything she had learned from investigating Lucy's murder. Was her ego so big that she wanted to solve the mystery herself? Was she so desperate to bond with her granddaughter that she was willing to risk her safety instead of letting the trained professionals do their jobs? And did she feel so guilty because she had found a woman—who she had known her entire life, but never liked—dead in her own backyard that she felt as if she needed to find her murderer to somehow right a wrong? Or had she just misunderstood Marion's question?

"I don't mean to pry, but you said you had a doctor's appointment this morning," he added.

"Oh! My appointment," Alberta replied, completely forgetting she had lied about needing to see her doctor so could have a diving lesson. "Yes, yes, it turned out to be nothing at all, just a little gas. I mean indigestion. My granddaughter has been trying out some new recipes and she hasn't been that successful."

"I'm glad to hear it wasn't anything serious," Marion said. "You're becoming quite invaluable around here and, dare I say, an improvement on my last secretary."

Alberta wasn't sure if Marion was using a dead woman's name in vain or just making an unkind remark about a former girlfriend who flew the coop, but the insinuation that she would take Beverly's place as possibly something more than his administrative assistant made her uneasy, as if she really was suffering from a bad case of indigestion.

"And I'm glad you feel it's working out," was all she could think of saying.

Luckily, she didn't have to say anything further because Marion's phone rang. She started to dash to her desk to answer the call when Marion beat her to it.

"Simon, thank you so much for returning my call," he said, pausing a moment before continuing. "And Antonio, hello, I'm so glad you could join us."

Marion placed a hand over the receiver and whispered to Alberta that he was going to leave after this call so she could call it a day as well. She would happily do that, but first she was going to have to deal with Joyce, who was standing at her desk.

"Hello, Lucy, I've been waiting for you."

It had been many years since Alberta had seen Joyce dressed up like the powerful businesswoman she once was, so she had to bite her tongue not to tell her how amazing she looked. She was dressed in head-to-toe red and wore a man-tailored jacket that had just enough soft curves to make it look feminine; a tight, straight skirt that landed an inch above her knees; patent leather pumps; and a wide-brimmed hat. Somewhere Alexis Carrington Colby raised a flute of Dom Pérignon in approval.

"I'm sorry, but . . ." Alberta started.

"Please, Lucy, let's not quibble," Joyce interrupted. "I've come here to discuss a business proposition with you and I don't have a lot of time."

In a move that would have made Alexis even prouder, Joyce slammed the silver metal briefcase she was holding onto Alberta's desk and patted the case with fingertips that had been painted the same shade of red as her outfit. Boy, Alberta thought, Joyce really pays attention to detail.

Finally understanding that Joyce wanted it to appear as if she thought Alberta was Lucy, she played along. But knowing Marion was undoubtedly listening to her every word while talking on his conference call, she still needed to make herself sound confused.

"I understand, but if you would let me explain . . ."

"No buts! I want to buy your *TV Guide* collection," Joyce said. "For one hundred thousand dollars."

Opening up the briefcase with the easy dexterity of a model from *The Price Is Right,* Joyce revealed that the briefcase was filled with cash. Alberta was so mesmerized by the sight that she didn't see Joyce tilting her head slightly to the left. Once she did, however, she realized Joyce wanted her to move out of the way so Marion could get an undistracted view of the cash. Walking toward Joyce, Alberta deliberately circled to the left and stood behind her desk. She didn't have to look sideways to know that Marion would have no trouble seeing the opened briefcase brimming with hundred-dollar bills.

Alberta had never seen that much cash all at once in her life and assumed the money had to be fake. Then again, Joyce was rich, so she could have made a pit stop at the bank to make a withdrawal. Would she really go so far as to take a hundred grand out of the bank simply to make her plan look legit? Alberta gawked at the money and tried to see if it was from a Monopoly game or if only the first layer was real or if the whole thing was actually one of Joyce's very life-like paintings. She couldn't tell, but it didn't matter. From where Marion was sitting he'd think the money was nothing less than cold, hard American currency.

"So, do we have a deal?" Joyce asked.

"I'm sorry, but you're mistaken," Alberta started. "I don't have any collection and I'm not . . ."

"Enough!" Joyce cried, slamming the briefcase shut. "I'll go up to a hundred twenty-five thousand, but that's my final offer."

She then took a business card out of her pocket and handed it to Alberta. Once again, Alberta was impressed with Joyce's commitment to every detail of her charade. Her maiden name—Joyce Perkins—was stamped on the card with the title Antiques Broker just underneath along with a phone number and e-mail address. In the upper right-hand corner of the

card was an embossed symbol of an owl, which Alberta
knew was Joyce's favorite bird.

"I have a buyer very interested in your collection,
but also too, he's very impatient, so you have forty-
eight hours to let me know your decision."

The only reason Alberta didn't laugh out loud at
Joyce's use of the phrase "also too," which belied her
impersonation of a high-powered businesswoman,
was that she was startled by the sound of a trumpet.
It was someone's cell phone ringing in the distance,
a familiar melody, but it stopped playing before she
could recall where she had heard it before.

Joyce, however, wasn't going to let a cell phone
ring ruin her tour de force, and she continued to play
out the rest of her scene. Grabbing her briefcase,
Joyce whirled around, but slow enough to catch
Marion staring at her. She glanced one last time at
Alberta, her hat perfectly slanted to create a red halo
over her head, and shouted, "Ciao!" over her shoulder. But even though she was gone, her performance
wasn't over.

Less than a minute later, Alberta received a fifth
text from Joyce with instructions to throw the business
card in her trash can and tell Marion she was leaving
for the day but to go to the ladies' room instead.

Alberta did what she was told and when she got to
the ladies' room she found Joyce was waiting there
for her in one of the stalls.

"Oh my God!" Alberta whispered excitedly, closing
the door to the stall behind her so they could have
some privacy. "Joyce, you were amazing! Absolutely
amazing! I'm not really sure what that was all about,
but you were really, really convincing. You should try

out to be part of the Tranquility Players, I think you'd be wonderful on the community theater stage."

"Thank you, sweetie, but first let's see if I convinced Marion."

"What do you mean?"

"When I first started working on Wall Street, I worked for a man named Seymour Hurwitz," Joyce relayed. "He was like a mentor to me, and one of the first things he taught me was *Dineri fanno dineri.*"

"A Jew told you in Italian that money makes money?" Alberta asked incredulously.

"In the mid-seventies, Wall Street didn't really lay out the red carpet for Jewish people, so Seymour told everybody he was Italian," Joyce explained. "I was one of the only ones who knew the truth."

"Okay, but what does that have to do with impersonating an antiques dealer who wants to buy Lucy's *TV Guide* collection?"

"If Marion knows anything about the collection and is desperate to sell it, he's not going to be able to resist taking the bait and retrieving my business card from your trash can."

Stunned by Joyce's brilliance, Alberta was speechless and just stared at her with her mouth open.

"I'm going to assume by your expression that you're impressed with my plan."

Finally regaining the ability to speak, Alberta said, "You're one of the smartest women I've ever known. And may I say for about the millionth time, I have no idea why the hell my brother ever cheated on you."

"Neither do I," Joyce said, shrugging her shoulders. "But let's see if I can judge another man's character better than I could judge my husband's."

Joyce instructed Alberta to go back to her desk to see if the business card was still in her trash can.

"What if Marion's still there?" Alberta asked.

"Well then, pick up something from your desk," she suggested and then added. "But as you're leaving, drop your purse in front of the trash can so when you bend down to pick it up, Marion won't see you looking to see if the card is still there."

Again, Alberta's jaw dropped. "Ah, *Madon*, your mind never stops working, does it?"

"Old habits die hard, sweetie. I'll wait here for you so I know the coast is clear."

While walking back to her desk, Alberta looked through her pocketbook as if she was searching for something to make her return appear more legitimate. When she turned the corner and glanced into Marion's office, she realized there was no need to keep up appearances; he was already gone.

She stood in front of her desk and took a deep breath before looking into the trash can. Part of her wanted the adventure to continue and see that the business card was missing, proving Joyce's belief that Marion indeed knew the location of Lucy's *TV Guide* collection and was desperate to make a buck off of it. But the other part of her wanted to disprove Joyce's theory so she could feel a bit more respect for Marion.

When she looked into the trash can, she saw that the business card was gone, along with her respect for her boss. Like the good little boy he was, Marion had wasted no time taking the bait.

# CHAPTER 20

*Chi cerca mal, mal trova.*

Marion didn't necessarily want to shoot the messenger, but he definitely wanted her out of his office. Jinx, however, wasn't ready to leave just yet.

As part of her plan to gain entry to the Wasserman & Speicher building carrying their scuba-diving equipment without being noticed, Jinx posed as a messenger. Wearing large sunglasses, her hair falling freely past her shoulders, and with a very large backpack strapped onto her back, she looked nothing like the saintly Sister Maria who had previously counseled Marion. But just to make sure he didn't recognize her, Jinx once again mimicked her grandmother's thick northern New Jersey accent and made it sound even thicker.

"But I wuz told ta bring dis to a Mistuh Krowzuh," she announced.

"I'm not Mistuh Krowzuh," Marion said, his patience wearing woefully thin. "I'm Mister *Klausner.*"

"Ohhhh," Jinx replied. "Ya sure?"

Marion's patience was now officially lost. "Yes! Now get out of my office!"

"Okay, calm yaself, I'm leavin'," Jinx said as she walked out of his office, the door slamming shut behind her. As she passed Alberta's desk, she turned to her grandmother and added, "Sheesh, some people get all huffy when I'm just tryin' to do my job, ya know?"

Before Alberta could answer, she saw Denise running down the hallway toward them. Marion's uncharacteristic shouting obviously prompted the nosy HR executive to investigate. Alberta needed to intervene quickly or else her investigation of the link between Wasserman & Speicher and Memory Lake was going to be thwarted before it even got started.

"Denise!" Alberta cried. "I need your help."

Ignoring Alberta, Denise asked Jinx, "Excuse me, who are you?"

"Lady, I'm just the messenger," Jinx replied, still in character, "Don't get yaself all excited."

Alberta could tell by the indignant look on Denise's face that she was about to make a scene, so Alberta needed to make sure that she was Denise's scene partner and not Jinx. Grabbing the first thing she could find, Alberta ran out from behind her desk and in front of Denise just as Jinx walked by her.

"What should I do with these?"

Naturally confused by the sight of Alberta holding up a pair of mint green espadrilles, Denise didn't respond immediately. She started to turn around to call after Jinx again, but Alberta waved an espadrille in front of Denise's face like a Payless salesperson desperate to make a sale.

"I still don't know what to do with the stack of shoes I found in Beverly's drawer."

Inspecting the merchandise closer, Denise replied, "Burn them, they're hideous. That woman has absolutely no taste."

Tugging on Denise's arm, Alberta dragged her back to her desk and opened a drawer to reveal a pile of shoes. She pulled out a black-and-white polka-dot pump and a hot pink slingback with gold embellishments to add to the collection she was holding. "Are you sure we shouldn't give them to charity?"

"The only charitable thing to do would be to use them as kindling for some homeless person's bonfire," Denise spat. "Beverly really did dress like a clown."

Dumping them back in the drawer, Alberta replied, "I think I'll just box them up and drop them off at Goodwill."

"Do whatever you want with them, I don't care," Denise said. "Now where did that messenger go?"

"She left," Alberta muttered indifferently, "Said something about having the wrong building."

Alberta could tell that Denise wasn't entirely satisfied by her answer, so she needed to distract her even further. "By the way, Freddy Frangelico says hello."

"Who?"

"The diving instructor."

After a moment, the name seemed to make more sense to her. "Oh, right, nice kid." Denise glanced over to Marion's office and Alberta followed her gaze to see that their boss was watching their every move. They both knew that it was time to get back to work.

"I have to get ready to leave for a benefits meeting with our new health-care provider," Denise announced.

"And you have to make some poor people look even more unfashionable."

*I'll get right on that,* Alberta thought, *but first I need to make sure my granddaughter made it to Phase Two of our plan.*

For the second time in as many days, Alberta found herself going to the ladies' room when she didn't really have to go. Ignoring the Out of Order sign taped to the bathroom stall, Alberta knocked on the door gently. "Jinx, honey, it's me, are you in there?"

Unlatching the door, Jinx opened it a crack. "We did it, Gram!"

Alberta couldn't help but smile at her grand-daughter's enthusiasm. However, she knew they still had a long way to go if they wanted to find the secret tunnel that led from the sub-basement of the building to Memory Lake without being seen. "Yes, but we still have a lot more to do."

"I know," Jinx said. "But if the security under-ground is as lax as the security upstairs, we won't have any problems finding the tunnel entrance. I mean se-riously, Gram, I was able to waltz right into Marion's office without anyone stopping me."

"Denise did almost stop you," Alberta reminded her.

"And look how easily you handled that situation! We really are a great team."

"Now Jinx, don't get like your Uncle Tony."

"Daddy's brother?"

"He was always *spavaldo . . . arrogante.*"

"Cocky?"

"Yes! He thought for sure Conchetta Minetti was going to wait to marry him just because she had a limp," Alberta explained. "So, he played the field. By the time he was ready to pop the question she had already run off with that orthopedic shoe salesman. He gave her one flat shoe and one with a three-inch platform heel so she could walk as steady as a tight-rope walker, never limped again. She's still happily married and your Uncle Tony? He's still a lonely bachelor."

"You and your stories," Jinx said, suppressing her laughter so she wouldn't make any unnecessary noise. "That's a good one . . . orthopedic shoes."

"Shoes!" Alberta cried, forgetting that she wasn't supposed to make any unnecessary noise. "Oh, *Madon*, I have to pack up Beverly's shoes."

"How much longer do I have to wait in here?" Jinx asked.

Alberta checked her watch as she started to run out. "Everyone's leaving at five today so just another half-hour or so. And remember if you have to go, don't flush, that toilet's not supposed to be working."

Shaking her head, Jinx closed the bathroom stall and sat on the toilet bowl. She wondered if being an investigative reporter could get any more glamorous.


An hour later, after all the employees had left the building, Jinx was still hiding out in the stall. When she heard the bathroom door open, she froze and held her breath until Alberta's whisper cut through the silence.

"Lovey, are you still in there?"

"Where else would I be?" Jinx asked.

Jinx unlocked the stall and Alberta got inside, both women trying to hide how nervous they were from each other. Now that they were so close to proving that there was a secret tunnel and, hopefully, finding out that Lucy's *TV Guide* collection was at the bottom of Memory Lake, they didn't want to make any mistakes that might get them caught on their way downstairs to the sub-basement, or worse, force them to have to turn over their investigation to the authorities.

"Do you think we've waited long enough?" Alberta asked.

"I think so," Jinx replied. "I haven't heard a noise since you got in here."

"Okay, do you have Sloan's map?"

Jinx unzipped a pocket of her jacket and whipped out the folded map. "Right here, but I practically memorized the thing while I was manning the john."

Suddenly the realization of what they were about to do struck Alberta and she was consumed with fear, delight, and anxiety. She definitely had a case of the jitters. "I'm not sure if I'm more excited or scared," Alberta declared.

"It's fine to be both, Gram," Jinx replied. "The most important thing is that we're prepared."

Jinx patted the backpack that contained their scuba-diving equipment—their air tanks, masks, fins, pressure gauges, and wet suits. She put her arms through the straps and hoisted the pack onto her back. Smiling roguishly, she said, "Let's do this, partner."

Pushing all of her nerves aside, Alberta smiled and beamed with pride.

Jinx slowly opened the bathroom door and, despite her bravado, part of her expected to find Marion, Denise, or a security guard waiting for them on the other side so she sighed with relief when she saw the hallway was not only dark but empty as well. She turned right, and Alberta followed directly behind her, making sure to close the bathroom door quietly in case someone was indeed lurking nearby.

At the end of the hall they went down a flight of stairs to the floor below and once they were sure it was also empty, continued on their way. A right, then a left, and soon Alberta realized she was in familiar territory. Straight ahead was the Safe Room. When they got to the double door, it was Alberta's turn to take charge.

"You need a password to get into this room."

"Are you kidding me?"

"Nope, it's called the Safe Room for a reason."

Throwing her hands up in the air, the map billowing in between them, Jinx said, "What are we supposed to do now?"

Beaming even more proudly, Alberta announced, "Allow Grandma to come to the rescue."

Alberta typed in the word "Duke" and they heard the door unlock. She pulled it open and gestured for Jinx to enter.

"You never cease to amaze me."

"Likewise, lovey."

Inside, Alberta looked around the room, which was chock-full of filing cabinets, while Jinx surveyed the blueprint to determine their next move. After a moment, Jinx looked straight ahead at a poster on the wall hanging above a small table. The poster was a blown-up photo of a string of small, adjoining buildings, each painted a different color along the banks of a huge lake. In the top left-hand corner of the poster, floating over fluffy white clouds, were printed the words "Lake Constance."

"There's a door behind that poster," Jinx announced. "Help me move this table."

The women grabbed the table from opposite sides and carried it a few feet away. They pulled off the poster that was Scotch-taped to the wall and saw that it was indeed put there to cover a door and not as a decoration to brighten up the space. There were a few tears at the edge of the poster on the bottom left side, indicating that it had, at some point, been pulled back to allow someone to exit the room, which was actually a very easy task. Where there should have been a doorknob, there was only a hole. Jinx put her fingers through it and easily pulled the door open.

"I guess Marion's mother didn't want to risk the chance of getting locked out from the other side," Jinx deduced.

"And she never figured someone would be able to get into the room who shouldn't be here," Alberta added.

"Talk about *spavaldo*."

The temperature on the other side of the door was several degrees colder than it was in the room. Alberta thought at first it was because they were so close to the computer room, which always had to be kept cold to keep the servers from overheating, but quickly realized it was because they were getting closer to the lake. To the right they saw an arched opening that led to a stairwell that only descended. According to Sloan's blueprint, the stairs led straight down to the sub-basement.

"There are some flashlights in the small pocket of my backpack," Jinx said. "Could you give me one?"

Alberta unzipped the compartment and pulled

out a flashlight made of heavy-duty yellow plastic. "Here you go."

With Jinx lighting their way, they moved slowly one step at a time down the narrow stairwell. The temperature seemed to drop with each step, and soon the sharp scent of mold and mildew filled the air. They were definitely getting closer to a source of water.

After descending about four flights they could see a clearing at the bottom of the stairs. When they were standing on solid ground again, they looked up and were amazed. In front of them and to the left it looked like they were staring at the outside of a building. The facade was weather-beaten, but clearly made of concrete. But to the right and behind them, it was as if they were standing next to the side of a mountain as the walls were smoothed out rocks and stone. And most unlikely of all, carved into the side of the rocks was an opening about eight feet tall and ten feet wide.

"I don't know how they did it, but they really did build a tunnel."

Surveying the man-made triumph, Alberta replied, "Say what you want about the Germans, but they're very crafty people."

Aiming her flashlight straight ahead, Jinx couldn't see much beyond the darkness and shadows, but since there was no other direction for them to go if they wanted to reach the lake, this was the path they had to follow.

With Alberta once again inches behind her, Jinx led the way through the tunnel, with each step marveling that such a structure could not only be built but kept a secret for so many years. After almost five minutes the darkness started to become claustrophobic as the air became thicker and ripe with the smells of the underground. Jinx's back and shoulders also began to hurt from carrying a heavy weight for such a long time. Just when they thought it might make more sense to turn back and abandon their madcap adventure, they literally saw a light at the end of the tunnel.

"I think we're here," Jinx whispered.

And they were. They finally emerged into an even smaller clearing that was completely empty except for a hole in the center of its floor.

"*Strabiliante!*" Alberta gasped. "This is absolutely amazing."

"Plus, it's exactly as Sloan described," Jinx said. "Look, those Germans are not only clever, but they're practical too. They built a plastic covering over the entrance to the lake so you wouldn't accidentally fall in."

When Jinx grabbed the handle and lifted the lid, both women gasped. Even though this is what they had come to see, they couldn't believe their eyes. They were looking down into a circular tunnel that would actually lead them directly into Memory Lake. All they had to do was climb down the metal ladder. Only three steps were visible, but peering down into the dark tunnel filled with what looked like ice-cold, black water, the surface seemed to be a million miles away.

This is why they took scuba-diving lessons, and this was the only way they were going to find out if Lucy's *TV Guide* collection was laying at the bottom of the lake, so no need to hesitate now. Unfortunately, all Alberta could think of was *Chi cerca mal, mal trova*. The unpleasant phrase roughly translated to "He who seeks evil, generally finds it." Was that what she was about to discover? Something evil? Or perhaps the complete opposite, an answer to the question of who killed Lucy Agostino? Yes, that had to be it. She couldn't be en route to meeting up with evil with her granddaughter in tow.

"Having second thoughts?"

Yes, Alberta thought, but she kept them to herself. "Not a one. Race you to the bottom of the lake!"

Quickly and quietly, the women dressed in their wet suits and fins, adjusted their pressure gauges according to what they read in an online geographical survey were the atmospheric levels of the lake, strapped on their air tanks, and donned their masks.

"Remember, stay close by me and if you experience any trouble at all, what's our distress code?"

"Three slaps to my left shoulder," Alberta replied.

"Good," Jinx said. "And what happens if I can't see you?"

"I turn my flashlight on and off three times."

"Who says you can't teach an old dog new tricks?"

Kneeling next to the hole, Jinx put on her mask and then lay flat on the ground. She held on to the ladder with one hand and tilted forward until her mask was submerged just underneath the water's surface. Rising back onto her knees, she looked up at Alberta and said, "The ladder goes pretty far down, but it's going to be hard to climb even a few steps in our fins. I think we should just go for it and jump, what do you say?"

Alberta wanted to say that she would like to go home and pour herself a very tall glass of raspberry-flavored vodka, but instead she took a deep breath and lied, "Stairs are for chickens!"

Standing next to the edge of the hole facing the

ladder, Jinx was about to bite down on her mouthpiece, but had some last-minute instructions to relay. "Remember, we're only going to dive for fifteen minutes, so let's synchronize our watches."

"I have six forty-two," Alberta announced.

"Me too," Jinx confirmed. "So at . . . um, six . . . oh my God, I hate math! What's fifteen minutes after six forty-two?"

"*Adio mio*, six fifty-seven."

"Oh right, okay, then no matter wherever we are, no matter what we find, we turn back at six fifty-seven." Jinx glanced at her watch. "Make that six fifty-eight."

"Will you just go before we spend all night here!"

"I love you, Gram."

Before Alberta could say that she felt exactly the same way about her granddaughter, Jinx had already jumped into the water. Momentarily frozen, Alberta felt her heart beat so loudly she thought it was going to burst out of her wet suit. If anyone saw her right now they would think she had completely lost her marbles and would haul her off to a mental institution. She could just hear her daughter, Lisa Marie, calling her an idiot for putting herself and Jinx in such danger. And she knew that wherever her husband Sammy was, he was shaking his head in disbelief. She could hear his gruff voice saying what he always told her when he thought she was about to do something stupid.

"I don't know who the hell you think you are, Berta."

"I'll show you who I am, Sammy," she said out loud. "I'll show all of you."

In quick succession, she made the sign of the cross,

pressed her finger into the crucifix underneath her wet suit, bit down hard on her mouthpiece, and jumped.

As she descended lower, she saw that Jinx was right and the ladder was about ten feet long. Staring ahead she felt as if she was simply floating to the bottom of the pool during her scuba-diving lesson. And then she turned around.

Everywhere Alberta looked there was nothing but water.

In the distance she could see Jinx moving gracefully like she was a mermaid. Her hair extended all around her head as her fins flapped up and down in slow motion so she really looked as if she were born to live underwater. That girl could do anything that she wanted to. Alberta chuckled to herself and thought, *Wait a second, so can I!*

Taking a deep breath and exhaling to make sure her apparatus was working properly and she could truly breathe underwater, Alberta swam in Jinx's direction. After only a few strokes, she let her body glide in the water and couldn't believe how liberating it felt. The sensation was far different from the several hours she had spent practicing in the pool. Here the darkness and the silence made her feel as if she was floating in space. She was completely free and completely at peace.

She could tell by the way Jinx was moving languidly to the left and then to the right, allowing the water to guide her wherever it wanted to take her, that she felt the same way. Upside down, Jinx looked at Alberta and waved. Then she did a somersault and just before she started to dive lower toward the bottom of the lake she beckoned her grandmother to follow her.

Alberta didn't need any prodding. She couldn't wait to explore this mysterious setting even further.

The lake was manmade. There wasn't much algae or underwater plant life that Alberta could see and there definitely weren't any fish. It was a little disappointing that the view wasn't more tropical and cluttered with sea creatures and botanicals, but what the lake lacked in biology, it made up for when it came to clues. Alberta's eyes grew wide when she saw four large metal boxes lying at the bottom of the lake.

She watched Jinx continue to swim farther away and realized she hadn't seen the bounty, so Alberta pointed her flashlight in Jinx's direction and turned it on and off three times. Immediately, Jinx turned around, thinking that her grandmother was in distress, and was relieved, but also confused, when she saw that she was perfectly fine. It wasn't until she noticed what Alberta's flashlight was illuminating that she knew their journey was a success.

Raising a fist triumphantly in the air, Jinx swam toward Alberta and together they did a sort of happy swirling dance round and round in circles. They actually did it, they found Lucy's *TV Guide* collection, or at least the boxes that they believed contained the collection. The only way to know for sure, however, was to bring them home and open them up. But first they had to get them out of the lake.

They dove down and each grabbed a side of one of the boxes, but when they tried to lift it up, it would hardly budge. They tried again and were handed the same result. Jinx pointed to the other box, thinking that they'd have better luck, but the third time wasn't a charm and they were still unable to lift the box any higher than an inch off the surface of the lake's floor. Clearly the combination of the box's contents, the water pressure, and their own inexperience was making what should have been a simple task impossible.

Jinx was going to suggest they try again when she noticed the time on her digital watch read 7:05. She couldn't add quickly enough, but she knew it was several minutes past their cutoff time and they needed to swim back to the ladder. She was reluctant to go, but as novice divers she didn't want to press their luck by staying underwater for too long. At least they achieved what they set out to do. They had found the boxes and were one step closer to finding out who killed Lucy.

Tapping her watch several times until Alberta nodded that she understood it was time to go, Jinx then turned around and started to swim back to the tunnel's opening. Alberta had every intention of following her granddaughter until she saw a handle on the side of one of the boxes. Maybe that would make it easier to carry. Only one way to find out.

Grabbing hold of the handle securely, Alberta pulled up with all her strength, but again was only able to lift the box an inch off the floor. Growing weary, she dropped the box, causing a little splash of mud to rise up to her knees. As Alberta raised her flashlight to guide her back to the tunnel's exit, she thought she saw something swim past her. Startled, she dropped her flashlight, but before she could pick it up, it hit one of the boxes and shut off. Suddenly, she was alone in the dark.

Before she could panic, she remembered what Freddy had taught her: If you close your eyes they'll adjust to the darkness so you'll be able to see shadows and the light coming from above. She did just that and lo and behold Freddy was right. When she opened her eyes it was still quite dark, but she could see there was another face staring back at her. Unfortunately, she could also tell that the face did not belong to her granddaughter.

# CHAPTER 21

*L'invidia prende non festive.*

During all of Alberta's scuba-diving classes, Freddy had never addressed the possibility of an underwater attack. She would have to remember to suggest that he amend his lesson plan, but until then, without any formal training in the matter, Alberta was forced to rely on instinct. And although she had vowed to stop being so passive and take a more active role in determining her fate, in this instance, her instinct told her not to fight back. It was a wise decision.

She didn't know who was pulling her in the opposite direction of where she wanted to go, but she knew it wasn't Jinx. For starters, her attacker didn't have long hair, nor did this person use their predetermined distress signal to indicate that there was some sort of emergency. However, the real reason Alberta knew she wasn't being forcibly dragged by her granddaughter was because she didn't think Jinx would rip out her mouthpiece and yank her air tank off her shoulders. Her daughter might do that to her, but never her granddaughter. Luckily, familial animosity had skipped a generation, but unfortunately Alberta had no choice but to hold her breath and go along for the ride. Where that ride was taking her, she had no idea.

Without a flashlight it was very difficult to see, but she could feel that they were swimming slightly to the right and definitely up toward the surface of the water, so despite the violent approach, this person wasn't trying to drown her. Although her vision was limited, it was definitely getting lighter and the water around her was no longer black but more of a light blue. She didn't know if the lake was being illuminated by the last stages of sunset or the first rays of moonlight, but she didn't care. As long as she wasn't swathed in total darkness, she was grateful.

She was also oddly grateful for her assailant's strength. Whoever was pulling her had to be strong, because her attacker had one arm around Alberta's chest and as a result only had one other free arm to breaststroke their way to the surface. Although Alberta's arms were being held down at her sides and were relatively useless, she was still able to use her legs and fins to give them additional speed and propel them upward much faster. One part of her brain hated working in tandem with whoever was kidnapping her—or was that lake-napping?—but the other part of her brain that contained her will to survive overruled any qualms she might have. The fact of the matter was that she was quickly running out of breath.

A sharp pain began to spread out from the center of her chest and she could almost see a thick rope start to wrap around her heart squeezing it as if it was about to burst. She could feel her throat start to twitch and expand involuntarily in a desperate attempt to take in oxygen that just wasn't there. She pressed her lips together as tightly as she could even though all she wanted to do was open her mouth and take huge gulps of air. But she knew that if she did that all she would inhale would be water, and after that the slow process of drowning. She remembered reading that drowning was a peaceful death, but she simply had too much life left in her to accept death, peaceful or otherwise.

Feeling herself getting light-headed from the lack of oxygen and gripping fear, Alberta kicked her legs wildly and was able to free her left arm from her attacker's hold. She raised her arm overhead and started stroking madly almost as if she was trying to pull herself out of the water. The second she broke through the surface of the lake, she gasped and allowed the air to reconnect with her aching lungs and flow all throughout her tired body. Still in panic mode, Alberta was breathing frantically, but she knew that if she continued she would hyperventilate. Willing the fear to remove itself from her mind, she forced herself to inhale and exhale deeply at a slower, more measured rhythm. Her heart was still racing, but soon she felt the pain in her lungs and head dissipate. She still didn't have the strength to break free from her attacker, but at least she wasn't going to have a heart attack.

Giving in to the motion, she allowed herself to be pulled to the bank of the lake. She didn't care if she was allowing someone else to have control over her body as long as it meant that she was going to be on a flat, dry, unmoving surface. Once she got there, then she could figure out her next move. Her assailant, however, had other ideas. The moment they got onto the grassy slope of land, Alberta's lake-napper got behind her, grabbed her underneath the armpits, and dragged her over the ground.

"Let go of me!" Alberta shrieked. She listened to her voice echo, but never heard a response.

Alberta's body banged into rocks, fallen branches, and jagged bumps in the earth. Flailing her legs, she tried to dig her heels into the dirt, but any attempt to slow her attacker down was thwarted by the fact that she was still wearing her fins. But so was her assailant.

Alberta couldn't grab on to the body that was dragging her through the woods surrounding the lake, but if she twisted herself far enough to one side, she might just be able to catch hold of one of its fins. Wrenching herself to the left, she reached out, but only grabbed the empty air. With her mask still on and the lens foggy from her heavy breathing, she could hardly see, but that didn't mean she was going to give up.

Hurling herself to the right this time, Alberta swung her arm out as far as she could and this time was able to grab on to a fin. She pulled as hard as she could until the person who was dragging her fell to the ground and was as horizontal as she was. Finally, they were on a level playing field so she could find out who wanted to cause her such harm.

Alberta whipped off her mask just in time to see the rock fly through the air and slam into her forehead. She saw a shadowy figure rise up in front of her, and then everything went black.

Jinx was crying so hard that everything around her was a blur. She sat behind the wheel of her car, still dripping wet from being in the lake, and quickly glanced to the right and then the left before driving through the red light. Her cell phone in the cup holder next to her bounced around as she accelerated, but it was on speaker so the connection wasn't lost.

"I'm so sorry, Aunt Joyce! I don't know where Gram could be!"

"Honey, I need you to calm down," Joyce said, forcing her own voice to remain calm.

"And *slow* down," Helen added. "We don't need another accident."

Joyce's phone was on speaker, and she was holding it between her and Helen so they could both hear Jinx's story. "When you realized your grandma didn't come out of the tunnel right after you, what did you do?" Joyce asked.

"I waited for a bit, but then I dove back down to where we found the boxes. I thought she might've still been trying to lift them up by herself."

"And she wasn't there?" Joyce confirmed.

"No, but I found her flashlight. It must've fallen somehow, so I thought she was swimming around in the dark and had lost her way."

"Then what did you do?" Helen asked.

"I started swimming and shining my flashlight all over the place to see if I could find her, and then— oh God!"

Helen and Joyce held each other tighter. "What happened then, Jinx?" Joyce demanded.

"I . . . I saw her air tank and her mouthpiece on the bottom of the lake. I've never been so scared in all my life!"

The sound of a car horn alerted Jinx that her car had drifted into oncoming traffic. She swerved the

Cruze to the right, barely escaping impact with a much larger SUV.

"Be careful, Jinx!" Joyce cried.

"Honey, maybe you should pull over," Helen suggested.

"No! I have to get to the police."

"What happened after you started looking around?" Joyce questioned. "Did you ever see her again?"

"Maybe . . . yes . . . I'm not sure!"

"Focus, Jinx!" Helen yelled. "What exactly did you see?"

Wiping the tears from her eyes so she could see the road better, Jinx instead found herself lost in a recent memory. "At first I thought I saw Gram swimming away from me, but when I adjusted my flashlight to get a better look I saw that she wasn't alone."

Helen and Joyce both screamed at the same time, "Someone grabbed her?"

"Yes! And dragged her up to the surface!"

"Why didn't you follow them?" Helen shouted.

"I got so scared that I screamed and my mouthpiece fell out! I was fumbling trying to get it back in, but I started swallowing water. I know I should've gone after them, but I thought I was going to drown, and I didn't know how far I was from the surface, so I swam back to the entrance of the tunnel. I'm sorry!"

"You did the right thing, Jinx," Joyce said forcefully. "Do you hear me?"

The only thing Jinx could hear, were her own sobs.

"Jinx, listen to me!" Helen barked. "You did exactly what you should've done and exactly what your grandmother would've wanted you to do. Do not blame yourself."

"But this was all my idea!"

"We're all in this *together*," Helen declared. *"Capisce?"*

After a few moments of silence, Helen thought she had to translate. "That means 'do you understand?' honey."

"I know. I know what it means, and yes, I understand, but— Gram's still out there somewhere . . . How are we ever going to find her?"

"Jinx, honey, I know exactly where Alberta is," Joyce declared. "Meet us in front of the house and I'll explain everything."


The first thing Alberta demanded when she woke up was an explanation.

"What the hell is going on here?"

The second thing she wanted to know was why she had a companion.

"What the hell are you doing here?"

"Trust me, Alberta, I'm more surprised to see you than you are to see me."

"But, Beverly," Alberta cried. "I thought you were dead."

"Lately, honey, I kinda wish I was."

So many thoughts were racing through Alberta's mind she thought her head was going to twist off, explode, and burst through the roof of the cabin. Beverly hadn't skipped town, which was good, or been murdered, which was better, but she was being held hostage, which wasn't ideal. Alberta couldn't really tell from her appearance if she had been here since the day she disappeared or more recently because even though she didn't look like she had been hurt in any way, she looked terrible. Her dark roots were showing underneath her bleached-blond hair, and her face, without the aid of makeup, was etched in a combination of weariness, fear, and anger.

She was sitting next to Alberta wearing a mismatched sweat suit and sneakers, and her hands and feet were tied to a wooden chair. Her hands were resting on top of the arms of the chair and her feet braced against the insides of each front leg. There was also a thick rope hanging around her neck, and Alberta felt a sickening pain in her stomach when she realized the rope was what her captor shoved in her mouth in order to silence her. Except for the wet suit and being barefoot, Alberta and Beverly were identical. They were both being held prisoner, and only one person could be their captor.

Alberta's eyes darted around the room. If Marion had kidnapped Beverly and tied her up here as his hostage, then the only logical conclusion would be that Marion had to be the one who attacked her in the lake.

"Come out and show yourself, you coward!" Alberta shouted.

Slowly a door to the adjoining room opened, and Alberta could feel her anger rise. She couldn't wait to tell Marion exactly what she thought of him for almost killing her. How dare he attack her! Didn't he realize she could've drowned? And why wasn't he the person standing in front of her?

"Denise?"

"Hello, Alberta," Denise replied. "So nice of you to finally wake up."

If Denise wasn't standing in front of Alberta wearing a wet suit and drying her hair with a towel, she would've thought that she was another one of Marion's prisoners instead of what she clearly was: the person who attacked her in the lake.

"What in the world is going on here?" Alberta asked. "Denise, why would you want to hurt me? You could've killed me out there!"

Folding the towel neatly into a square, Denise rolled her eyes. "Oh my God! You old Italian women are all the same, so friggin' dramatic. Seriously, Alberta, if I wanted to kill you, you'd be lying on the bottom of the lake right now."

"But you took out my mouthpiece and made me lose my air tank!"

"How else was I going to get you here?" Denise asked. "I knew you wouldn't come willingly so I made sure you didn't have a choice."

"But how did you even know that I was going to be in the lake tonight?"

"I know that I sometimes come across as gossipy and maybe a little airheaded, but down deep I'm a very smart woman," Denise bragged. "And I'm pretty good at picking up clues."

"Such as?"

"Such as your sudden interest in diving lessons and your private sessions with the old fart at the library."

"Sloan?"

"How do you think he got copies of those blueprints to the tunnel?" she asked. "They were on loan to the library from the Wasserman & Speicher archives, so he had to request permission from me to duplicate them. When he told me that a reporter from *The Herald* wanted them for background for an article about the Tranquility Waterfest, I found out that you're related to that same reporter. Oh, and you might want to tell Jinx to get a better disguise next time. Her dark sunglasses and heavy accent didn't fool anyone."

Alberta watched Denise sit down at the wooden table on the other side of the cabin, cross her ankles, and lean forward just like she did at her desk at work. She placed the towel on the table, folded it once more, smoothed out some wrinkles, and then pushed it to one side. Denise was acting no differently than she normally did, but somehow, in this queer setting, her movements were disturbing.

Taking a deep breath, Alberta realized that she wasn't going to get any answers if she became hysterical, so once again she forced herself to remain calm.

"So where is this place?" she asked.

"I think you already know that, Alberta," Denise replied. "Or should I say Little Miss Private Investigator?"

Clearly, Denise knew that she was doing more than secretarial work at Wasserman & Speicher, but just how much did she know? Alberta needed to make sure that she didn't give away too much information in case Denise was on a fact-finding expedition.

Glancing at the clock on the wall above the table, Alberta saw that it was only seven thirty-five, roughly a half hour since she was abducted. She remembered looking at her watch right before Jinx swam back to the tunnel's entrance and it was only a few minutes after seven. She didn't know exactly how long it took to swim to the surface of the lake, get dragged through the woods, and reach the cabin, but in that short amount of time they couldn't have traveled very far. This must be the cabin Sloan had told her about, the one Marion's mother originally built, and the one that was near the tunnel exit that was only recently boarded up. If Marion brought Beverly here, it made perfect sense that this was his cabin.

"It doesn't take a genius to know that we're in the Klausner family cabin," Alberta said, trying to sound smug and not frightened. "Which is on the northwestern side of Memory Lake."

"Very good," Denise said, clapping her hands together. "For an old broad you're not so dumb. Not like this one here."

"Shut up!" Beverly shouted. "If I'm dumb, then you're certifiably insane!"

Denise sprang up, slammed her palms onto the table, and leaned forward. "Says the *idiot* who's tied to a chair!"

"That's the part that doesn't make any sense," Alberta said. "Why would Marion tie you up and keep you hidden out here? I thought that you and he were a couple."

Denise pounded her fist so hard onto the table that Alberta thought for sure it was going to split in two. "They were *never* a couple!"

"That isn't true!" Beverly cried. "Marion loves me!"

"If he loved you, you stupid *bitch*, do you think he would've tied you up here? No, the two of you would be married by now. If you could just understand that, none of this would've had to happen!"

"He would've married me years ago if you weren't constantly throwing yourself at him every chance you get!" Beverly snapped.

"I never threw myself at Marion!" Denise retorted. "I can't help it if he wanted to upgrade to a younger model."

"Oh please! You practically had to hit him over the

head for him to notice you! You're such an obvious, common tramp!"

"Tramp? If I'm a tramp then you're a whore!"

"At least I was first!"

"*Ah, Madon! L'invidia prende non festive,*" Alberta muttered under her breath.

"What?"

Alberta didn't think two jealous women such as Denise and Beverly would want to hear that envy never takes a holiday so she ignored their question. "Never mind, but if you're going to keep me hostage, would you mind explaining to me exactly what happened?"

"It's all her fault!"

Since Beverly and Denise spoke at exactly the same time, Alberta had no idea who to believe. "How about we go one at a time?" Alberta suggested. "Denise, since you're sort of in charge, why don't you go first?"

Sitting back down and smiling, Denise replied, "It would be my pleasure. It all started when Beverly stole Lucy's *TV Guide* collection."

"I didn't steal it," Beverly interrupted. "I only borrowed it."

"In order to plant incriminating evidence in it in order to get revenge against Marion because he refused to marry you," Denise explained.

"What kind of evidence?" Alberta asked.

"Proof that Marion is using the tunnel and this cabin to smuggle drugs out of the building and into the hands of international drug dealers," Beverly said. "You know that computer room that he keeps locked up? Well, it's no computer room, it's where he stores all the drugs."

"*Dio mio!*" Alberta exclaimed. "But the computer room doesn't lead to the tunnel, the Safe Room does."

"Correction, both rooms do," Denise interjected. "It wasn't part of the original design, but when Marion realized his side hobby was way more lucrative than the family business, he needed to make some changes. So, he turned the computer room into a drug lab and needed to build a secret passageway from that room to the tunnel as well."

"So that's the real reason he outsources the IT department," Alberta said.

"Unless you know of a computer technician who moonlights as a drug dealer, it's really the only option," Denise quipped.

"I can't believe there's a drug lab right in the building!" Alberta exclaimed.

Tilting her head from side to side and frowning, Denise replied, "Well it's only a small lab and really more of a storage unit, but in a pinch you can whip up some good stuff in there."

"And you knew all about this?" Alberta asked. "And never said a word to the police?"

"Like you never kept a secret for your family or for someone you loved," Denise scoffed.

Yes, Alberta thought, she had definitely kept secrets, but never something of this magnitude. And never something that could have such a harmful effect on so many innocent lives. The more the layers of this onion started to peel away, the more complicated the whole situation was becoming. She needed to go back a bit and focus on things that she could comprehend.

"So, Beverly took the collection from Lucy, put incriminating evidence in it, and blackmailed Marion," Alberta reiterated.

"And I couldn't let her destroy Marion like that," Denise confirmed.

"So why not just destroy the evidence instead of hiding it in the lake?" Alberta asked. "If Marion's such a shrewd, unscrupulous businessman, why would he do such a thing?"

The women were going to answer for Marion, but when he entered the cabin they allowed him to speak for himself.

"Because Marion never got the chance, Alberta," he announced. "Beverly hid the collection and very selfishly wouldn't tell me where it was, which is why I tied her up here. I was hoping she would eventually come to her senses, but thanks to you, I know exactly where the evidence is. And now I can get rid of all the annoying women in my life. Just like I got rid of Lucy."

# CHAPTER 22

*Non ha il dolce a caro, chi provato non ha l'amaro.*

Even though Alberta long suspected that Marion had killed Lucy or at the very least was on the short list of suspects, hearing him actually say he took her life was monumental. Like when she heard herself say, "I do" to Sammy. She had known she was going to say those words to him during the six months that they were engaged, but until she uttered them in front of her entire family being married was nothing more than a possibility, a dream, and not an unchangeable reality. That's how she felt after hearing Marion confess.

"Marion," Alberta said, her voice small and shaky. "Why would you do such a thing?"

For a moment when Marion looked into Alberta's eyes, he was the same shy teenager she once knew, hungry for affection and friendship, but the moment was fleeting. Quickly, a darkness filled his eyes. They didn't change color, of course, but it was as if someone had pulled down the shades to keep out the sunlight so that all remained was an unsettling shadow.

"Because she left me no choice," Marion stated. His answer was simple and his voice was steady, and still Alberta was confused.

"Lucy?" she replied. "But she didn't do anything to you."

"No, not Lucy," Marion corrected. "Beverly."

Twisting her chair violently so she could face Marion, Beverly lashed out, "Don't you blame this on me!"

His calm reply was even more unnerving than Beverly's outburst. "Why not? All of it is your fault."

"How can you say that?" Beverly asked, her voice shrill and filled with disbelief. "You know I never meant for any of this to happen!"

Slowly Marion walked toward Beverly's chair. The closer he got, the farther she tried to lean back in a vain attempt to get away from him. He grabbed the arms of the chair, his thumbs pressing deep into Beverly's fleshy wrists, bent forward, and glared at her silently for a few seconds before lifting her a few inches off the ground. He was the cat and she was the mouse he was taunting. When he had enough, he slammed the chair back down on the floor, causing Beverly to shriek in fear. "And yet the fact remains that your friend Lucy is dead because of you."

"Stop saying that!" she screamed. "Please . . . stop it!"

Unable to listen to Beverly's cries any longer or follow the cryptic conversation, Alberta needed even more facts. "I know that I can be a bit of a *stunod* sometimes, but I'm not following the thread here," Alberta said. "Could someone please tell me exactly what happened and how Lucy died?"

Still holding onto Beverly's chair, Marion turned his head to the side and smiled at Alberta. His expression sent a cold chill down her spine. She couldn't comprehend how such a friendly, handsome face could belong to a murderer. But when she looked over at Denise, who had been conspicuously silent the past few minutes, it was as if her spine had turned into one long icicle. Denise was glaring so viciously in her direction that if looks could kill, she, along with the entire population of Tranquility, would be annihilated. It didn't make sense, but even though Marion was a confessed killer, Alberta didn't fear him nearly as much as she feared Denise.

"I guess you've earned an explanation, Alberta, after all the trouble you've gone to in order to get to this point."

Marion released his hold on Beverly's chair with such force that the frightened woman teetered back and forth for a few seconds before she was able to steady herself. Pacing from one end of the cabin to the other, Marion clasped his hands in front of him, one knuckle pressed into his chin as if he was about to begin a lecture and was searching for the perfect opening line. Alberta was fascinated by his actions, the calmness and the control, and she couldn't believe he was about to offer the details of such a heinous and deplorable act. The only sound in the room other than the muffled beat created by Marion's footsteps was the drumming of Denise's nails on the table. Alberta thought for sure that Denise already knew the tale Marion was about to tell, but she appeared to be just as interested in the story as she was.

Finally, but without ending his continuous stride,

Marion began. "As you know, Beverly and I had what you could call a . . . *relationship*. One that I desperately tried to convince myself could graduate from the vulgarities of the superficial and physical into the more sophisticated realm of the intimate and permanent. I tried to create that transition, I truly did. I searched my heart and soul for the strength to overlook Beverly's faults and convince myself that she could be the right woman for me. But, alas, it was an exercise in futility."

Gazing out the one window in the room, Marion stopped moving as he continued to share his story. Alberta couldn't see his face, but his back was straight and his hands were now clasped behind his back like an army drill sergeant overseeing his platoon's calisthenics. "Instead of doing the right thing, the decent thing, and bowing out gracefully, Beverly kept badgering me to marry her. Her true colors shined so brightly they were blinding, and she proved herself to be insistent, almost grotesque in her attempts to become my wife. And then, when I didn't think she could stoop any lower, when I didn't think she could become any more *indecent*, thanks to Lucy she found what she thought would be the perfect solution to get me to marry her: blackmail."

"Well, you know what they say, *Non ha il dolce a caro, chi provato non ha l'amaro*." Beverly quipped.

"No, Beverly," Marion replied, turning to face his audience. "Not all of us know what *they* say, because not all of us speak in primitive tongues."

Clearing her throat, Alberta said, "Nothing ventured, nothing gained."

"What?" Marion asked.

"That's what it means!" Beverly shouted. "'To taste the sweet, you must taste the bitter' is the direct translation, but in English it means 'Nothing ventured, nothing gained.' My mother always told me that and you of all people, Marion, should know how important it is to listen to your mother."

At the mention of the word "mother," Marion seemed to lose a bit of his control. His eye twitched, and his lips were clasped together so tightly in a fake smile that he was breathing loudly through his nose. Denise's body language changed as well, and she sat up straight with her feet planted firmly on the floor. Her gaze was fixed on Marion, and it was clear that she wasn't sure how he was going to respond, either emotionally or physically.

"What my actions really meant, Marion," Beverly said, "Is that I loved you!"

Ramming his fist into the wall, Marion shouted, "But I didn't love you!"

With his fists still clenched, Marion resumed pacing the cabin floor. He started muttering something to himself, but he was talking so quickly and quietly that it was incomprehensible.

"You had to bring up the *M* word, didn't you?" Denise whispered.

"I'm sorry," Beverly said, "with all that's going on I kinda forgot."

It took a while for the rage to leave Marion's body and for his mumbling to stop. When he finally spoke loud enough to be heard and understood, his voice was so calm it was as if the tantrum never happened. The only evidence of the violent outburst that remained was the broken, bloody skin on his knuckles.

"And I told you how I felt, Beverly, many, many times, but you couldn't comprehend that very basic concept. So, what did you do to deserve my love? To secure my hand in marriage? You stole Lucy's *TV Guide* collection, planted incriminating evidence in it, and hid it someplace where you said I would never, ever find it. And then you told me I had a choice: marry you, or force you to turn over the collection and the evidence to the police."

"I would never have gone through with it, you know that."

The anger returned and once again Marion's voice reverberated throughout the small room. "The only thing I knew, Beverly, was that you had threatened me! And Mother always told me that once a woman threatens you she can never be trusted!"

Clearly Helga Klausner had a strong hold on her son, because when Marion mentioned his mother, Alberta could tell that he was being pulled back to the past, to a preferable, more comfortable time. She needed to stop him from making that journey and focus on the present. "What did you do next, Marion?" she asked, quietly, but sternly. Mechanically, he turned his head in Alberta's direction. He heard her, but she wasn't sure that he was firmly back from stepping onto memory lane, so Alberta needed to pull a little harder. "What did you do after Beverly black-mailed you?"

It took him a few more seconds to respond, but Alberta's goading did the trick. "After Beverly called in sick for a few days, I went to her condominium for one final attempt to reason with her. I was re-signed to give her whatever she wanted. Enough money to relocate, buy herself a bigger and better house somewhere far, far away, and live out the rest of her life without a financial care in the world."

"But the only thing I wanted was to marry you, Marion!" Beverly exclaimed. "That's what you could never understand."

"Which is just like a woman! You always want the one thing you cannot have!"

Alberta could see Marion regressing again and she needed to reel him back. "What happened when you got to the condo, Marion? What did you say to Beverly?"

"Nothing, because she wasn't there," he replied. "But Lucy was."

"Lucy?" Alberta asked. "What was she doing there?"

"For the same reason I ventured into enemy territory, to confront the shrew," Marion explained. "Lucy had only told one other person about her collection, and that was Beverly. When it went missing there could only be one culprit."

So Enza was right, Alberta thought, Lucy couldn't keep a secret if her life depended on it, and she did tell someone else about the collection. If she had kept quiet, she might still be alive.

"I was convinced that Lucy must know about the evidence, because Beverly is what is known as a blabbermouth. The woman gossips about everything, but in this instance I was wrong and she hadn't told Lucy about my peccadillo," Marion continued. "For all of Beverly's faults, and it must be acknowledged that she has many, many faults, she truly can keep a secret when she wants to, I must give her that."

"Oh please!" Denise cried. "Beverly's mouth was

as big as Lucy's! You know that the moment she found out about Lucy's collection and how it would make the perfect repository for her revenge against you, she just had to spill her guts . . . to me!" Denise explained. "And me being the trustworthy and empathetic HR executive, I had no choice but to listen to every word she said."

"Watch your temper, Denise," Marion chastised. "Didn't Mother always say that no matter what the circumstances a lady must always control her temper? And it didn't matter that Beverly told you because you already knew about my side business."

"I only told Denise because I knew how she felt about you, and I figured the two of you were having an affair, so I thought if I told her about you and the drugs she would break up with you," Beverly conceded.

It was Marion's turn to lose his temper.

"Just like a woman!" Marion spat. "Always thinking about yourself, never thinking that if Denise spoke to the police what that would've done to me."

"But Denise would never speak to the police, because her ex-husband was in on the scam too!" Alberta shrieked.

Finally, Alberta connected the mayor's criminal relative—Johnny Kaplan—with Denise Herb-Kaplan. Joyce had uncovered information from Marion's e-mails about Johnny Kaplan, who was indicted for drug smuggling. Alberta knew the name rang a bell, but didn't make the connection until now.

"Good for you, Alberta," Marion beamed. "Tranquility really is more closely knit than the sweater-vests Mother used to crochet for me."

"But Marion, that still doesn't explain how you

went from accidentally bumping into Lucy at Beverly's condo to killing her?" Alberta reasoned.

Once again Marion turned into the lonely, misunderstood teenager from Alberta's youth, all furrowed brow and wide eyes in search of lost innocence. "You have to believe me, Alberta, I didn't want to do it. But I kept asking Lucy about the evidence and the drugs and the location of the collection, and she kept repeating over and over again that she didn't know anything. And do you know how infuriating it is when a woman doesn't answer you and just says 'I don't know' over and over again? It's like a record that skips repeatedly for hours. Just scratching and repeating incessantly! The next thing I knew I was slapping Lucy and hitting her and before I knew it she fell to the floor. She must have hit her head on the coffee table because she wouldn't get up, she just lay there, dead. I didn't mean to do it, but I killed her."

Watching Denise roll her eyes, Alberta realized that she wasn't such a *stunod* after all.

"Marion, you didn't kill Lucy," Alberta announced.

"I appreciate your trying to assuage my guilt, Alberta," Marion replied. "But if I didn't kill Lucy, then who did?"

"Denise."

The three other people in the room cried out at the same time. "What?"

"It's true, isn't it, Denise?" Alberta asked.

Trying to act as nonchalant as possible, which was difficult sitting cross-legged while wearing a wet suit, Denise replied, "I don't know what you're talking about."

"You didn't care about the drugs or about Marion's affair with Beverly, those things you could live with,"

Alberta began. "But you couldn't live with being the other woman if Marion gave in to Beverly's demands and married her. So, you followed Marion to Beverly's condo and when he left you barged in thinking you were going to have it out with your nemesis and the future Mrs. Marion Klausner once and for all, but instead you found Lucy lying on the floor."

"Denise . . . is that true?" Marion asked, his question filled with stunned disbelief. "Answer me!"

Rising suddenly from her chair, Denise walked a few steps to the left, then to the right like a caged lion. "How stupid can you be?" she shouted. "If you had been a man and waited a few seconds longer instead of running out of that condo like a frightened little boy you would have known all along that you didn't kill her!"

"Oh dear God, it's true," Marion said, his voice sounding very much like a frightened little boy's.

"Alberta's right, I knew there was still something going on between you and Beverly and I knew that you would crawl to her on your belly, cave in to her demands, marry her just to get the evidence back, and make sure she couldn't destroy your future," Denise seethed. "And there was no way in hell that I was going to play second fiddle to that old, overweight, bleached-blond . . . how do your people say tramp, Alberta?"

Shyly, Alberta replied, "*Putan.*"

"To some *putan!*"

"Watch it, Denise!" Beverly shrieked. "I am a natural blonde!"

"So, I followed you to her condo," Denise explained. "When you ran out, I went in and saw Lucy on the floor, but she wasn't dead, Marion, she was just unconscious."

The revelation was so shocking to Marion that he had to sit down. "I cannot believe this."

"Well, believe it!" Denise shouted. Crouching down next to Marion, she grabbed his hands. Marion still looked terrified, but he didn't have the strength to pull away from Denise's grip. "And believe me when I tell you that I did what I did because I love you, Marion! Do you remember what *I* always told *you*? Unlike your mother and unlike Beverly and Alberta and all the other women in your life, I would never put any demands on you. I accepted you the way you are, but even that wasn't enough for you."

"Denise, what exactly did you do?" Alberta asked.

Releasing her hold on Marion, Denise stood up and this time paced the full length of the cabin. "When Lucy came to, she immediately started screaming that she was going to press charges against Marion for attacking her and against Beverly for stealing her collection, and I could not let that happen," Denise said. "If the police came after Beverly she would spill her guts and tell them where the collection was and exactly what was in it. Lucy held all the cards and there was no way I was going to let that selfish bitch destroy the life of the man I loved and, along with it, my only chance of happiness."

"You killed her?" Alberta asked.

"I grabbed the nearest thing I could, which happened to be the letter opener on Beverly's desk, and stabbed her right through her heart," Denise proudly recalled. "It was almost too quick, you know what I mean? I was prepared to get down and dirty to kill her, but all it took was one perfectly aimed thrust."

Marion looked at Denise in shock, his mouth open, his head slowly shaking from side to side. "And all this time . . . I can't believe you let me think that I was the one who killed her."

Abruptly, Denise stopped her pacing. "How else do you think I was going to keep you in my life?"

"You're insane!" Marion cried.

Denise's laughter was so loud it was like a banshee's shriek. "Said the overgrown mama's boy!"

Alberta ignored their outburst as she still had more investigating to do. She knew most of the story, but not all of it, and there was one element to Lucy's murder that she never quite understood. "But why did you change Lucy's clothes? That doesn't make any sense."

"Because the bitch started to bleed . . . a lot," Denise explained. "If the cops found her covered in blood, they'd be able to figure out how she was killed, so I needed to buy some time. I started to clean her up and undress her, but I knew I couldn't leave here there naked or else they would see the puncture wound. The cops around here aren't bright, but they're not idiots, so I went into Beverly's closet and grabbed the first thing I could find."

"Which was her navy blue suit," Alberta said, finishing Denise's explanation.

"Not the most attractive ensemble ever designed, but it served its purpose."

"But why didn't you just leave her there and go?" Alberta asked. "Why take the risk of being seen leaving Beverly's condo with a dead body in broad daylight?"

Denise smiled approvingly at Alberta just like she did during Alberta's interview. "You're pretty good at this detective thing, Alberta, I have to give you kudos for that," Denise replied. "By that time it was dark and Beverly still hadn't shown up, so I realized luck really was on my side and I could buy myself even more time. They were doing some construction outside, planting trees and putting in a little patio, so there was no one around in the front. I carried Lucy through the garage, backed my car into the driveway, dumped Lucy in my trunk, and then tossed her body into the lake without anyone seeing me. Pretty clever plan, don't you think?"

"If my nosy neighbor, Ruthanne, hadn't been away visiting her sister in Barnegat," Beverly said. "She would've heard everything."

"And if only you would've picked a different color suit to dress Lucy in, you might've gotten away with it," Alberta said.

Denise looked at her with an expression that morphed slowly from satisfied to sinister. "What are you talking about? I did get away with it."

"Not really, hon," Alberta said. "At first, Vinny did think Lucy committed suicide or accidentally drowned in Memory Lake, and he wasn't even going to have an autopsy performed until I pointed out that Lucy would never in a million years be caught dead wearing navy blue. She hated the color, and if you knew anything about Lucy, you would've known that. I told him that if Lucy was wearing that outfit somebody must have changed her clothes and there definitely was foul play involved. The autopsy confirmed my suspicion that Lucy died from a puncture wound to the heart, so the police are indeed looking for her murderer. And it's only a matter of time before they find out that it's you."

"Now who's the idiot?" Beverly asked, laughing heartily.

"You're the one who convinced the cops to do an autopsy?" Denise shrieked. "If it wasn't for you there wouldn't be an investigation. No one would care that the old crone was dead and we wouldn't have to worry about the truth coming out!"

"I never *had* to worry about the truth coming out, Denise, because I'm innocent," Marion announced, "I never killed Lucy. I can't believe that you let me believe that I did. This is how you treat someone you love?"

Once again Denise crouched down next to Marion and grabbed his hands, but this time she applied much more pressure. If Marion hadn't winced and yanked his hands away, it would've been a very tender scene.

"I had to, Marion," Denise pleaded. "It was the only way to get your full attention and to make you understand just how much I love you. I would do anything for you."

"Even go to prison for me?" Marion asked.

Stunned, it was Denise's turn to wince and turn away. "No one has to go to prison, Marion, thanks to me! I made it possible for the two of us to live free and rich for the rest of our lives."

"Really?" Marion cried, standing up and walking as far away from Denise as possible, which in the small confines of the room meant he was only about thirty feet away. "And just how did you accomplish that magical feat?"

"By getting rid of Lucy for you, dumping the body away from the scene of the crime to avoid linking her to anyone you know, *and* retrieving the business card from that woman who wants to buy her stupid *TV Guide* collection!" Denise declared.

When she pulled Joyce's business card from the small pocket in her wet suit Alberta realized that she was the one who retrieved it from the trash can and not Marion. The trumpet, of course! The cell phone Alberta heard ringing while Joyce was impersonating a brash and sassy businesswoman determined to make a deal was Denise's. She knew she had heard the melody before and now she realized why.

"This antiques broker, this Joyce Perkins, is willing to pay over a hundred grand for it," Denise explained. "All we have to do is get the collection from the bottom of the lake, sell it to her, and you'll be able to pay off what you owe the drug dealers. *Then* you and I can finally begin our life together."

"You think it's that simple?" Marion asked. "We're not the only ones involved."

Calmly, Denise replied, "So I'll shut them up permanently."

"Marion, say something!" Beverly screamed. "Tell the crazy HR lady that you aren't going to let her kill us! You didn't kill Lucy, she did, so you haven't done anything wrong."

"Except keep you tied up as his prisoner for a week," Denise reminded her.

"I'll tell the police I was here of my own volition, taking a bit of a vacation to deal with the emotional stress of Lucy's death," Beverly bartered. "You said so yourself that I can keep a secret if I really want to."

Marion remained silent, but his faraway gaze was evidence that he was weighing his options, and it didn't take Sherlock Holmes or Miss Marple to be able to read his mind. Alberta Scaglione had a good idea of what he was thinking, too. If he revealed that he had a physical altercation with Lucy, but that it was Denise who had killed her, he might be the subject of small-town gossip for a time, but soon it would be forgotten. However, could he really trust Beverly to keep her end of the bargain and lie under oath that he hadn't kidnapped her? That he kept her as his prisoner to make her tell him where the collection was? A collection that contained proof that he was involved in drug smuggling, which would guarantee his arrest and put him behind bars possibly for the rest of his life. That was a big gamble. And even if Beverly played by the rules of their elaborate game, there was still one wild card.

"What about Alberta?" Marion asked. "Even if Beverly remains quiet and I agree to continue my . . . *dalliance* with you, Denise, there's still Alberta."

"There's an easy solution for that, Marion," Denise replied. "Let me take care of her like I took care of Lucy."

Despite it being the answer Alberta was expecting, it was still a shock to hear it spoken. Could this woman who up until this morning Alberta thought was a bit unprofessional, but sane and definitely moral, be willing to kill her in cold blood just so she could have the man of her dreams? Could she be that obsessed with him? Or did she cross over to the point of no return when she killed Lucy? Could one spontaneous, mindless act make it possible for her to commit another deliberate and calculated offense? Alberta didn't have any of the answers, but erring on the side of caution, she didn't want to find out.

"Marion, don't listen to her!" Alberta screamed. "Don't listen to either of them. You haven't done anything wrong. Okay, maybe kidnapping Beverly wasn't the smartest or the most legal thing you've ever done, but it won't put you on trial for murder. Plus, I'm friends with Vinny! Let us go and I'll help you explain everything. With a good lawyer, you probably won't get more than a slap on the wrist."

"Don't forget all the drug-smuggling charges," Denise said, reminding her of his other offense.

"Well, yes, there's that, but selling drugs is nothing compared to committing murder," Alberta rationalized.

"The drug lab and storage facility set up in the fake computer room could be emptied very quickly," Marion reasoned. "It was designed that way, of course, so with enough lead time it could be turned back into some sort of file room and no one would know the difference."

Relying totally on instinct, Alberta wasn't sure if she could reach Marion by talking about his own life and the redemption of his own soul, but she knew of someone he wouldn't want to disappoint. "What would Helga think?"

"Shut up!" Denise cried. Incensed, she lunged for Alberta and would have slapped her across the face, if Marion hadn't grabbed her arm in the air. The way he practically snarled at Denise, Alberta knew that her instincts were right.

He pushed Denise so hard that she stumbled backward, her shoulder slamming into the wall. Marion loosened his tie and tried to undo the top button of his dress shirt, but had a bit of trouble, so he started pulling at the cloth as if it were strangling him. Finally, he tugged on his collar with such force that he ripped the button right off the shirt. "Mother was always right, you know."

"I know that, Marion," Alberta said, "She was a very smart woman."

"She was the best!" Marion screamed. "No one was as good as she was! Or as wise! She always told me to beware of women! She always told me that women were no good and they were nothing but trouble, and she was right! Every single woman that I have ever known has been nothing but trouble. Starting with that lying whore in college who tried to ruin me."

"You mean the girl from Rutgers who accused you of date rape?"

Astounded that Alberta was aware of his past indiscretion, his face grew white. "You know about that?"

"Yes, and I also know that you were innocent."

Marion's face softened and tears formed in his eyes. Alberta could tell that he was reliving the long-ago incident. She had no idea if he was guilty or innocent of the crime, but he was damaged and humiliated by it, and he still felt ashamed all these years later.

"You have to believe me, Alberta. I would never do that to a woman."

"I know that and so did your mother," Alberta placated. "You're a good man, and that's why I know you aren't going to hurt us or let Denise do anything that you'll regret."

Slapping away his tears, Marion let out a guttural cry that frightened all three women. "I don't know what to do! And it's all your fault! All of you!"

"Let me help you, Marion!" Denise sobbed. "If you would just listen to me, we could have everything. Your mother would be so happy for us."

"Don't you talk about my mother! You have no idea what she would want!"

"I know that she wouldn't want you to give up your life because of an unworthy woman," Alberta said. "And if you give in to Denise's demands, that's exactly what you'll be doing."

"Stop talking! All of you stop talking and let me think for a minute!"

Denise grabbed Alberta by the shoulders and started to shake her, "Do you see what you've done? Why couldn't you just mind your own business? If it weren't for you, Marion and I would be getting married and planning the rest of our lives by now."

"Oh, for Crise sake!" Beverly shouted. "Just because Marion refused to marry me doesn't mean he was going to marry you. Face it, we both fell in love with a man incapable of loving any other woman except his mother!"

Marion flipped the table over, and if one of its legs hadn't broken, it would've careened right into Alberta and Beverly. "Shut up! You've all left me with no other choice," Marion said. If his voice wasn't frightening enough, the gun he pulled out of his jacket pocket was worse. "Mother was right, women only get in the way, so it's time I got rid of all of you."

The door to the cabin swung open, and the only reason Marion didn't shoot was because his hand was shaking so hard.

"Looks like you're going to have to get rid of a few more women."

"What the hell are the antiques dealer and the nun doing here?" Marion asked, confused as to why Joyce and Jinx were standing in the doorway.

"Don't forget about the crotchety older sister,"

Helen said, entering the cabin and standing between them. "We kind of work as a team."

Marion looked at the six female faces staring at him—Denise, Beverly, Alberta, Jinx, Joyce, and Helen—and felt like he was living his worst nightmare. Everything his mother had warned him about—the fury of women, their unpredictability, and their desire to make a man's life a living hell—was all coming true. He had only one choice: get rid of them all.

"Then prepare to die as a team," Marion said.

# CHAPTER 23

*Crepi il lupo.*

"Grandma!" Jinx squealed. "Thank God you're all right!"

"Yes, I'm fine, lovey," Alberta reassured. "Despite, you know, being tied up."

"Your forehead! You've been cut."

"Oh, it's nothing," Alberta said, already having forgotten that Denise threw a rock at her head and knocked her unconscious. "Hazard of the job."

"Hold on for just one second," Marion ordered. "Sister Maria is your granddaughter?"

Ignoring Marion's command, Alberta wanted to make sure that Jinx was also unharmed after their scuba-diving expedition was so rudely interrupted. "You're okay too?" she asked. "And don't lie to me."

Jinx placed her right hand over her heart and swore, "I'm perfectly fine, I swear. I've just been so worried about you. What happened?"

"I asked you a question!"

"Lovey, you wouldn't believe it in a million years."

Marion and Alberta spoke at the same time and

even though he was brandishing a gun, Alberta still garnered all the attention.

"Try me!" Jinx demanded.

"I was attacked underwater!" Alberta cried.

"Because of the *malocchio*!" Jinx shouted, "You see, Aunt Helen, Grandma was right, all of this is because of Lucy and the *malocchio*!"

"Lucy isn't the only one who has an evil eye," Alberta said. "My attacker isn't all that innocent either."

Turning to face Marion, Jinx screamed, "Marion, how could you?"

"Not him, lovey," Alberta corrected.

"Then who?"

"Me!"

Everyone turned to face Denise and slowly, but surely, the shock of her announcement settled in. But since Denise was the only other person in the cabin wearing a wet suit other than Alberta and Jinx, it made total sense that if there was a nautical altercation, Denise would have instigated it. Still it was hard to comprehend that someone who looked so sweet, wasn't.

"I've known some duplicitous, cutthroat HR executives in my day," Joyce shared. "But one that would stage an undersea attack on an employee? That's a new one."

Dismissing Joyce's comment with a wave of her hand, Denise obviously didn't care what Joyce thought about her. She was more interested in why and how she was here. "Why don't you keep your opinions to yourself and tell us who you really are?" Denise said. "You're not an antiques dealer, are you?"

Marion stomped his foot on the floor several times

to try to regain control of the room, but everyone was more interested in hearing Joyce's explanation.

"Officially, no," Joyce said. "However, I have traded stocks on Wall Street and currently I'm a landscape painter. Also too, I'm Alberta's sister-in-law."

"I knew it!" Denise hollered, pointing a finger at the Ferrara women. "You're all related! And all four of you have been working together to solve the mystery of Lucy's murder. I hope it was worth dying over."

"I hope it was worth spending the rest of your life in jail!" Jinx spat back.

"Enough!"

This time Marion didn't rely on the stern tone of his voice to assure that the bickering would come to an end and he would control any further conversation, he took matters into his own hand and fired a warning shot that went right through the ceiling. A few of them shrieked and several cowered, not knowing exactly where the shot was fired because they weren't looking at Marion when he pulled the trigger. However, after hearing the gunshot, the women in the room did finally take notice that there was a man in their presence, a man who no longer wished to be ignored.

"Nobody talk!" Marion shouted, his hand holding the gun shaking a little bit less than it was when the unexpected company arrived. "Nobody say a word until I say you can."

He surveyed the group of women staring at him and smiled when he realized that, at last, he was being taken seriously. Now, maybe he would get some answers. Pointing the gun at Jinx, he asked, "So you're not a real nun?"

"No," Jinx replied. "Neither am I a messenger."

"A messenger?"

Throwing her hands up in the air in disbelief, Denise yelled, "She was the messenger this afternoon in your office! Don't you recognize her? Don't you get it? They're all working with Alberta! And they're here to bring you to the police so they can destroy you."

Looking wounded and self-righteous, Marion faced Alberta. "Is this true?"

Alberta opened her mouth to respond, but quickly shut it. Facing Marion on her own was one thing, but now that the rest of her family was in tow, she needed to choose her words carefully. Marion was definitely a loose cannon, and if she said the wrong thing there was no telling how he might react. Maybe it was naïveté or narcissism, but she still believed that Marion wouldn't hurt her. She wasn't as confident, however, that the rest of the women in the room were equally as safe.

"Yes and no," Alberta finally replied. "Yes, they're with me, but no, they don't want to destroy you."

Turning to face the three intruders, Marion asked, "Then why are you here?"

"To make sure my grandmother is okay."

"To close that deal I offered to buy Lucy's *TV Guide* collection."

"I had a couple of free hours, so I'm just along for the ride," Helen added.

After the first two comments, Marion just nodded his head in agreement to show that he understood. The final comment, however, made him burst out laughing. "Helen Ferrara!" Marion exclaimed. "You are still as funny as you were in high school. I can't believe you didn't become a comedienne, you would've been more famous than Totie Fields."

Jinx turned to Joyce and whispered, "Who?"

Shrugging her shoulders, Helen replied, "I *was* the laughingstock of my family for a while after I announced that I was joining a convent, but a girl's gotta do what a girl's gotta do."

Once again Marion nodded in agreement. "The same holds true for some of us boys."

Alberta looked around the room and knew that everyone was thinking the same question, even Denise, but no one wanted to ask the only boy present what it was that he had to do. When Marion pointed the gun at Joyce and spoke, his intentions became clear.

"Are you serious about wanting to buy the *TV Guide* collection?" Marion asked. "Or were you just trying to set a trap to capture me?"

"As serious as Robin Leach was about maintaining a lifestyle of the rich and famous," Joyce remarked. "And to prove it, I have the briefcase full of cash in the trunk of my Mercedes."

"Then you, ma'am, have got yourself a deal."

Just as Marion was walking toward Joyce, Denise jumped in front of him to block him from sealing the deal. "Not so fast!"

"What the hell are you doing, Denise?" Marion hissed. "Isn't this what you wanted? For us to get the money for the collection and pay off the smugglers?"

"Yes, that's exactly what I want," Denise confirmed. "But first I want to know how Nancy Drew and her two elderly sidekicks found us here. This cabin is isolated, and it isn't public knowledge that it's owned by your family."

Stepping around Denise, Marion aimed his gun directly at Jinx and this time his hand was no longer shaking. "That's a very good question, and there really is only one good answer," he said. "You contacted the police and they're waiting for you outside."

The vision of seeing a gun pointed at her granddaughter was almost too much for Alberta to bear. She twisted her body and tugged at her ropes desperately trying to free herself. What she was going to do once she got free she had no idea, but she would have a much better chance at protecting Jinx if she had full use of her body. In this instance, however, Jinx didn't need her grandmother's help; she was surrounded by other family members who didn't hesitate to be Alberta's backup.

"I would come to the same conclusion if I were in your position, but I'd be wrong," Joyce said. "We didn't need the police to track you down here, we just needed my business card."

"What are you talking about?" Marion asked.

"I assume you have the card I left with Alberta at your office."

"You assume wrong."

"That's . . . that's impossible," Joyce stammered. "You must have it."

"No, I don't," Marion replied. "But Denise does."

Turning to look at Denise, Joyce looked both surprised and impressed as Denise took the card out of her wet suit. "See that little embossed logo on the upper right-hand corner of the card?"

"The picture of the owl?" she replied, examining the card.

"It's really a GPS device," Joyce replied. "I have a friend who still works in the tech industry and he was able to put in a little tracker that led us right to your cabin door."

"How many friends do you have?" Helen snapped.

Ignoring the comment, Denise replied, "Remind me to thank your friend, because now you're going to lead us straight to your hundred grand."

"Well, well, well, cutthroat *and* money hungry."

"Also too, she's the one who killed Lucy," Alberta announced.

Cries of "*What?*" "*Are you serious?*" and "*I thought for sure the* mammone *did it!*" rang through the cabin as Joyce, Jinx, and Helen came to terms with the fact that Denise and not Marion, their prime suspect, killed the woman whose murder they were trying to solve. They shouted even louder and with more enthusiasm when Alberta announced that she figured it out before Denise actually confessed.

They had done it! They solved Lucy's murder. They couldn't believe Denise was the murderer, she wasn't even on their short list of suspects, she was supposed to help people, not kill them. They'd contemplate the details later, now all that was left was to inform Vinny of the news so he could take over and arrest the guilty parties. But first, they had to find a way out of the clutches of a psycho wielding a pistol. Fortunately for them, the psycho was more interested in Joyce's money than he was in detaining his prisoners any longer.

"Let's go," Marion said, waving his gun in Joyce's

direction. "The *TV Guide* collection is at the bottom of Memory Lake. Give me the cash and it's all yours."

"Don't you mean 'give *us* the cash'?" Denise corrected.

Moving quickly, Marion positioned himself in front of the cabin door facing the women. Jinx had moved to stand next to her grandmother, while Helen and Joyce were standing on the opposite side of the door. Since Beverly had no choice but to remain seated next to Alberta, that left Denise standing directly in front of Marion. Right in the line of fire.

"I've made a decision to live the way my mother always dreamed I would—*without* a worthy woman by my side," Marion announced. "Which means, Denise, there's no place for you in my life any longer. I'd like to say that I'm pained by this resolution and that I'll miss your company, but I can't, because I have never been happier in my entire life and it's all because I'm going to be rid of you."

Watching Denise react to Marion's callous kiss-off and the sudden demise of all her hopes and fantasies of becoming his wife was like watching a volcano erupt. First, her shoulders started to heave, then, her body began to shake, followed by tears falling from her eyes, and culminating in her dropping to her knees and unleashing a cry that was more primitive and painful than any that the women in the room had ever heard or uttered themselves. What was even more devastating was that each of the women felt sorry for her. Because despite knowing that Denise had taken a life and was willing to take even more lives in order to fulfill her romantic and delusional quest to wed the man of her dreams, watching her crumble so completely because of unrequited love reminded them that she was human and, most disturbing, that they were all similar. They each had emotional scars from the men in their lives and carried with them the baggage from previous relationships so they understood Denise's pain. They, of course, didn't agree with or condone how she used her scars as an excuse to wound others, but they could sympathize, which made it all the harder to despise her. Especially when she got a taste of her own medicine.

"You can't do this to me! I won't let you!" Denise screamed. "Not after everything I've done for you!"

Running forward, Denise leaped in the air toward Marion. The only reason her hands never reached his throat was because Marion pulled the trigger while she was in midair. It wasn't clear if he was a poor shot or was just taken by surprise, but when Denise rolled over and blood started to race down her wet suit from the inside of her left thigh, it was obvious that she wasn't mortally wounded. What was clear was that Marion had made the decision to use brutal force if necessary.

"You son of a bitch, you shot me!"

"Keep shouting and I'll shoot you again to put you out of your misery and get you completely out of my life!"

"I wouldn't do that if I were you," Joyce said, "Isn't that an Erika?"

Holding up his pistol, Marion replied, "You know what this is?"

"Looks to me like it's a Pfannl Erika pistol made in Germany right after World War I," Joyce noted.

"Typically considered a ladies' gun, but the handle is different than most—was it specially made?"

Smiling as if he and Joyce were discussing dog breeds and not mass-produced weapons of destruction, Marion confirmed Joyce's suspicions. "Mother didn't like the way it looked, it reminded her of the guns the soldiers used back home, so she had them redesign it with an alabaster finish."

"It's quite beautiful," Joyce added.

"You shot me with your mother's lady gun?" Denise bellowed. "You couldn't even shoot me with a real man's gun?"

"Do you want me to shoot you again?"

"Don't some of those models only carry four bullets?" Joyce asked as innocently as possible. "You've already used two. You might want to save the rest, you know, for an emergency."

Which was exactly what Marion was about to be faced with. While he and Joyce were reminiscing about the good old days of German gun manufacturing, Jinx was slowly loosening the ropes around Alberta's hands and feet. By the time their conversation was over, Alberta was freed. She and Jinx were about to tackle Marion from behind, but he must have seen them out of the corner of his eye just before they were going to throw themselves onto his back because he whipped around and shot blindly. A framed picture of snow-covered mountains on the far wall fell to the floor, the glass shattering into tiny pieces.

"And that makes three," Helen said. "Looks like you only have one more bullet to go."

"You should use it on yourself!" Denise shrieked as

she pressed down harder on her thigh trying to lessen the flow of blood.

"Will you just give the *forsennato* the money so he'll get out of here?" Helen suggested as she ran over to Denise to help apply more pressure to her bleeding wound. "This one needs to get to a hospital."

Looking around the room frantically, Marion was searching for a way out. From his point of view he had only one. "You wanted your freedom, Alberta. You're coming with me."

"No!" Jinx cried.

Grabbing her granddaughter by the shoulders, Alberta said, "Lovey, I'm going to be fine."

"But he's crazy," Jinx whispered.

Hiding her fear, Alberta smiled. "So are we . . . a little bit anyway. And look how far it's taken us."

"But it has to take us even farther," Jinx sobbed. "We've only just begun."

Refusing to cry in front of her granddaughter, Alberta swallowed hard and bit her lip. "*In bocca al lupo.*"

"*Crepi il lupo.*"

"Don't you worry about me," Alberta said. "I'm going to be just fine."

Unable to control her tears, Jinx hugged Alberta and over her grandmother's shoulder, looked directly at their captor. "You hurt my grandmother and I swear to God I'll hunt you down and kill you myself."

A bit thrown by the ferocity in Jinx's voice, Marion took a moment to reply. "After I get the money I've been promised, none of you will ever see me again. Now give me your cell phones."

"I don't have mine with me," Jinx declared.

"I don't believe you!"

"I'm wearing a wet suit, where do you think I'm going to hide it?"

Helen took out her phone from her jacket and slid it toward Marion as Joyce did the same

"And you, Denise?"

"I don't know where it is, I must have dropped it . . . *when you shot me!*"

His eyes darted around the room in search of her cell phone and, even though the room was sparsely furnished, he couldn't find it. Not wanting to waste any more time, he slammed the heel of his shoe into the two cell phones on the floor, shattering them into several pieces, and decided to give them one last warning. "If I hear sirens or see a police car, I'll use this last bullet on Alberta. Now, let's go."

Marion ushered Joyce and then Alberta out of the cabin and once outside closed the door behind him. He saw a thick branch on the ground a few feet from the door and jammed it into the door handle. It wouldn't prevent the women from leaving, but it would make their escape that much slower.

He followed Joyce to her Mercedes, and just as she was lifting the trunk, he grabbed it with his free hand and said, "If this is a trick, I'll kill your sister-in-law right in front of you."

Raising her hands in surrender, Joyce said, "No tricks, just cold hard cash."

She opened the trunk and revealed the briefcase that she had brought to the office a few days earlier. She took it out, closed the trunk, and placed the briefcase on top of the car to open it. When Marion saw the stacks of hundred-dollar bills, his eyes glazed over. He was so close to putting this whole nightmare behind him. All he needed to do was get out of town and he could start his life over again. The only thing he needed was a chauffeur.

"My car is right over there," Marion said, pointing to the black Volkswagen Passat parked a few feet away. It wasn't easily seen because the cluster of trees and bushes on either side created the perfect camouflage. Marion aimed his gun from Alberta to the car and ordered, "The keys are in the ignition. Get in the car and drive."

Alberta wasted a few seconds trying to find the courage to reach out and grab the gun from Marion's hand. By the time she was brave enough to act, he had stepped back and there was too much space between them for her to take action without devastating consequences. Marion might not be the most accurate shot, but she doubted he would miss his target if she were less than five feet away. She might've lost her courage, but Marion apparently had found his. Looking at Joyce, he said, "This is to make sure you don't try to help your friends."

He slapped her hard across the side of the head with the barrel of the gun and Joyce collapsed to the ground. She rolled over, and Alberta could see blood start to trickle from the open cut on her temple.

"Joyce!" Alberta screamed.

"Forget about her or you'll be next."

Resigned to her fate, Alberta got into the driver's seat and it felt like she stepped into a time warp. The dashboard contained a cassette player, a cigarette lighter just underneath, and on the sides of the doors there were handles that opened each window. Alberta was hardly a car buff, but even she could tell she was sitting in a vintage model and she shuddered when she realized it was more than likely that the original owner of the car was Marion's mother.

She didn't have long to contemplate that she was sitting in the same seat Helga once graced, because Marion jumped in the car next to her. He placed the briefcase between them and pointed the gun at Alberta's head. "Drive."

The last thing she saw through the rearview mirror as she pulled away was Joyce's still body in the dirt. She couldn't imagine it was a good omen of what was yet to come.

# CHAPTER 24

*Non avere peli sulla lingua.*

Silence was not something that Alberta had ever gotten used to.

Growing up in a large Italian family, there were always loud relatives whichever way you looked, always too many people crowded around the small dining room table eating and/or arguing, always people coming and going from their house at all hours of the day and night. Even now that she was living alone for the first time in her life, her moments of solitude and quiet were rare, and most of the time was spent in the kitchen with Jinx, Helen, and Joyce or some combination of the three. She loved their company and, truth be told, would have been incredibly lonely without their frequent visits.

Almost always being surrounded by noise, however, made her treasure the moments when she was alone sitting by herself gazing at the lake or sitting in her favorite chair drinking a cup of tea, Lola purring softly and snuggled close by. The silence during those moments was welcomed and offered comfort and a chance to contemplate the past, the present, and the future. The silence in the car was different. It was filled with fear, doubt, and questions. What was Marion going to do to her? Why had she allowed herself to come down this path? Was her life going to end just as surely as Lucy's had?

Alberta wasn't ready to die; she definitely wanted to spend more years getting to know Jinx and even herself. And it would be nice one day to reconnect with Lisa Marie. But the longer Alberta drove, the longer she felt the silence was a sample of what was to come.

"Mother always liked you," Marion said.

The comment not only startled Alberta away from her thoughts, but struck her as odd, because she could only remember meeting Helga Klausner once and that was at their high school graduation. Alberta and her friends were discussing what parties they were going to attend that night, and she saw Marion standing by himself a distance away with his mother. She felt sorry for him, and he looked so lonely and ill at ease that she was compelled to go over and talk to him.

It was a brief conversation and she stopped short of inviting him to any of their parties, because she knew her friends would kill her if she extended an invitation to the social misfit. Alberta couldn't remember anything more about what they discussed except that they were interrupted by Marion's mother.

Helga Klausner looked like the stereotypical German matron: square face, ample bosom, thick body adorned in a short-sleeved cotton print dress, white gloves, sturdy shoes, and a hat with a small white veil that hung like bangs on her forehead. "Hello

Alberta," Helga had said. "It's nice to finally meet you. I've heard so much about you."

At the time Alberta had focused on her strong German accent and how it sounded very much like Marlene Dietrich if she had starred in a Nazi propaganda film. What shocked her now was not how Helga looked, but what she remembered she had said, "I've heard so much about you."

"I didn't think your mother knew me," Alberta said.

"Well not directly, but she knew so much about you because I talked about you all the time," Marion confessed.

"Really?" Alberta replied, trying hard to keep her eyes focused on the dirt road that ran along the north side of the lake. "Why did you talk to her about me?"

"As much as Mother didn't want me to socialize with girls or make the mistake like so many young men my age did and become trapped by them, she didn't want me to be lonely," Marion explained. "So, she was happy to hear that you and I were friends even if we never fraternized."

What a complicated woman Helga Klausner was, Alberta thought. The more she heard about her, the less she liked her, but the more she wanted to know about the woman. And how Marion truly felt about her. "Did you love your mother, Marion?"

Alberta kept looking straight ahead, so she couldn't see Marion's expression, but out of the corner of her eye she saw his grip tighten on the pistol.

"What kind of question is that?" Marion asked. "She was my mother. Of course I loved her."

"I guess maybe what I meant to say was did you like

her," Alberta said. "I love everyone in my family, after all they're my family, but I don't like them all."

"Oh . . . well . . . yes, I know what you mean," Marion said, his voice softer and less angry. "There are certain people we're linked to by blood that we have to accept and love for that reason alone, but just because you share the same DNA with someone doesn't mean you have to like them."

"Exactly," Alberta agreed. "So, did you like your mother?"

Quickly, Alberta turned to look at Marion and saw that all the color had drained from his face and he was contemplating her question very seriously. His response was exactly what she expected.

"No."

She expected it because it was the same way she felt about her husband.

"I know how you feel."

"You do?"

"*Non avere peli sulla lingua*," Alberta said in her native tongue.

"What?"

"Sorry, it's a saying . . . without hair on the tongue . . . the honest truth," she translated. "Yes, I feel the same way about my Sammy as you do about your mother. We both loved them, we both would have done anything for them, but *only* because we loved them and felt obligated, not because we liked them or wanted to make them happy. The fact was that there was nothing I could do to make my Sammy happy, because he didn't love me. He married me because . . . well, I'm not entirely sure why he did. I was available and a good catch, I guess, but definitely not because he loved me. It didn't matter how hard I tried, my actions wouldn't make him happy. I think it's the same with your mother."

While she spoke Alberta eased her bare foot off the gas pedal so the car would slow down. She didn't want to get too far from the lake and onto the highway because then it would be much harder for anyone to catch them. Here they stood out, a lone car on Memory Lake Road, but on the highway they would be just another vehicle. Fortunately, her words pushed Marion into such deep thought he didn't even notice.

"Mother always said she loved me and only wanted the best for me, but I always knew she wasn't telling me the truth," Marion pondered. "I was like a prized possession to her, like one of her Hummel figurines, perfect and completely hers. My father stopped trying to connect with me before I learned how to walk because he was tired of fighting with my mother for my attention. She would always interfere with his attempts and push him away—it's no wonder he buried himself in his work." Marion smiled at Alberta and said, "Thank you."

"For what?"

"For making me face the truth," Marion confessed. "My entire life has been spent trying to please my mother and make her happy, but you've shown me that was an impossible task. You've released me from her hold and given me freedom that I never had. You're amazing, do you know that?"

"Well, I don't know about that," she said. "I only suggested . . ."

"You did more than that," he said. "You listened to me and you asked me questions. You asked me how I felt. Do you know that no other woman has ever done that? Not Beverly or Denise. They never cared about how I felt, they only cared about how I made them feel, just like my mother. Like your husband."

"I guess we are similar, Marion," Alberta acquiesced. "You lived under the shadow of your mother, and I lived under the shadow of my Sammy."

"Now we can live outside the shadows! We can push them both aside and live together," Marion declared. "I have enough money and connections that we can start over, just the two of us, just like it was always meant to be."

"Always meant to be?"

"Oh, come on! You can't possibly think that your moving to Tranquility, where I happen to live was a coincidence, can you? No! It was destiny, *our* destiny. We're going to have such a wonderful life together, just you and I."

"I think you're right, Marion, moving here was my destiny."

"So, you agree, the two of us are destined to be together."

"No, Marion, what I mean is that I refuse to allow history to repeat itself."

A few hundred feet before the entrance to the highway, Alberta slammed her foot on the gas. There was a dip in the land leading into the lake where rowboats and canoes used to dock until a more modern mini-marina was built closer to the residential area, and it was exactly what Alberta was aiming for when she turned the steering wheel sharply to the left so the car could drive off the road. It hung in the air for a few seconds before plunging into the lake.

Alberta could hear Marion screaming, his voice riddled with terror and shock, but it was as if she were in a trance and the sound was coming from far away instead of from the seat next to her. A second before she swerved the car off the road she had no idea she could do something so drastic. Never before had she acted so impulsively, deliberately putting her life in danger. But knowing that Marion had no intention of willingly letting her go and could at any moment end her life, something in her brain and in her heart clicked. If she was going to die, she was at least going to be in control of how.

Looking out the front window, she saw only black because the car was completely submerged. Marion was still screaming, but now she saw that he was frantically trying to roll down the passenger side window. She looked over at him and it was as if he was moving in slow motion, his right hand struggling to crank open the window with the old-fashioned handle allowing water to start to seep into the car, his left tightly clutching the handle of the briefcase that held over a hundred thousand dollars. In the darkness, the pistol was nowhere to be found, Marion must have dropped it accidentally or decided he would have to let go of his mother's antique if he wanted to survive.

Turning her focus to her own survival, Alberta used both hands to crank open the driver's-side window and soon a rush of cold water started to flood the car from both sides. She started doing the breathing exercises Freddy taught her as if she were preparing for another scuba dive so she would be ready when she had to take one last deep breath and swim through the car window and up to the surface of the lake.

Although she was focused, she was starting to become afraid and wasn't sure if the fear was making the water feel colder than it had before. It could be the cooler temperature outside, but the water was freezing and as it poured into the car and quickly rose up to her waist, she started to shiver.

"Why did you do this, Alberta?" Marion asked, unable to mask his own fright. "We could've had the perfect life together."

"My life was already perfect, Marion," Alberta replied. "There was nothing you or any man could do to make it better."

Even if Marion wanted to continue the conversation and persuade Alberta that she was wrong, he wasn't able to because at that moment they each had to take one last, huge breath as the entire car filled with water.

Marion deftly maneuvered his body out the car window, his briefcase still in his grip, and Alberta could see his legs flick back and forth to assist him with his ascent to the surface. But when she pushed herself up in her seat to escape she immediately felt a tug against her waist and was pushed back into her seat. She looked down and couldn't see anything, but when she felt her lap she realized that her seatbelt was still buckled, she didn't even realize she had put it on. But of course she would have put her seatbelt on because that's what good little girls do.

Tugging and pressing down on the seatbelt latch, she finally felt it release. She grabbed onto the roof of the car and hoisted herself up so she was standing on the seat with half of her body wedged inside the window frame. Then she crouched down and pushed off, propelling her body upward, her hips and thighs scraping against the sides of the frame. This time Memory Lake offered no sense of peace and freedom, only desperation: She had to reach the top of the lake before she ran out of breath. And that moment was quickly approaching.

All sense of reason left her brain as her mouth was fighting to open and take a deep breath. Kicking her legs and thrashing her arms wildly, Alberta pushed herself up higher and higher until she could see the dark black water lighten in shade to navy blue. *No, not navy blue,* she thought, that was what started this whole adventure. Lucy's damn navy blue suit. She'd have to remember to rid her wardrobe of that color once she was able to wear dry clothes again.

Finally, Alberta burst through the water for the second time in one night and started gasping for air. She looked over and could see Marion silhouetted against the moonlight, one arm stroking as he swam toward the edge of the lake, the other extended at his side, still attached to the briefcase that followed him like a persistent buoy.

"Help me!" Alberta screamed.

She didn't wait to see if Marion turned to look at her, but threw her arms up in the air and let herself sink. Opening her eyes underwater, she couldn't see if he was swimming toward her, all she could see was darkness.

Rising up again, she thrashed herself from side to side and screamed even louder, "Help me! I'm drowning!"

Taking a deep breath, she let her body submerge under the water, and this time when she opened her eyes she saw the faint image of Marion, still clutching the briefcase, swimming toward her.

"Hurry!" Alberta screamed, water spitting from her mouth. "Please Marion, hurry!"

This time Alberta allowed her body to submerge even deeper and didn't put up any struggle. Arms out to her side, legs unmoving, she was starting to drop to the bottom of the lake. And she would have, had Marion not reached out to grab her.

He wrapped his right arm around her chest and together they broke the surface of the lake, but when he tried to swim to safety with only his feet to motor them, it became evident that he would need both arms to be successful.

They floated there for a few moments, Alberta's body pressed close to Marion's, neither of them speaking, their choppy breathing making the only sound, and finally Marion made the decision Alberta was confident he would make: he opened his hand and let go of the briefcase. It was a turning point because they both knew that he wasn't just letting go of the money, but also of any hope he had of starting a new life.

With both arms free, he was able to hold Alberta tightly and swim toward land. He was a few feet away before he saw the twirling red light in the distance and the people standing along the shore. The intrusion surprised him so much that they switched roles, and Alberta had to pull a dumbfounded Marion to the banks of the lake or he might have been the one to sink to the bottom.

"Grandma!" Jinx screamed, running toward her. "Are you all right?"

"I'm fine, lovey," Alberta panted as she dragged Marion's unhelpful body behind her. "But how in the world did you find us?"

"Aunt Joyce put a GPS tracker in the briefcase," Jinx explained. "Just like the one on her business card."

"*Ah, Madon*, that one's full of surprises, ain't she?"

On his knees, Marion sat back on his haunches and looked at the spectacle in front of him. He looked as if he was bearing witness to one of the great wonders of the world, not members of the Tranquility police force. "But I said no police."

"Didn't your mother ever tell you that women don't do what they're told?" Jinx asked. "My cell phone was in Aunt Joyce's car. You should've checked before kidnapping my grandmother!"

Still lost in his own reality, Marion turned to Alberta and said, "But you were the only one Mother would ever approve of."

Not knowing whether to laugh in Marion's face or hug him tenderly, Alberta replied, "Well, you know what they say? Mother does know best."

Even when Vinny told Marion that he was under arrest for kidnapping, drug smuggling, and attempted murder, and Detective Miyahara handcuffed him and started reading him his rights, the faraway look never left his eyes. He didn't resist arrest, he didn't scream to the heavens that he was innocent, nor did he break down and cry for Mommy, he accepted his fate like the good little boy that he was. And even after everything he did and all that he wanted to do, it still almost broke Alberta's heart.

"Don't hurt him," she said watching Kichiro walk Marion to a waiting police car.

"Don't worry about him, we're doing this one by the book," Vinny assured. "Now, Alfie, did he hurt you?"

Shaking her head dismissively, she said, "No, not at

all. The only thing he did was point a gun at me and make me drive his car off into the sunset so the two of us could live happily ever after."

"And how did the car wind up in the lake?" Vinny asked.

"Oh, I swerved off the road."

"Deliberately?"

"How else was I going to snap him out of it?" Alberta asked. "He was determined to run off with me, and I knew the cops would be after him and it would not end well."

"You could've gotten yourself killed!" Vinny exploded. He shrugged his shoulders and threw his arms out in front of him with his palms up. "*Quanto stupido si può essere?*"

"That's what I'd like to know," Helen said joining the group near the edge of the lake. "Just how stupid are you, Berta? How'd you know that Marion wasn't going to let you drown so he could run off with all that cash in the briefcase?"

Alberta wrapped the thin gray blanket that one of the policewomen had given her tighter around her still wet body and shook her head. "First of all, Helen, I didn't *need* Marion to save me from drowning because I'm a damn good swimmer, thank you very much. Second of all, I knew that deep down he would make the right choice. Marion's *guasto* . . . damaged . . . but in his own twisted way I knew that he cared about me and wouldn't hurt me. Yes, I know that he hurt Lucy, but Denise is the cold-blooded killer. You know that, Vinny, don't you?"

"Yes, Alberta," he replied, gritting his teeth. "Your fellow *detectives* filled me in on that."

"Good! She's the evil one," Alberta stated. "Even though Marion did all those other things, I knew that in his heart there was still some goodness left."

"*Ashpet!*" Helen cursed. "You think deep down everybody's good! Looks like I have to teach you some things about the world."

Helen turned away from her sister, but not before Alberta saw her wipe away the tears that had gathered in her eyes. Joyce put her arm around Helen and for once the woman didn't try to escape the embrace.

"Oh, Joyce!" Alberta cried. "How's your head?"

"I'm fine," she replied. "A bit of a headache, but it'll go away."

"Maybe you'll feel better when they pull your hundred grand out of the lake," Jinx said, trying to console her aunt.

It did the trick, because Joyce roared with laughter. "Oh honey, that money's fake! My friend keeps it as a decoy in case she needs to impress a client with how liquid her cash flow is."

Stunned, Alberta replied, "You bet my life on a briefcase full of fake money?"

Still laughing, Joyce replied, "Sometimes, Alberta, you have to take a really big gamble to fully appreciate life."

"Next time, let's roll the dice with *your* life, okay?" Alberta said, shaking her head, but unable to resist laughing right along with Joyce.

The laughter proved infectious, and soon Jinx and Helen joined in. The four of them wrapped their arms around each other, thankful that their adventure, while not going *exactly* as they had planned, had ended safely. Vinny watched the women in disbelief, but couldn't hide his admiration.

"I have to hand it to you, Alfie," he started. "If it weren't for you, we would've thought Lucy's death was just an accident and Denise would've gotten away with murder. And Marion would have kept on selling drugs to those international dealers."

"If that's your way of saying thank you, Vinny," Alberta replied, "We accept."

"Chief, what's going to happen to Beverly?" Jinx asked.

"Well, even though she set all of this into motion, technically the only thing she did was steal Lucy's *TV Guide* collection," he conveyed. "I think in light of the ordeal she's been through, we can forget about charging her with theft."

"The real question is, will she be able to forgive herself?" Helen asked. "If she hadn't stolen Lucy's property and tried to get a marriage proposal out of it, Lucy would still be alive."

Helen's comment made the air so thick it was difficult to speak. But as with all of life's events, no matter how terrible the situation, there's always another way to look at things.

"At least now Lucy can rest in peace knowing that her killer has been brought to justice," Alberta said.

"Thanks to her worst enemy," Jinx added.

"You mean thanks to all of us, lovey."

Clearing his throat loudly and assuming his no-nonsense chief of police stance, Vinny added, "And about that, Alfie. Promise me that you and your cohorts aren't going to try anything like this again. You got lucky this time, but in the future leave the crime solving to the professionals."

Holding Jinx's hand and flanked by Helen and Joyce, a mischievous smile slowly formed on Alberta's lips. "The only thing I can promise is that we'll try very hard not to make the *professionals* look bad," Alberta said. "But it looks to me like the Ferrara family detectives are just getting started."

# EPILOGUE

*Finché c'è vita c'è speranza.*

Memory Lake looked so much different basking in the morning sunlight. It looked calm and peaceful, majestic and strong, nothing at all like the setting of fear and chaos from the previous night.

Alberta and Jinx sat next to each other in the Adirondack chairs drinking coffee and sharing the silence. Lola couldn't decide which lap was the ideal napping spot, so she chose to lay on the grass between the two chairs, her eyes half-closed, and every once in a while letting out a throaty purr to let the women know she enjoyed their company.

"You must be tired, lovey," Alberta said. "Staying up all night to finish your article."

"I guess I'm still too excited," Jinx gathered. "It'll be my first real byline, shared of course with Calhoun, but my first published news article about something really important. And Wyck's promised that I can start to work on more hard news stories and not just fluff pieces now that I've proven myself."

"I'm so proud of you."

"Thanks, Gram, but I couldn't have done it without you. Or Aunt Helen and Aunt Joyce. Lucy's been vindicated and Denise and Marion are in jail because of the four of us."

"And Beverly gets the chance to start her life over, I'm happy about that," Alberta added. "Vinny said she's selling her condo and moving to South Jersey to be with her sister. Family really is the only thing you can count on when you hit rock bottom."

"Unfortunately, you can't always count on them to do the right thing," Jinx sniped. "Lucy's worthless daughter, Enza, didn't care about her mother for years, but she'll still get to benefit from selling Lucy's *TV Guide* collection now that they retrieved it from the bottom of the lake."

"Maybe Olive Berekshnyav will decide not to buy the collection after all," Alberta mused. "And even if she does, I don't think the extra cash is going to make Enza any happier. Some things even money can't buy."

Like a new romance. Or two.

Lola didn't move from her sunshine-soaked location, but raised her head and purred loudly to greet Freddy and Sloan as they entered the backyard. They had not arrived together, but they came with the same thought in mind.

"I'm so glad to hear that the two of you are all right," Sloan said. "The entire town is talking about how you ladies single-handedly found out who killed poor Lucy Agostino."

"And took down the local drug cartel!" Freddy exclaimed.

"For a quiet little town, gossip sure spreads quickly around here," Alberta joked.

Laughing along with her, Sloan replied, "Oh you'll soon learn that nobody around here minds their own business."

"Speaking of business, Jinx," Freddy said. "I kind of have to work the Waterfest, you know, giving scuba lessons and all that, but I was hoping you'd be my date for the Aqua Ball Saturday night."

Until that moment, Jinx had absolutely no intention of attending the party that was going to close out the Waterfest celebration, thinking that the entire event was ridiculous and small-town nonsense. But when she looked up into Freddy's blue eyes and saw his big ears practically flopping in the wind, she suddenly knew there was no place she'd rather be than dancing in Freddy's arms on Saturday night.

"I'd love to," she said.

"That's quite a coincidence," Sloan said. "Because the real reason I came here was to ask you the same question, Alberta."

Before Alberta could even process that she was being asked out on her first date in over forty years, Jinx shrieked. "Oh, say yes, Gram! We'll go on a double date!"

She felt the same tingling feeling in the pit of her stomach when she looked into Sloan's smiling eyes as Jinx did when she looked at Freddy, and her response to the invitation was the same: "I'd love to."

"If the couples are done contaminating the fresh air with romance, we have some business to attend to." They all turned to see Helen and Joyce standing behind them. Joyce was carrying a bottle of vodka and four red plastic cups and Helen was wearing her usual disgruntled expression. "Sorry, fellas, this is a girls-only party," she barked.

Having succeeded in achieving what they had each come for, Sloan and Freddy instinctively knew not to push their luck. They quickly said their good-byes and left. Once the men had gone, Helen pulled two more chairs closer to Alberta and Jinx and Joyce started pouring the vodka into cups.

"Joyce, it's ten in the morning!" Alberta cried

Handing Alberta a cup filled with vodka, Joyce replied, "Since when have we ladies played by the rules?"

"Plus, it's bacon-flavored vodka," Helen said, allowing Lola to move languidly in between and around her legs. "So, consider it your breakfast."

Alberta had pushed the boundaries of her comfort zone lately, but when she smelled the vodka, she wasn't sure she was adventurous enough to taste such a concoction. "Ah, *Madon*, this doesn't smell so good."

"*Basta!* It's no worse than anything Jinx has ever made us eat," Helen said. "Drink up!"

The four women raised their plastic cups in a silent toast and then sipped their vodka. To their surprise they all enjoyed the taste. Looking straight ahead they enjoyed the sight as well. Slowly they watched Marion's car being removed from its watery grave so it couldn't pollute the lake with its rust or its reminder of recent events.

"*È fantastico!* It's like cleansing a body and starting all over," Alberta remarked. "Getting rid of the trash so only the good parts remain."

She reached out to grab Jinx's hand and was so grateful to have her back in her life. Sitting in the company of her family, she realized she had been so wrong. She whispered to herself, *"Finché c'è vita c'è Speranza,"* and for the first time understood the power and the truth of those words.

Where there's life, there really is hope.

## RECIPES *from the* Ferrara Family Kitchen

### ALBERTA'S HOMEMADE MEATBALLS AND GRAVY

**MEATBALLS**

1 pound chopped meat, 70–77 percent lean

1 pound ground pork

1 cup of grated pecorino Romano cheese—*Locatelli brand, that's all I ever use*

2 eggs

2 slices of bread soaked in whole milk or water

Garlic—*not too much, but just enough—you'll know when it's right by the smell*

A couple of pinches of parsley

1. Mix everything together in a large bowl.
2. Roll into meatballs about the size of golf balls— remember they're Sicilian, not Swedish.
3. Fry them in a large pan in about ¼ inch extra virgin olive oil—Partanna if you can find it, or Colavita. I don't know for how long, but practice and you'll figure it out.
4. Drain on paper towels—not the cheap brand either!

**GRAVY**

2 28-ounce cans of crushed tomatoes—*Cento brand,
    do not use Hunt's no matter what my sister Helen says*
1 6-ounce can of tomato paste—*again, only use Cento*
Garlic—*as much as you want, but remember a little goes
    a long way*

1. Put everything in a large pot, cover, and bring
   to a boil.
2. Add in your meatballs and let it simmer.
3. Cook on a low simmer for at least 45 minutes. I
   cook the gravy for 60 minutes, no less, because
   I like a thick gravy.

## Jinx's Vegan Meatballs

¼ cup couscous—*Bob's Red Mill brand is my favorite*
¼ cup water
1 15-ounce can of chickpeas
½ cup of chopped onions
3 tablespoons of ketchup
Some pinches of Italian spices—*McCormick works,
    but I only use Oh My Spice gluten-free spices*
A pinch of black pepper and sea salt
½ cup of brown rice flour

1. Bring a small pot of water to boil and stir in the
   couscous until it gets to a crazy boil.
2. Remove the pot from heat, cover, and let it sit
   for five minutes.
3. Blend the chickpeas, onion, and everything
   else, except the couscous and rice flour, until
   it's chunky—do not overblend.

4.  Add the mixture to a large bowl—I like my Gram's big green Pyrex bowl with the daisies on it—and add in the couscous and rice flour.
5.  Stir everything until it's sticky.
6.  Chill in the fridge for about 20 minutes.
7.  Preheat the oven to 375°F and line a pan with parchment paper.
8.  Roll the meatballs into tight balls and place them on the pan.
9.  Bake for 30 minutes, turning them over once.
10. Enjoy a healthy alternative to an Italian favorite!

### GRANDMA MARIE'S WEDDING COOKIES

6½ cups of flour
6½ teaspoons of baking powder
1 cup of sugar
2½ sticks of butter, softened
6 eggs
Bottle of anise or lemon extract—*I prefer lemon, but Grandma Marie likes a little anise*
1 cup of whole milk—*don't you dare you use skim or 2%!*

*For the icing:*
4 cups of confectioners' sugar
Food coloring
5 tablespoons of milk
Decorative candy sprinkles

1.  Preheat oven to 350°F.
2.  Line a cookie sheet with parchment paper.

3. Mix butter and sugar in a bowl for about five minutes until light and fluffy, adding in the eggs one at a time, mixing after each one.
4. Add in the anise or lemon extract.
5. Blend flour, salt, and baking powder.
6. Start adding about a third of the dry ingredients to the butter/sugar in your mixer.
7. Add 1 tablespoon of milk, another third of the flour, and another tablespoon of milk.
8. Mix in enough of the remaining flour until your dough is like brownie batter, but still soft. You can refrigerate the dough for a few hours for fluffier cookies or just continue on.
9. Roll out the dough like a rope and cut into pieces and twist each into a knot.
10. Bake for 10 to 12 minutes until they're brown on the bottom.
11. While they're baking, prepare the icing by mixing the sugar, milk, and food coloring to make a sugar glaze.
12. When the cookies are cool, turn them upside down and dip the top half in the glaze. Turn them over and immediately top them with the sprinkles so they'll stick.
13. Do not bring these to someone's house in your good Tupperware because you will not get it back!

## JINX'S GLUTEN-FREE SNICKERDOODLES

1½ cups of sugar
2 sticks of unsalted butter—*I like Earth Balance, but feel free to experiment*

2 large eggs

½ teaspoon gluten-free vanilla extract—*I find Simply Organic brand to be . . . simply the best*

3 cups of gluten-free flour—*King Arthur or Krusteaz are my faves*

1 tablespoon of baking powder

A couple pinches of sea salt

*For the topping:*

¼ cup of sugar

2 teaspoons of cinnamon

1. Preheat the oven to 400°F.
2. Line two baking sheets with parchment paper.
3. Mix sugar, butter, eggs, and vanilla extract.
4. Mix flour, baking powder, and salt in another bowl and stir into the butter/sugar mix.
5. In a separate small bowl, mix the sugar and cinnamon.
6. Scoop out the dough into large balls and roll them in the cinnamon sugar.
7. Place on the tray.
8. Bake for 10 minutes or until golden brown—do not overcook!
9. Enjoy!

# Connect with

Visit us online at
**KensingtonBooks.com**
to read more from your favorite authors, see books
by series, view reading group guides, and more.

Join us on social media

for sneak peeks, chances to win books and prize packs,
and to share your thoughts with other readers.

**facebook.com/kensingtonpublishing**
**twitter.com/kensingtonbooks**

## Tell us what you think!

To share your thoughts, submit a review,
or sign up for our eNewsletters, please visit:
**KensingtonBooks.com/TellUs.**